THE

PROFESSOR

LISA SELL

Published by Continue Books, 2024.

Copyright © Lisa Sell, 2024.

The right of Lisa Sell to be identified as the Author of the Work has been asserted by her in accordance with the Copyright, Designs and Patents Act 1988.

Apart from any use permitted under UK copyright law, this publication may only be reproduced, stored, or transmitted, in any form, or by any means, with prior permission in writing from the publisher or, in the case of reprographic production, in accordance with the terms of licences issued by the Copyright Licensing Agency.

This book is a work of fiction. Names, characters, businesses, organisations, places, and events other than those clearly in the public domain, are a product of the author's imagination or used fictitiously. Any resemblance to actual persons - living or dead -, events, or locales is completely coincidental.

Print ISBN: 9798339629894

This novel is dedicated to all those who love to read,
whether it's a classic novel, psychological thriller,
romance novel, fan fiction, a magazine,
or anything else with words in it.
I hope reading always brings you joy
and book snobbery never wins.

CHAPTER 1

Then

"Eat me, drink me, love me."

He'd read the words and made them his own. His victims had feasted, drunk poison, and felt his devotion. The love was for literature, though, not the dead women.

Christina Rossetti would've been horrified at his interpretation of her poem, "Goblin Market". For him, tarnishing a woman's writing was sweeter than the fruit pulp staining the bodies of those he'd killed.

When he discovered Alice had a sibling, he believed in fate. Alice and Dinah answered the call for sisterly victims. Even better, they were twins studying at the local university. Twins had always fascinated him.

He wondered what the girls' parents were thinking when naming their daughters after characters from *Alice in Wonderland*. They were likely excited about their children attending Oxford Carroll University, named after the author, Lewis Carroll. The pretentiousness of naming people after literary characters annoyed him. It was an impossible standard to live up to. Only he was allowed to steal names from books.

Research made him aware halls would be quiet that evening. Slipping in unseen was easy. The sisters had been getting ready together for a party off campus. Instead, they had a last celebration with the man many feared, The Professor.

He reflected on how Alice often avoided talking about her English Literature degree. She stated it must be boring for him. Knowing her end was coming, he dampened his rage at her judging him as stupid. Rather than following his dangerous impulses, he educated her in sex.

While smoothing Alice's hair, he remembered its silkiness whenever he playfully tugged it. Now, golden strands wrenched from her scalp, stuck to his gloves. He flicked away the evidence.

On the floor, Alice didn't stir. The dead don't move.

Looking down at her corpse, he read the quote from "Goblin Market", torn from a book, and pinned to Alice's top.

"Hug me, kiss me, suck my juices
Squeez'd from goblin fruits for you,"

He was the devious goblin, offering delights and sending females into frenzied desire. Like Laura from the poem - seduced by goblin men with forbidden fruits - Alice seized his sexual wares. Lustfulness makes girls more than peep at wicked men.

Thumbing cherry skin from Alice's cheek, he smiled at the memory of her reading while they laid in a hotel bed. She received his gift of a Christina Rossetti anthology as a sign of affection. For him, it was more of a warning. As Alice read aloud of the poem's Laura, literally dying for another fix of the goblin's offerings, he visualised Alice's death.

In "Goblin Market", Lizzie rescued Laura. Lizzie tricked the angry goblins into pelting her with their fruit. The juices revived her failing sister, who licked them from Lizzie's skin. The Professor's targets *never* get a second chance at living.

He had shown kindness in staging the sisters in a last embrace, as per the poem's description, "Like two pigeons in one nest".

There wasn't much he could do about the filthy carpet, though; a casualty of years of students living in the room. He'd brightened the scene with a fruity rainbow decorating the corpses. Splashes of glutinous purples, yellows, oranges, and greens were almost cheery. Smashed strawberry smeared Alice's mouth, mocking her usual scarlet lipstick.

THE PROFESSOR

The work done, he grabbed his rucksack and turned to leave. After switching off the music that had drowned out cries, he heard a sound. A soft groan became a scream to his ears.

Dinah wriggled, fighting against the effects of drugged wine and cannabis. Her rattling breath sought life-giving air.

The Professor moved closer. Dinah's eyes flickered open. A fearful stare fixed upon him. She clung to her twin as his hands tightened around her neck. When Dinah finally let go, a smile formed on her face. It was too much. Surely, Dinah mocked him, even in death? He'd become careless.

The Professor resolved to bring his killing spree to a temporary end. Mistakes lead to capture. When he returned, he would be better than ever. For a while, female students could live freely, but he'd always be there, watching and waiting.

One day, The Professor would be back to kill again, and again.

CHAPTER 2

Jane

Now

'Jane, can you get your bloody nose out of that book and help me?'

I look up to see Kate buckling underneath an enormous box. She veers to the left, threatening to wipe out a shelf of folders. The shop's narrow aisles are obstacles on delivery days.

I steer her straight. 'Sorry, boss. I was reading the juicy part where Jane and Mr Rochester kiss.'

Kate drops the box, narrowly missing my toes. 'How many times have you read *Jane Eyre*? Aren't you bored of it by now?'

How can I explain that my mum hugs me when I read? Holding a book brings me closer to the person who passed on a love of literature.

'Take that back!' I wink. 'You can never have enough of *Jane Eyre*.'

Kate strips parcel tape from cardboard, balls it up, and throws it at me. 'Reading will have to wait. If you don't start unpacking this lot, you're fired.'

I roll my eyes extra hard. Whenever she threatens me with the sack, we both know it's in jest. I've worked in her stationery shop

THE PROFESSOR

for years. If Kate gets rid of me, she'll be on her own. Neither of us wants to lose our friendship either.

We begin placing pens in their specific sections. When I started working here, endless plastic holders, arranged by manufacturer and type, were my nemesis. Previously, I thought pens were only ballpoints or the fancy glittery ones we had at school with a fluffy topper. Now I'm aware there's a pen for every purpose and occasion. Despite being a mind-numbing job, I don't mind it. The distraction helps clear my head for a while from unexpressed thoughts and aspirations.

Kate frequently sighs while hurling pens into holders.

'I'll finish this,' I say.

'No, it's fine, absolutely fine.' Her teeth are clenched.

'What's he done this time?'

'Nothing. Come on.' She claps her hands. 'Stop slacking.'

I flick a ballpoint, which glides past her ear.

'Spill it,' I say. 'You'll keep feeling crap otherwise.'

Kate puts a handful of pens back into the box. 'It's Sam, as always.'

I don't reply. Sam is her husband, although he regularly needs reminding of the fact. When Kate's annoyed with him - which is often - I've learned not to bitch about him. They always make up after arguments. Sharing my opinions on Kate's deceitful other half makes things awkward later.

Her jaw trembles. 'I think Sam's having another affair. He's going out at strange hours.'

'He *is* an estate agent.'

She glares back. 'No one views a house at 10pm.'

'Where does he say he's been?'

Although I'd rather not be involved, Kate wants to talk. Most of her mum friends are toxic perfectionists whose husbands *never* stray, their children's lips only touch organic products, and these women *never* fail. Sometimes, Kate needs good old, single, full of additives, straight-talking Jane.

She shakes her head. 'Sam says he's going to the gym. Since the doctor said he's at risk of having a stroke, Sam's trying to get fitter.

He's worried he'll make me a widow. If he's cheating on me, I will voluntarily become bereaved.'

I lean against a wall. 'It could be true. Sam's too young to have those kinds of health issues. Perhaps he's trying to do something about it.'

'Maybe.' She slumps to the floor and clutches her head. 'I can't think clearly. I'm thirty-five, but sleep deprivation makes me feel more like sixty.'

Ignoring marks and stains made by customers' footfall, I join her on the carpet.

'Tell me about it,' I reply. 'I'm approaching thirty and already becoming a knackered housewife.'

'Sorry to say, but you already are.'

I hold my copy of *Jane Eyre* to my chest. 'It can't be helped.'

Kate squeezes my knee. 'I'm sure your mum never expected you to fill her shoes. Your dad's big enough and ugly enough to look after himself.'

Tending to Dad is my thing. Since Mum died when I was eighteen, Dad and I only have each other. Grief keeps us close. The house we live in is our mourning glue, sticking us together with memories of Mum.

Kate grabs my book. 'What would Jane do? *This* Jane, I mean.' She taps a finger on the stern-looking woman on the cover.

'Fall in love with a wrong 'un.'

'You're already an expert in that. Takes one to know one, by the way.' Kate laughs for the first time today.

She has a point. Most of the men I've dated needed saving, slaying, or silencing. My taste is lousy, which is why I'm not looking for a relationship at the moment. The biological clock is silent, whereas my desire for knowledge ticks so loudly I can hardly hear myself think sometimes.

'You always put others' needs above your own,' Kate says. 'Do you want to work in a poky stationery shop for the rest of your life?'

This shop, nestled in a row of businesses near the Cowley centre, is a second home. There's nothing I don't know about where an item is or how it works. Helping set up and run Kate's business used to be satisfying. Now, I want more. Speaking my truth is scary. Everything will change.

'But I enjoy working with you.'

She smiles. 'I love having you here, but that brilliant brain needs more challenges. You have so much potential and deserve more than waiting on your dad. Must admit, though, if I had access to Larry's gadgets and gizmos, I'd never leave home. Still, that's his stuff. Even though she's gone, the house is still your mum's. You're living Viv's life. Maybe she wanted more when she was alive. Don't forget, she read books to you about amazing, adventurous women. I'll ask again, what would Jane Eyre do in your situation? Viv named you after her for a reason.' Kate hands the novel back to me.

I open the book to one of many pages I can recite by heart. I hand it to Kate to follow. This quote has been bouncing around my mind for ages. As I speak the words, I know they're an instruction.

'"I am no bird; and no net ensnares me; I am a free human being with an independent will, which I now exert to leave you."'

'*Jane Eyre*, Chapter 23.' Henry Glynn enters the shop.

CHAPTER 3

Jane wonders if she's making the most of her life. The Professor can relate. Jane worries about the future. So does he. This is where the similarities end. It's obvious Jane wants more. He needs her to have less. She has a potentially great future, where she'll steal everything from him. He won't allow it to happen. The Professor will take charge the best way he knows, killing in a Victorian literature style. His murder scenes must mirror the themed rooms of Glynnholme. Evangeline Glynn's favourite era is his murder motive.

The Professor originally planned for his killing hiatus to be short. Jane's existence made him behave for years. The thought of her now crackles in his veins as a vengeful electricity. He's been away too long. Women have freely studied and gained qualifications in English Literature. Oxford Carroll University's female students have been undisturbed since the murders ten years ago. It is time for The Professor to resume his teaching.

Today's students try to delve into the tortured mind of the governess from Henry James' novella, *The Turn of the Screw*. They won't consider Karin, though; a former au pair and part-time student. Current students are too young and self-absorbed to care about someone who died a decade ago. They probably don't know her corpse was discovered dressed in a replica Victorian governess' gown. Sourcing the outfit was a true labour of love. The Professor takes pride in his planning and research. The vision of Karin's bludgeoned head, leeching blood into a carpet, is an eternal reward.

Feminism has a lot to answer for. Women think they're brave and confident, hating men. They read into novels, rooting out fake patriarchy and crying, "Not fair!"

Feminists question why a male narrator ends the story of the female governess from *The Turn of the Screw*. Silly girls don't consider the author was a man. *He* owns his work, not them.

The bra burners further rage that the governess is unnamed. Even worse is her being left holding the dead boy she was supposed to protect. When The Professor staged Karin's body, embracing a boy mannequin - he'd never kill a child as only sick people do that - he laughed at the prospect of women getting their knickers in a knot over a misogynistic murder. It was fair to say he hated most females. Why do they have to make everything about them?

Karin had to die, protecting a terrified child, like in the novella. While Miles seemingly died of fright, the governess lived. Karin could not. He had no qualms with altering the plot to show his intellect. The last thing Karin saw before dying was more terrifying than a ghost. She saw The Professor in all his killing glory.

He scrolls through a mental spinning file of his kills. Resentment ripples under his skin at the world's forgetfulness. It saddens him to think of the forgotten Phoebe, once Evangeline Glynn's protégé. Evangeline didn't get to have everything.

Phoebe's death not only ended her life, it destroyed her research project with Evangeline. He granted Phoebe some greatness by immortalising her as Miss Havisham, albeit less charred. The charity shop polyester wedding gown licked up the flames, but he didn't let them take hold. Identification was important. The Professor needed others to understand he knew Charles Dickens' *Great Expectations* well. Also, Phoebe's end was a personal message to Evangeline. *He* was the Victorian literature expert, not her.

When people now study Anne Brontë's *The Tenant of Wildfell Hall*, they likely won't know about the long-dead student, Brooke.

She fancied herself more of a painter than an English Literature scholar. After viewing Brooke's attempts at art, he hid his disgust. Splatters of paint resembled the crap an angry chimp throws in its cage. With a scalding tongue, he applauded her artistic "talent" and then crept into her life.

Brooke was obsessed with painting a masterpiece. The Professor fed her ideas while enjoying her hunger for his body and artistic recognition. She delighted in his proposal to paint a double-sided canvas. The self-portraits would be of who Brooke felt she had to be and who she really was. With each brush stroke, she unwittingly created the centrepiece of her murder landscape. The night she unveiled her work, The Professor later added finishing touches of quotes and death.

The extract from *The Tenant of Wildfell Hall*, attached to the front of Brooke's portraits, was apt, "I perceive the backs of young ladies' drawings, like the postscripts of their letters, are the most important and interesting part of the concern."

Those words exposed Brooke's one-sided and idealised version of herself. This first quote he'd chosen directed the viewer to turn over the canvas, to see the real Brooke. The other quote was vicious, "She's the very devil for spite! Did *ever* any mortal see such eyes - they shine in the dark like a cat's."

Brooke was often hateful about other people. She was also an ungrateful little bitch, throwing away the privilege of studying books to make terrible art.

Arthur Huntingdon, husband and provider in *The Tenant of Wildfell Hall,* is a misunderstood man. For his wife Helen's good, Huntingdon keeps her in place. How does she repay him? By taking his son and finding a new love interest! Like Helen, Brooke forgot her place and pursued a fantasy. The Professor was happy to shatter her dreams.

Huntingdon and The Professor are both sinful men, but sin is fun. Besides, when you have assets, particularly of extensive book knowledge, they cover a multitude of sins.

CHAPTER 4

Jane

Henry Glynne takes the copy of *Jane Eyre* from me. I fidget, searching for a substitute comforter.

He opens the book and then points at something written inside. 'Was this your mother's?'

I get up from the floor where Kate and I were chatting, needing to be on Henry's level. Seeing the name, *Viv*, in Mum's handwriting provokes many emotions: sadness that she'll never own another novel; joy from well-read pages; and happiness at Mum claiming this novel for both of us.

'Are you here for your order?' Kate asks as I help her stand.

Henry gives his customary wink. 'Yes, please.'

There's no disputing that he's a handsome man who's aged well. Kate teases me that he doesn't want stationery or could just buy it online. Someone like Henry doesn't do his own fetching and carrying. Kate thinks he comes to the shop to chat with me. Despite his cockiness with women - I've seen Henry in action with Kate and female customers - he doesn't act the lothario with me. There's a sense of respect between us. I admire his intellect as an academic doctor. I'm not sure what he sees in me.

'Fancy a cuppa, Henry?' Kate asks.

'Love one, gorgeous.'

She rolls her eyes before leaving.

Henry favours the finer things: Montblanc pens; reams of thick embossed paper; and leather-bound notebooks. Kate's grateful for the custom. Giving him a caffeine fix is the least she can offer. Henry's close to being told to piss off, though, for the suggestive comments and eyeing her up.

Squeezing past more boxes piled high, I stand behind the counter. There's no need as Henry's the only customer, but the divide eases my nerves. Whenever we discuss books, I worry I sound stupid. Henry has a PhD, gives lectures worldwide, and is obscenely rich. He never makes me feel like an idiot, but I'm always waiting for it. Kate reckons my working class inverted snobbery shows too much. Dad has a lot to answer for in how his views rub off.

Kate soon returns with a tray of drinks and a tin of biscuits. Henry's visits are always welcome because she upgrades from the usual custard creams. Kate gives Henry a box with a decorative bow added only to his orders, at his request.

'Here you go,' she says. 'It's on your account. Excuse me. I've got paperwork to sort out.'

'Good to see you.' Henry cranes his neck, watching her walk to the back office.

'She's not a piece of meat,' I say.

He laughs. 'Just appreciating the view.'

'Don't.'

'Yes, Sir!' He salutes. 'Jane, do you like working here?'

I grab a duster by the till and flick it around. 'Of course. I wouldn't do it otherwise.'

He takes out a hip flask from an inner jacket pocket and adds the usual whisky to his coffee.

'Care for a tipple?' he asks.

'No thanks.'

After taking a sip of super-charged coffee, he grins. 'Don't tell the principal I'm daytime drinking.'

It's well known Henry often annoys people at the university with his loose behaviour. Gossip states - Kate states - he's almost been fired many times. The Glynn fortune offers reprieves. Henry lives in a fancy old house in a picturesque Oxfordshire village. The Glynns have an enormous fortune from their confectionery empire. Some of the money is pooled into Oxford Carroll University. Despite Henry's stereotypical roguish behaviour, I kind of like him. He doesn't make me feel inferior and has a surprising belief in me. Also, he challenges me to read new books I hadn't considered. Since we met, my library loans and bookshop visits have increased.

Henry flourishes a theatrical hand. 'My dearest Jane, I must be brutally honest. You're far too set in your ways. Expand your horizons.'

'You don't know me well enough to make that assessment. For all you know, I could've travelled the world.'

'I bet you haven't.'

I swish the duster over the same spot, determined not to share I've never been abroad and don't have a passport. Family holidays were in the UK because of Mum's fear of flying. Perhaps I should see more of the world. I add it to an ever-increasing bucket list.

After Henry gulps his drink, it dribbles down the side of a chipped mug. I try not to laugh at this posh bloke, more used to champagne, drinking coffee that comes from a jar.

He leans over and grabs my hand. Henry's never touched me before. If he tries it on, I'll boot his arse out the door.

'Get an education, Jane. Stop wasting your brilliant brain.'

I wrench free of the vice grip. 'Brilliant brain? You're having a laugh. I spout whatever's in my head.'

'Can't you see? From our chats, it's clear you analyse literature with a flair many will never possess. I haven't encountered such raw brilliance since, well, me.'

'Are you saying I should go to university?' I seek permission to explore an unmet ambition.

'I think you've known for a while what you should do. Literature and academia are calling to you, my dear. Don't silence them. You weren't made for a humdrum life. Greatness awaits you.'

He winces as I snap the duster at him.

'Knock it off. I'm nowhere near as accomplished or knowledgeable as you.'

'No, but you could be. Come and study at Oxford Carroll. Nothing would give me greater pleasure than teaching and moulding you.'

I bang a stapler on the counter, just missing his fingers. 'I don't want to be moulded, thanks very much.'

'Bad choice of words. What I meant is I can play a part in shaping your knowledge. Recently, I've set up The Henry Glynn Scholarship for a student who shows great promise. It covers tuition fees, books, and some personal expenses. I choose who gets it, so it's you.'

'I haven't applied yet. Besides, I'd rather pay for it.' I cross my arms and then have a silent word with myself for being a sulky cow.

Henry smiles. 'Do you have several thousand pounds? You might get a student loan, but it won't cover everything. Afterwards, you'll be saddled with debt, too. Look, I'm not trying to disempower you. I applaud independence, but don't let stubbornness be your undoing.' He snaps open his leather briefcase and brings out a wedge of paper. 'These are the forms to fill in for the scholarship. Part of the process, unfortunately. The principal insists.'

I glance at the first page. My name could be there: Jane Unwin, English Literature student.

'Surely it's too late to apply.' I begin. 'Doesn't the academic year start soon?'

'It does, but I'm in charge of this. There are clearing procedures. A few haven't got in because of overestimating their intellect. I trust you have A-levels and one of those subjects is Literature?'

'Yes. I received *A* grades for English Literature and Language.' My chin rises. I'm a puffed-up peacock. Oh, stop it, Jane. You did well at school. Plenty of others did too.

Henry picks up his box of stationery. 'Advance your bildungsroman, Jane.'

'What's a bildungsroman?'

THE PROFESSOR

'Look it up and we'll discuss its relevance next time. I need that application as soon as possible. Never let go of your dreams.'

After he leaves, I consider if this *is* my dream. I've spent so long looking after Dad I lost sight of what I want. He didn't ask me to give up some of my life for him. It just happened. I've been sleepwalking into a role that was never mine. Wake up, Jane!

'Tell me you're doing it,' Kate says as she joins me.

I jab at her arm. 'Have you been listening?'

'Never mind that. You're going to take up Henry's offer, right?'

'Can I work part-time here?'

'Absolutely. You don't get away from me that easily. I'll take on someone else for the other shifts. Sam's cousin has been asking about a job.'

Knowing I can still contribute to the household helps. Dad has his carpentry job, along with selling dolls' houses, but he won't be able to do it forever. Also, I enjoy paying my own way. Even with Henry's scholarship, I'll keep working.

I seize the forms. Kate offers a pen. This Jane is becoming the "free human being" Jane Eyre taught her to be.

CHAPTER 5

Jane

The chair creaks as Dad leans back. 'You'll wear the lino out with your pacing,' he says. 'Sit down and have a natter with your old man.'

'The washing up needs doing.'

I turn on the tap, trying to drown out my worries. From the window I check the flowerbeds bursting forth a rainbow of pansies. They'll need watering. There's always something to be done around here. Dad reaches behind me and turns off the tap.

'Jane, I can tell when you're worried. You walk the length and breadth of the house. I know you're not sleeping well either.'

We sit opposite each other at the kitchen table. Three people used to sit here, but it seems smaller with only two. Dad insists we have evening meals together as much as possible. Continuing to live with him at my age doesn't feel weird. We're both busy with work and socialising - him more so than me, at the pub - we're sometimes more like housemates than relatives.

Raking my hands down my face, I realise I should hide my worries better. Dad knows insomnia returns when I'm stressed or anxious. My tactic of coming downstairs and watching TV must wake him up. I make a note to use my phone and headphones for future night-time box set binges.

THE PROFESSOR

Dad rubs his emerging stomach; a product of good living with home-cooked meals and beer. Lugging heavy blocks of wood for his job forms part of his fitness regime. Sometimes I wonder why the exercise genes missed me. Then I put my feet up on the sofa and am thankful they did.

'Don't think I haven't noticed you made my favourite dinner,' Dad says, 'although I'll never complain about having steak and ale pie.'

'I never want to let you down. Do you know that?' I ask.

'You never have and I can't see how you ever could.'

'Since Mum died, I've tried my best to look after you.'

I look at the patch of floor in front of the fridge. The well-trodden section of lino bears marks of hunger and domesticity. It's also where I found Mum, curled into a ball, against the attack of an unknown blood clot on her lung. No matter how I try, I can't erase the image. It's strangely comforting, though, knowing she hugged herself as she died alone.

At first, I wondered if I'd ever enter the kitchen again. I couldn't go near the fridge, fearing treading on a desecrated place. Dad offered to sell the house, but I wouldn't let him. This is where our memories of Mum are. She permeates the walls.

For eleven years, we haven't changed a stick of furniture. Our house in Cowley is becoming a museum to outdated décor and furnishings. I'm certain Dad will never change it. Mum shopped like a whirlwind to make her house show home worthy. It was always a bone of contention between my parents about how Mum liked bargains, whereas Dad wants the best. In the end, he left her to it. Scouring the internet and shops was a second job to her first, working in the local school's canteen.

The landscape around Dad and me must stay the same to keep Mum with us. Wallpaper is peeling but papering over it would be like erasing her. As he always does whenever he's in this room, Dad won't look at his wife's death spot. He still blames himself for being asleep when she died. We don't discuss it. Mum's death is a dirty, open secret.

I had to face my fears of the kitchen and the horror of what I discovered after returning from my eighteenth birthday party. I'm grateful I didn't have a party on my actual birthday. At least I'm spared the reminder when I should be celebrating. I decided if I ever wanted to eat or drink again, I had to be in this part of the house. Now the kitchen is my domain. I bake and cook here, keeping Dad fed and nurtured. Food is my language of love. The cupboards are full of baking ingredients and cookbooks.

Dad lays his hand on mine. Sandpaper callouses rough against the back of my hand.

'No one ever expected you to take your mum's place.'

'Someone has to look after you. We're all we've got.'

'True, but I keep saying I can look after myself. It makes me feel bad when you rush home from work to put dinner on the table. Not a day has passed without you cooking, washing, ironing, and cleaning.'

'I'm glad you've said that because I won't be able to do as much around here soon.'

Here it comes. This is the moment.

'Why?' he asks.

'I've applied to do an English Literature degree and…' My fingers drum roll against the table. 'I've been accepted.'

Dad's smile takes an age to creep across his face.

'That's great news!' A wobble threatens his enthusiastic tone. 'Where are you doing it?'

'This is the best bit. I don't have to leave home. It's at Oxford Carroll. One of the professors, well, doctor I suppose, since he has a PhD, has given me a scholarship. No need to worry about the fees either.'

Dad snatches his hand away. A fire of red rises from his neck and into his cheeks. 'Who's giving you this money?'

'Henry Glynn. He's a regular in the shop and he says I—'

'No! You can't go there.' Salt and pepper pots clink against each other as he slams his fist on the table.

My Jane Eyre independence rises. 'I *am* going. I don't need permission.'

Chair legs grate into the lino as he stands. 'You can go to any university in the country, but not there, not with Henry Glynn. He's a monster.'

CHAPTER 6
Jane

The water reaches boiling point. I snap my fingers away from the flow of the tap. From the window I watch Dad stomping across the lawn, deep in a telephone conversation. The last thing I want to do is the washing up. Let him do his own chores. How dare he dictate what I can and can't do? When I finally want something for me, he's trying to forbid it. Good luck with that. I'm not a kid. Also, I'm not a timid daughter from the classics I love to read, expected to obey her father.

I add cold water and plunge my hands into the sink. Dad goes into his shed at the bottom of the garden. Inside are dolls' houses in various stages of construction and decoration. As a child, I loved entering Dad's den when he allowed it. Dolls' world was a magical place. It still is. He's never made a dolls' house for me. I can't remember ever asking for one. In our family, they're viewed as his work - creative visions rather than toys. Dad won't let me look at his creations before they're completed. I understand. When I bake, I hate anyone checking on my progress. I'll only reveal the finished product.

When Dad wheels a dolls' house through on a trolley into our home - ready for a new owner - it's a huge moment. Mum and I always applauded him while he took a silly bow. I'll never tire of seeing what he produces. His skills in creating miniature worlds are unsurpassed. Sometimes, I wish I could shrink into the rooms and live there.

A dinner plate slips from my grip into the soapy water.

'Damn it!'

My soggy T-shirt clings to my skin. Will nothing turn out right today? Why is Dad being such a dick? What's his issue with Henry Glynn? Dad's never mentioned knowing him when I've mentioned Henry's visits to the shop. I grab a glass in the sink. That slips, too, smacking against a mug, and shattering. Blood trickles down my finger.

'I'm sorry. Of course, you should go to university.'

Dad's voice makes me jump. His head skirts the top of the back door frame. Usually, he's not so stealthy. Heavy treads around our home form part of the daily soundtrack.

'What have you done?' He points at my bleeding finger.

'A glass smashed while I was washing up.'

After grabbing the first aid kit, he leads me to the kitchen table.

'It's usually me who has the cuts and bruises from working,' he says.

I allow him to attend to the wound. In the silence, we're both inevitably considering how to fix our argument. It will take more than a plaster.

'How do you know Henry Glynn?' I ask.

'I've heard about his reputation. Despite its size, Oxford is small if you've lived and worked here all your life.'

'Are you concerned Henry will be inappropriate with me? He's never done that and I'm sure he never will.'

Scarlet blotches form on Dad's cheeks. 'Henry and his mother are well known for manipulating others. They use their money to make people perform for them like circus animals. The local newspaper is full of what they get up to.'

'So, you don't want me to go to Oxford Carroll because of them?'

'While I'd prefer it if you didn't, a friend has set me straight.' He taps his mobile. 'I was chatting with Stan from the pub. His daughter's your age. She's got a family and is running a business.

THE PROFESSOR

Stan told me to stop being so selfish, and you should live your life the way you see fit. Take the Glynns' money and attend university.'

'Wow, Stan should do a side-line in counselling, along with being a… What *does* he do?'

'Since he retired, Stan spends his days supping pints, shouting at the football on the tele, and giving good advice.'

'How about I come with you to the pub later and thank him?'

Dad laughs. 'You'd do better than going in there.'

'I won't show you up.'

'An English man's pub is his castle, although admittedly that place is a bit of a dive. It suits me, but you prefer trendy bars. So, Jane, you're off to uni. I'm pleased for you, love. Who's to say people like us can't take advantage of the Glynns?'

'This isn't about class struggle. I just want to study literature.'

'What do you think gaining knowledge is? It's the ultimate tussle for power. Learning makes you powerful.'

'You're pretty smart yourself.'

He stands. 'Not all wisdom is found in books. Now, Jane, you show the Glynns what you're made of.'

CHAPTER 7

Jane going into further education is a beacon lighting The Professor's dangerous impulses. The Victorian literature-inspired murders will resume. It starts here. Why wait for the new term when a suitable victim is waiting for him at the university?

The Professor is beginning with the novel, *Middlemarch*. He'd intended to use it ten years ago, as the next text after the "Goblin Market" murders. Now he'll destroy the male pen name of George Eliot and annihilate Mary Ann hiding behind it.

This academic year will be even better than his first killing spree. The Professor's knowledge of Victorian literature is deeper, his plans more detailed, and the vigour for killing is renewed.

He's set to reveal the truth about educated women; they masquerade as men. Females are fools to believe they've progressed from times when female writers adopted male pseudonyms. This is a man's world, all of it. Jane must learn this, not study literature. One day, The Professor will give her the most painful lesson she's ever received.

Clementine is the best victim to begin again. The pretentious name fits the owner, although the way she lords it over others can be amusing. Before the academic year begins, she's working as a cleaner at Oxford Carroll to earn some money and get free board in halls. Her formerly wealthy parents scrabble for pennies as a

THE PROFESSOR

consequence of her father's risky games with the stock market and poker.

In the bustle before a new year, staff are planning courses, advanced students continue projects, admin wade through enrolments, and the cleaners keep things clean for everyone. The Professor is always in the background.

Clementine's mouth puckers as she eats lunch in the canteen. She sneers at the food, cutting it into morsels, likely remembering the fine dining she can no longer enjoy.

'I'm surprised you're allowed to work here, Clementine,' one of the cleaners says. 'Students don't usually get jobs here.'

Clementine waves a fork towards her colleague. 'How many times do I have to tell you? Call me Clem. Shortening names is what "you people" do, isn't it?'

The Professor tries not to strangle her right there.

She continues. 'Daddy thinks working is character building. The principal agreed, not that anyone cares what he thinks. That man's no more educated than you. Daddy's seen his CV. The principal is a business manager, not an academic.'

The cleaners and kitchen staff give each other knowing looks. Since Clementine's employment began, they've held their tongues. In private, they mock her posh voice and endless tales of living in an enormous house in the country. What they don't know is her family now live in a terraced house on a residential estate.

Clementine's colleagues punish her snobbery by giving her the worst jobs. Scrubbing the toilets and hooking smelly gunk out of the shower traps are often on her task list. The domestic staff's hatred makes The Professor like them even more.

Dinner over, Clementine takes her plate to the kitchen. As usual, she leaves it in the sink for someone else to wash.

'That girl's too big for her boots,' a cleaner says after Clementine has left. 'She needs taking down a peg or two.'

Near the open door, The Professor smiles, willing to please. He will be seeing Clementine later to teach her a lesson.

* * *

Automatic doors swish open as The Professor enters a building. Clementine is right about one thing. The principal *is* an idiot. The lack of security across the campus is startling. Anyone can walk around without being questioned, although it's fair to say on this evening in the holidays hardly anyone is around.

Once again, The Professor considers why he's both drawn to and repelled by this place. Female students are the barrier to him truly belonging here. They steal his deserved spotlight as a knowledgeable man.

The sign for the library always makes his heart skip. Here is his domain. The library is the only area that has a key code to enter. It's not hard to get, considering it only changes once a year. Earlier that day, he was in here, making sure the cameras didn't work.

The fustiness of old books is like smelling salts to his stagnant mind. He skulks past familiar shelves boasting an array of books. Dust motes waltz in the air after he closes a copy of *Middlemarch*. In his hand is the treasured quote, ripped from the novel. Not adding his name to the bottom, as he used to, is excruciating. Pride could catch The Professor out, though, if he claims this death as his own too soon.

Clementine is closeted in a carrel. The wooden walls line the edges of the room, offering students privacy. He's seen heads bobbing over the slats to chat and do anything but study. Ungrateful bastards. Clementine always sits in the last carrel on the left. She shuts off from others, as if they're unworthy of looking at her. Her Converse-clad feet, shining with diamantes shaped in the letter *C,* swing across the floor.

As part of her job and being on site, she's responsible for locking up the library at night. Most evenings, Queen Clementine is here, acting as if she owns it. Wherever there are books, he belongs. She will no longer claim his property.

As he approaches, Clementine flicks her hair away from her shoulders. He pauses, visualising Jane's similar long brunette hair. Even when she's not there, Jane makes The Professor stop and consider his actions. He replaces the image with the hated Evangeline Glynn and advances towards Clementine.

THE PROFESSOR

After turning around, she says, 'Oh, hi', drawing out the sentence, as if talking to him is a chore.

They go through pleasantries about how they are and what they've been up to. He remembers to nod and offer acceptable sociable noises. Clementine then points at a picture on her laptop.

'Doesn't Bali look amazing? Daddy will say we can't afford it, but I know he'll find the money from somewhere. I'm adding it to my travel plans.'

At the mention of her altered plans, he can hear his blood whooshing inside his head. Previously, she told him in confidence about her family's fall from grace. She further confided she wanted to give up studying to travel. As he thinks about Clementine's selfishness, he holds his hands behind him, waiting for the best moment to strike.

With a click, Clementine opens an email she's composing. 'I'm telling my parents I'm quitting uni. They won't like it, but I have to follow my heart. Daddy keeps saying I must do well here, considering he scraped together the fees. Why can't he see I'm a free spirit? Read this and tell me what you think.'

The Professor scans the email. It's the final plot point of Clementine's death narrative. In her writing, she's offered a sob story about hours spent crying alone and feeling out of place. What she intends to be an explanation for leaving university could be read as a suicide note. It just needs a few more touches. He leans over, typing some extra wording.

'Why are you wearing gloves?' Clementine asks.

He smothers her mouth. Her body spasms. Frenzied hands flail. The clock on the wall warns someone will be here soon to lock up. The Professor locks his other arm around Clementine's throat and squeezes. She is still, but death is never the end for him. There's always a scene to complete. A scalpel slices along Clementine's wrist. Blood still flows at this early stage of death. It is glorious. White letters on the keyboard turn crimson.

He places the knife in Clementine's hand and lays the *Middlemarch* quote next to her head, slumped on the desk. It is perfect for a young woman who had no right deciding literature isn't enough.

"It was wicked to let a young girl blindly decide her fate in that way, without any effort to save her."

Young women aren't mature or masculine enough to make their own decisions. They need a teacher - a professor, to save them from making more mistakes. Now she's dead, Clementine will never mess up her life again.

The police will consider this suicide until The Professor warms up his murdering skills. Later, he'll willingly claim responsibility for this murder.

He regards Clementine's email and then presses *Send*. Her parents will cherish these last words from their daughter. Words are powerful. They make The Professor want to kill. And so he does.

CHAPTER 8
Jane

At university, I'm still fighting imposter syndrome, waiting for someone to tell me to leave. Dad keeps saying the other students aren't better than me. The rants about working-class people being better start whenever I share my fear of being out of my depth. Dad won't tolerate any affront - perceived or real - to his position. He's worked hard to build his businesses. Even this university has traces of his work in extensions, restorations, and patch-up jobs.

Oxford Carroll has been part of the local landscape for a long time. Before studying here, I'd never been inside. It doesn't have the town and gown stigmas linked to the much posher Oxford University. Oxford Carroll offers night classes and hires out rooms for meetings and activities. I've not had a reason to be here before, though.

Scanning the dining area, I assess those around me. A crescendo of shouting, laughter, and heated debates takes some getting used to. The food servers already look weary at this early stage of the academic year. After doing stints in pulling pints and waiting on tables, along with working in retail, they have my sympathy. Customers can be dicks sometimes.

My fears about being the oldest person here are unwarranted, despite most students being fresh out of sixth form or college. At twenty-nine, I'm in the middle place. Thankfully, this means I don't stand out. It also means I'm too young for the really mature students and too old for the kids. I wondered if I'd ever fit in. Then along came Leah, who's now walking towards me, balancing a full plate of food.

'How's it going?' She sits at my table.

I hold up my copy of Bram Stoker's *Dracula*. 'Oh, you know: blood; vampires; and bad ass women. The usual.'

Leah spears a sausage with her fork and takes a bite. She points to her mouth, rapidly chewing.

'Sorry. I'm starving,' she says after swallowing. 'I can't function without a second breakfast.'

'You're such a hobbit.'

She glances at my novel. 'I haven't started reading that yet. Guess I'll have to watch the film before tomorrow's seminar.'

'Henry will know. Remember how he shouted at Tom last week?'

Leah laughs. 'Yeah, but Tom deserved it for such a rookie error. Henry's face when Tom described the plot of *Twilight* was priceless.'

'I nearly pissed myself laughing. Henry's a hard taskmaster, though.'

'You have nowt to worry about. How come he's always extra nice to you?'

'I guess he's protecting his investment, considering his scholarship's paying for me to be here.'

'No. I think it's more than that. I've heard Henry's got a reputation for sleeping with students.' Leah pops a mushroom into her mouth.

I scrunch up my face. 'Ew. There's no way Henry thinks of me like that. He can be a bit of a perv with some women, though. Are you going to offer a juicy Bible quote about seducers and their sinful ways?'

She vigorously shakes her head. 'I believe in God, but I'm not a religious ranter. Flamin' well annoys me, seeing them in town, wearing sandwich boards and yelling that everyone is damned through a megaphone.'

THE PROFESSOR

'This is one of the many reasons why I like you.'

She picks up her phone from the table. 'Did you hear the latest on Clementine's death?'

'No.' I'm struggling to keep my voice controlled. 'I've already had to convince myself that coming to this university was safe after a student died here before the year started. I'm trying not to think about it too much.'

Since I was a child, death and I are enemies. Sometimes a random sickening panic at the nothingness of being dead takes over. Terror fills my lungs whenever I consider ceasing to be. The sneaky death phobia attacks when I'm at my most vulnerable, usually drifting off to sleep. Insomnia then thrives on the continuing dread.

Leah's cutlery clangs against an empty plate. 'A cleaner has returned after having time off. Right traumatised she was. She discovered Clementine's body. Now the cleaner's sharing what she found online.'

'You always have the gossip.'

'Don't tell my vicar. He'll give me one hell of a sermon.' She sniggers. 'The cleaner says there was a torn piece from a book next to Clementine. People have worked out it's from *Middlemarch*. I'll never read it again in the same way. Actually, I don't think I *have* read it. It's a bloody big book. Anyway, everyone's on social media saying Clementine's death wasn't suicide, but the police aren't taking it seriously. Makes me wonder exactly what the cleaner saw.'

Acidic coffee scratches down my throat. 'Seeing a dead body isn't something you can erase from your mind.'

Leah's eyes widen. 'Sorry. I should've thought before letting my big gob run away. Finding your mum like that must've been awful.'

Although we've known each other for a short while, we've shared many details of our lives. When this bouncy nineteen-year-old pocket rocket sat next to me on the first day, I thought we wouldn't have anything in common. It turns out she's more mature than I expected. We bonded over being down-to-earth and a love of baking. Leah's parents own a bakery in Haworth which is

Brontë country. She states bread, bakes, books, and the Brontës are her lifeblood.

'If Clementine didn't die by suicide, it means—'

'She was murdered.' Leah's tone is subdued. 'Sad as it is, it was most likely suicide. Don't let that put you off being here. Apparently, Clementine was right complicated. Talking of complicated…'

She tilts her head to indicate Henry approaching us. I've never seen him in the cafeteria before. Surely hob-knobbing with the students is below Henry Glynn.

He stands over Leah. She pulls her chair away.

'Dearest Jane and the lovely Leah! How are you both?'

'Fine,' Leah mumbles into the rim of her mug.

'Good, thanks,' I say.

Although I don't want to, I feel I owe him something, at the very least, politeness. In seminars, I rein myself in from giving the right answers, seeking his approval. No one likes the know-it-all who monopolises class time. Despite this, Henry often asks for my opinion. Last lecture I heard bitches sitting in the back calling me *the teacher's pet*. The double death stares from Leah and me made them stop. I'm determined not to be Henry's project. Dad's comments about how I'm beholden to the Glynns aren't helpful, either.

Henry checks his watch. Of course, it's a Rolex.

'Jane, could you come to my office at 3pm? We haven't had a tutorial yet.'

'Okay.'

I try to hide the disappointment at not being able to go to the library. Coming here is worth it for that building alone. Several floors filled with books are my idea of paradise. It's sad the death of Clementine lingers over it.

'I will see you, anon.' Henry marches away.

A group of female students giggle as he approaches. One of them pushes a pen off their table and exaggerates a gasp. Henry picks up the pen and hands it to the hunter. His fingers linger over her hand. He licks his lips in response to her doe eyes and gushing thanks.

THE PROFESSOR

Leah grimaces. 'Eurgh. It's like a nightclub around here, with people trying to get it on with each other, even the lecturers. Jane, mind how you go when you're on your own with Henry. I'm not convinced his intentions towards you are good. He's far too interested in you. It's kind of like an obsession.'

CHAPTER 9
Jane

Henry takes a seat. I check the door isn't shut behind me. Leah's warning about him lingers in my mind. University policy states all office doors remain open when the staff are with students, not that Henry cares for protocol. I've often walked past and seen through the windowed section of the closed door him with a woman in his office.

Pushing away a mountain of essays, Henry places his elbows on the desk. The antique piece, complete with a green leather top and blotter, isn't a surprise for someone who regularly takes his expensive stationery orders. The lecturers' offices probably have standard university issued furniture. There's nothing Henry can do regarding the smallness of the rooms, though. I bet it pisses him off. I can't help but feel a little pleased about it.

'Apologies for my lateness.' Henry glances up at the clock that confirms he's kept me waiting for thirty minutes. 'I had other business to attend to, which took longer than expected.'

'No problem,' I reply, although it is. I'm never late. In fact, I'm always at least ten minutes early. It's something Dad has instilled in me.

Henry forms his hands into a prayer position and rests his chin on his thumbs. 'How are you finding university?'

THE PROFESSOR

Despite wanting to be cool, I can't help bouncing in the plastic chair. 'I love studying and wish I'd done this sooner.'

'Sometimes we have to wait for the most fortuitous moments. This is part of your destiny, dear Jane.'

Henry has a habit of inflating sentences. Previously, I found his flowery language interesting. Since I've begun studying, I'm gradually seeing him in a different light. Henry's qualifications and knowledge are still impressive, but my learning is exposing the façade he's created. What I once believed was sophisticated speaking now seems affected. The hip flask he regularly swigs from isn't jaunty. It hints at a drinking problem. The designer and tailored clothing screams of wanting to be noticed as rich. Henry's bookshelves still have the power to amaze me, though. Being in here is always a treat. First editions of classics whisper to open them and read. Sadness washes over me. They'll never be mine and they're wasted here as ornaments.

'Are you enjoying *Dracula*?' Henry grabs a copy from on top of a filing cabinet.

I take the novel out of my rucksack. 'It's brilliant! After watching a lot of horror films, I thought it might be more of the same, but they have nothing on this. *Dracula* is steeped in beauty, longing, and the painful passage of time.'

'Wonderfully grasped!' He claps. 'Indeed, it's a text that reflects upon endings and if they ever truly are the end.'

'I've never been comfortable with endings.'

The room feels hotter. I suspect it's not only because I'm practically sitting on the radiator.

Henry leans in across the desk. 'Do tell.'

'Endings are sad. I struggle with letting go, finishing things, or saying goodbye. As a child, I sometimes cried when Mum finished reading a story. I'd hold the book to my chest, wanting it to dissolve into me so we'd always be together. Mum said a book never ends. It moves from the pages, into the mind and heart. She told me to close my eyes and asked what pictures I could see after reading. So many visions swam around in my head. Books *are* inside me.'

Henry throws his arms up. 'What a wonderful way of perceiving literature! Your mother was an astute woman. I expect you miss her terribly.'

Have I ever told him she's dead? Perhaps I mentioned it in conversation or he's noticed I refer to her in the past tense.

'Mum gave me my love of books.' I speak against the lump in my throat. 'Without her I wouldn't be here, studying.'

Leather squeaks as Henry reclines into his chair. 'I believe you were born for books. It's in your blood. The energising force of it is in you, Jane. Embrace this first module on Victorian literature. I want it to become as important to you as it is to me.'

I turn away from his stare. 'Are there any useful resources to help with my analysis of *Dracula*?'

'I have a list, but enough of that. Let's discuss you. What do you want from studying and life?'

'I'm not sure. As my sponsor, I guess you need to know your money won't go to waste.'

He smacks a paperweight down on the desk. 'Damn the money. It's not about that, despite Mother insisting I look after our investments. I'm interested in *you*.'

'But why? I'm just me, nothing special.'

'Oh, but you are. You're very important indeed. One day, the world will sit up and take notice of you.'

I offer a nervous laugh. 'I really don't think so. Besides, I hate being in the spotlight.'

Henry gets up and stands beside me, placing a hand on my shoulder. I try not to flinch.

'You have no choice. I know what's best for you. See this?' He taps a finger on my copy of *Dracula*. 'Learn more about the character, Mina Harker. Despite my difference of opinion with your friend, Leah, in the last lecture, I accept Mina is powerful. *You* are the modern Mina, with a man's brain and a woman's heart. Dearest Jane, you will become the perfect example of the educated female.'

CHAPTER 10

Jane is thriving. For now, The Professor allows it. The higher she rises, the harder the fall. She must not know her education makes him feel lesser. He will reveal his feelings through killing rather than directly to Jane. Every murder brings him closer to showing her the truth. For ten years, he's played a role of normality. He can't contain his true nature any longer.

Fiona is in his sights. Since freshers' week, when she showed compassion and talked excitedly about her dissertation, The Professor knew she was perfect. He prepares to meet with his very own Mina Harker from *Dracula*.

* * *

Spindly fingers of fear creep along the back of Fiona's neck. An empty student union creates an eerie atmosphere. Her annoyance with a lazy staff member increases. They'd agreed never to work alone. The pastoral team should be advocates of personal safety. Once again, Fiona's colleague hasn't turned up.

The broom cupboard masquerading as an office in the corner of the building is always dark. The extra lamps are useless. Despite her love of Gothic Horror, Fiona's a self-confessed coward. Being away from the bar and dance floor is a bonus in busier times. In the silence, though, it adds to the spookiness.

Since the academic year began, Fiona's mopped up students' tears and listened to their woes. The problems are often due to homesickness, heartbreak, or choosing the wrong course.

In the second year of her degree, Fiona became head of student pastoral care. She knows about her peers' issues because she's had many of them too. She came from Wales to Oxford Carroll to study history, but the lure of literature was impossible to resist. Soon after beginning studying, she switched to English Literature and enjoyed the best of both worlds. Books are steeped in history. Fiona never tires of researching the eras in which novels and poetry are written and set. Her Masters studies in the Victorian Gothic are endlessly fascinating. She envies the first-year students discovering Bram Stoker's writing. For a natural scaredy-cat, she adores *Dracula*.

A firm knock on the door makes her startle. She considers the wisdom of allowing the visitor to enter. Vampires need an invitation. While opening the door, she laughs.

'Hi there,' Fiona says. 'This is a nice surprise. Come on in.'

A creature of darkness enters.

CHAPTER 11

Fiona is drifting. Words become gibberish as he continues sharing his woes. Checking if she's real, she pinches the web between her thumb and finger. She can't feel anything.

An overwhelming urge to sleep overcomes her. Falling asleep on someone in need is rude. He's been hospitable, inviting her into his home. It's not Fiona's usual practice to take pastoral care outside of the university, but he's not a student. She's well-versed in safety procedures - particularly for women - but he wasn't comfortable being in the student union. She understood why. Also, he promised they wouldn't be alone in his house.

He sits across the room at a respectful distance. Fiona knows him. It should be fine.

And yet.

They *are* here alone. Will he be offended if she asks why? The emptiness of the house resurrects the earlier chill she felt in the office. Trepidation rose before he appeared. What does it mean? In response to a fleeting, dangerous thought, Fiona sharply inhales. The warning travelling to her mind dissolves.

Merlot sloshes in the fishbowl glass, swaying like choppy sea waves. The momentum is hypnotic. Fiona's head bobs along. His hand is there, propping up her chin. How rude he must think her having to check if she's awake. She takes another sip. His chatter becomes an unfamiliar language. The sofa offers an embrace. His voice is a soothing lullaby. She drifts and keeps drifting.

Fiona knows him. They've spoken many times. It should be fine.

And yet.

* * *

The saying to never return to the scene of the crime doesn't apply here. As The Professor regards the dilapidated mansion, his heart borders on bursting. Beauty can be found in decay. Moss feasting on stone mirrors his voracious appetite for ravenous revenge. Dank corners are dwelling places for his dark thoughts and deeds. Most of the roof has gone, exposing them to the sky. It allies with his uncontainable desire for murder.

Holding an unconscious Fiona in his arms, he shouts into the night sky. 'I'm back and this time I'll win!'

The damp reception room comes to life as he recalls laying a different woman's body there; Karin, his *The Turn of the Screw* governess. As he carries Fiona over his shoulder, The Professor remembers the silkiness of the black Victorian gown in which he dressed Karin. The plain, cotton nightgown Fiona wears is nothing in comparison, but everything has to be correct. In this part of *Dracula*, it's how the woman is clothed. Fiona is Mina Harker, Dracula's great love and nemesis.

Nostalgia from a former killing isn't the only reason for being in this place. The police need clues. A second death of a female student - linked to Victorian literature - isn't a coincidence. Clementine's demise won't be considered suicide any longer. The police will associate the recent killings with those that happened a decade ago. Can The Professor trust them to work it out, though? The detectives probably haven't read a book since they left school. Returning here and the effort it involves better not disappear into uneducated ignorance. Murder isn't fun if no one notices it.

Fiona's sleeping form lies on the floor where rugs purchased from the Orient once spread. He's seen photos of this mansion in its former glory. Now, he'll make it noteworthy again by recreating the scene where Dracula ravages Mina.

Not being able to use a bedroom tests his anger. Authenticity is compromised, but he's learned to adapt. Earlier visits confirm the stairs won't hold their weight. Time and woodworm have crept in. Only the hardiest of ramblers battle through the weeds and tall grass to come here. The pathway The Professor created is secluded enough to remain a secret.

He sends silent thanks to the eccentric, long-dead owner who led a solitary life. His will stated the building be left to ruin. If he couldn't enjoy it, no one else would. But someone *is* enjoying it very much. A stately building, at least eight miles away from anywhere else, feels like a gift.

The Professor splashes red wine on Fiona's virgin-white nightdress as if performing an exorcism with holy water. She's certainly not chaste or worthy of wearing pure white. The boyfriend who often stays overnight confirms it. Things were getting serious between them. Fiona shared this as sleeping tablets thickened her tongue. He wondered if mentioning her partner was a precautionary measure, a warning that there's someone out there who will notice her absence.

Merlot blots on the gown mimic bloodshed. While Dracula craves blood, The Professor isn't keen on making a mess. He'll make others bleed if it's necessary, though.

Life disappearing through his clasping hands is a thrill unsurpassed, but every detail has to be right. He must delay gratification. Mina's nightdress is stained with wine, mimicking blood drunk from the breast of a vampire. Mina had a thirst for Dracula as he offered himself to her. The Professor thirsts for Fiona to become his Mina.

A tool fit for the purpose punctures Fiona's neck. Behold the vampire's bite! Fiona's rousing groans make him smile. She will die here, within a setting so seamless he could cry at its beauty. He regards two torn-out quotes from a copy of *Dracula* he'll pin on Fiona's clothing.

"Her white night-dress was smeared with blood,"

"From her throat trickled a thin stream of blood. Her eyes were mad with terror."

The Professor will stake his claim. He laughs at the pun on how such a thing slays a vampire when stabbed in the heart. Nobody can ever kill him.

He signs his name underneath the quotes, confirming The Professor is well and truly back.

He cradles Fiona's jaw and thanks her for accomplishing the role. She has Mina's "woman's heart" with a pastoral care position, filled with kindness. The "man's brain" sealed her fate. Women have no business harbouring intellect and a passion for learning. The Professor is taking what's rightfully his.

The Professor grips Fiona's neck. She flails and then fails.

He smears wine-blood on Fiona's lips and cheeks. Then, he seizes her wrists to create the marks of Dracula's "terrible grip". It is done. Another female is destroyed for seeking knowledge.

The Professor is killing off Jane, one educated woman at a time.

CHAPTER 12

Jane

Henry bangs his fist on the wooden lectern. Even the snoozers in the back row of the lecture hall sit up.

'How can you possibly claim Mina is the most important character in *Dracula*?' Henry shouts. 'Where's your evidence?'

A student called Meredith - Henry's adversary - cracks her knuckles. Two seats along from her, I wince at the sound. Leah nudges me in the ribs. This will escalate. It always does. Rottweiler Meredith never lets go of an opinionated bone. Whenever Henry asks if there are any questions near the end of lectures, everyone groans. She not only has a list of questions but will give an in-depth analysis of her thoughts, too. Batting away Henry's anger, Meredith waves a copy of *Dracula* in her hand. Leah leans into me to avoid being smacked in the face.

'Mina's the New Woman role model Victorian females desperately needed,' Meredith begins. 'She symbolises elements of what the later suffrage movement aimed for: independence; not caring about staying slim; and not being defined by sexuality. Furthermore, Mina's relationship with Jonathan Harker is seriously lacking in passion. Yes, the era expected women to be chaste, but we all know many Victorians were secretly sexual. Not Jonathan, though. Mina would've got more seduction and satisfaction from a vibrator.'

Sniggers sound across the room.

Leah rubs her hands together. 'This is getting interesting,' she whispers to me.

Henry leans over the lectern and fixes Meredith with a penetrating stare. I can tell what he's doing. My discomfort rises at witnessing it.

'Meredith,' he says, 'while your activities with sex toys are fascinating, save it for home time.' He offers a wink and a sly smile.

She whacks her book down on the fold out desk in front of her, already in danger of snapping off its hinges. 'Stop objectifying me or other women! Mina's intelligent and savvy. She deserves respect, as do all women pursuing an education.'

Henry leaves the stage and marches towards her. 'Mina is submissive. She bows to the wants of men, telling them how brave they are, like a damsel desperate to be led. Her knowledge derives from what Jonathan knows, too. Do you understand, Meredith? Mina's learning comes from a man.'

'But she's smart in her own right.'

I almost fall out of my seat at Leah's contribution. Her usual activities in lectures consist of being quiet, making notes, and leaving as soon as possible.

Leah continues. 'The conventions of the era limited Mina, but she did the best she could. Despite Van Helsing admiring what he considered the male part of her brain, we now know, biologically, that's bollocks… I mean *incorrect*. Mina's cleverness is clear throughout, while Jonathan is easily seduced by the brides of Dracula. Mina becomes a smarter lass - er, woman - ready to confront Dracula. Men don't always have autonomy in education. Don't forget, Bram Stoker was a man who created a strong female character. He wasn't threatened by her, unlike some fellas.'

Cheering and applause break out. Leah puts down the pen she's waving and slumps. I know how hard it was for her to speak. She's uncertain about her ability to analyse literature. She earlier confided that being surrounded by "posh" southerners made her

THE PROFESSOR

feel insecure regarding her northern speech. Meeting other students from the North, and me confirming I'm far from sophisticated, has helped.

'You were brilliant.' I squeeze her arm.

Leah grins. 'I stayed up all night reading the novel rather than just watching the film.'

Henry moves even closer. 'Well, well, Leah. You're positively an academic. It's good to hear from you at last, with that "charming" northern dialect. Although, that outburst was akin to 1970s feminists burning their bras; overrated and outdated.'

Leah lowers her head.

Henry cracks his knuckles. 'Mina may have a mind that's trying to be like a man's, but it's the male who finally overcomes her. Dracula's feeding upon her body is him deriving power. For all her attempts at forging a New Woman identity, the man takes from Mina. Dracula overcomes her with his sexual potency.'

Before speaking, I take a breath. 'Doctor Glynn, firstly you're bordering dangerously close to supporting and advocating sexual violence. I'm sure you didn't mean that, right?' I pause.

Henry reddens. 'I… well… of course not.'

I nod. 'Glad we got that sorted. Also, I'm surprised at how rude you're being about female students. You might want to look around this room. Have you noticed how many of us there are?'

Leah and I look behind us. Waves and smiles from other women give me the courage to continue.

'Dracula isn't a man. He's a creature. When faced with something evil, *anyone* would be overpowered, whatever their gender or orientation. The novel shows they often are. We *can* fight back, though. Women have been doing so for centuries.'

'Not every woman lives to tell the tale, Jane.' Henry grabs his laptop and slams the door against the wall on his way out.

Lecture over.

CHAPTER 13

Velvet covering a wing-backed chair is smooth under The Professor's touch. It reminds him of a woman's soft skin. Still, it brings no comfort. The excitement of killing agitates his mind. Throughout planning, he lives in a state of unrest. After the release of a kill, it takes days to unwind. He doesn't want to forget, though. The Professor thrives on reliving the details of his murders, even if he can only do so alone. Fiona's death, as Mina from *Dracula,* was the greatest yet.

Jesus and the Virgin Mary judge him from a wall in Glynnholme's The Madam Mina Room. Religious symbolism aside, he's always hated the painting. It's fair to say The Professor and God aren't close. The pious, assessing eyes of mother and son bother him. He considers scratching their eyeballs out with a knife, like he did as a child with faces in newspapers. Unfortunately, the precious paintings are out of bounds. Everything in Glynnholme must be as Evangeline Glynn decrees. Much as it pains The Professor to abide by her rules, he accepts it's for a purpose. He can still claim Evangeline's rooms by giving them a new, deadly meaning.

If she hasn't already, Evangeline will eventually realise The Professor is back doing what he does best. Each Victorian literature-themed room in her house fulfils his agenda. Victims unknowingly await their role as characters in the rooms' stories and the texts after which they're named.

He regards the brides of Dracula caressing Jonathan Harker in an orgy of sex and violence. It's a picture he often admires. Evangeline asserts it depicts a man's downfall. She refuses to acknowledge Jonathan's ecstasy at the awakening of his sleeping lust. With the chaste and prudish Mina as his fiancée, the man was begging to get laid.

The Professor rests his hand on the mantelpiece but feels no heat from the fireplace. Instead, the inferno rages inside him. Clementine and Fiona have proved he's a better killer than before. The time away was occasionally unbearable. He feared he'd go mad with longing. Patience was indeed a virtue. His Victorian literature-related murders will never be forgotten again.

There's a detailed outline for future killings. Soon, The Professor will progress to the next novel. Above this room is Cathy's Chamber, the impetus for his next murder based on *Wuthering Heights*. The perfect trio of interior design, literature, and revenge will end in death.

CHAPTER 14
Jane

Lecture cancelled due to bereavement. Please go to the student union at 2pm if you wish to attend the memorial for Fiona Birch. The pastoral care team and university staff will be there to offer support.

I read the notice taped to the door of the lecture hall. Fiona Birch. The name sounds familiar. Has another student died? How? My mind races through possibilities.

Leah sidles up next to me. 'It's awful news about Fiona. This is getting right scary.'

'Who's Fiona?' Aware of other students milling around, I keep my voice hushed.

Some have red eyes and faces betraying sleep deprivation. Whether it's from grieving or too many nights out is uncertain. Stragglers whispering and lowering their heads replace the usual buzz. Leah leads me to a bench outside.

'Fiona was the head of student pastoral care,' she says.

As I place my bag on the ground, it tips over. Leah grabs my copy of *Dracula* and shoves it under her coat.

'What on earth are you doing?' I ask.

'I swear you don't hear uni gossip because you're always reading. This,' Leah becomes a flasher as she points at the book under her coat, 'is the reason Fiona died.'

THE PROFESSOR

'Don't tell me you believe in vampires!'

'Of course not, but some wrong 'un out there does. Fiona's body was discovered yesterday. She'd been missing for a few days, but her gormless boyfriend didn't report it. They'd had an argument. He thought he was getting the silent treatment.'

'What happened to her?'

Leah turns towards me, as if forming a shield. I wonder if it's against eavesdroppers or to protect us from the horror of another death.

'A man who travels across the country, photographing abandoned buildings, found Fiona's body,' Leah begins. 'It was in a derelict mansion in a little village you lot have loads of around here.'

'Says the person who lives in Haworth.'

'Yeah, yeah, but we've got the moors, too.'

As she gazes into the distance, I consider if she's mentally transporting to her special place. The moors are so entrenched in Leah's heart she could be a Brontë.

She continues. 'You'd expect when the photographer found Fiona he would've phoned the police straight away. The cheeky beggar took photos of that poor woman's body and the scene. It was all over social media. The principal's threatening to kick out anyone who shares the pictures. They've been deleted, but screenshots are still going around. I'll tell you this for nowt, stay offline for a while. You'll never unsee it.'

'What's the *Dracula* connection?'

Leah grimaces. 'There were puncture wounds in Fiona's neck. Someone was obviously trying to make it look like fang marks.'

'It might not specifically link to *Dracula*, though. Perhaps it's a weirdo who wants to be a vampire. I read an article in a magazine once. They drink each other's blood.' I screw up my face.

Leah scans the area before speaking. 'Fiona's body was staged like Mina when she's bitten by Dracula and then he makes her feast on him. The killer even dressed Fiona in a white nightgown with blood in all the same places as described in the novel. There was an extract left with the body; the one about Mina having a man's brain and a woman's heart. Makes me shudder thinking about how we were discussing it in our last lecture. I'm still right pissed off with how Henry lost his shit with Meredith and us for daring to tell him he's wrong. He was being such a sexist shit.'

'I agree, but surely you're not thinking Henry killed Fiona?'

Leah shrugs. 'I don't know. No, probably not. What's frightening is the name that was typed underneath the quote: *The Professor*. I looked it up online. He was a serial killer who killed women studying at Oxford Carroll a decade back. Lasses back then couldn't go anywhere, fearing for their lives.'

Why didn't I research this? In true Jane style, I looked into the university while filling in the application. Adding "serial killer" to the internet search terms wasn't something I considered, though.

'Perhaps it's a one-off,' I say. 'Maybe it's someone playing copycat, horrible as that is. Ten years is a long time to wait to kill again.'

'I don't know how those nasty bastards operate.' Leah's volume rises. 'Maybe The Professor was taking a break for some reason and has made a comeback. Two recent deaths of women from this university are worrying. The cleaner who found Clementine in the library doesn't believe it was suicide. The news is already focusing on how Fiona and Clementine's bodies both had literature quotes left with them.'

'I've just remembered who Fiona is,' I add. 'At an open day, she was so helpful. She made me feel better about being a mature student, explaining she began studying in her late twenties. Fiona spent ages chatting to parents, encouraging them to contact her whenever they needed.'

'She was good to me, too. At the beginning, I was homesick. Fiona contacted my parents. They sent stuff from home. Mum told me to give the teacakes to Fiona to say thanks. I ate them.' Leah blushes. 'Now I feel crap.'

She uses her sleeve to blot her tears. I hold her close, needing the comfort too. Our growing attachment makes me sad at being an only child. I've always wanted a sibling. I would love to have a younger sister like Leah.

'Let's go to the memorial,' I say. 'It's the least we can do for Fiona.'

THE PROFESSOR

After Leah hands over my copy of *Dracula*, I drop it into my bag. The killer's not only taken a life, he's stolen my love for this novel. A murderer called The Professor. How pretentious. Is he an academic or a wannabe? As we walk to the student union, it's not the snap of winter making me shiver.

CHAPTER 15

Gossip focuses more on the victims than The Professor's killing successes. Clementine and Fiona have received sympathy and dominate the media. He must not make mistakes based on pride. Eventually, the sensationalism of all the murders will take over. Years later, people will struggle to remember the victims' names. The Professor won't forget them, though. From the moment of choosing his prey, he lives and breathes them. They become part of his daily routine. He whispers their names when showering, eating, and as he drifts into sleep.

Fiery ashes rise into the night. He stokes the bonfire, watching it destroy Fiona's clothing. It reignites a murderous passion when recalling his version of Dickens' Miss Havisham. The memory of how Phoebe met *his* great expectations is always a delight.

* * *

Then

Mature students weren't any more difficult to fool than their younger counterparts. The "mature" aspect was often more of a label than a personality trait.

The Professor hadn't considered Phoebe until Evangeline Glynn's demands increased. She was so obsessed with lineage she refused to take her former husband's surname. She's a self-made academic and self-made bitch. Killing an infatuated student in the vein of *The Tenant of Wildfell Hall* and the student au pair, *The Turn of the Screw* style, weren't enough. Evangeline needed to receive and understand his message. The Professor was destroying her through the studious women who emulated her.

Like an answer to a sinful prayer, Phoebe entered his life. Satan was once a prominent angel in heaven. The Professor related to falling and being cast out. Self-proclaimed goddess, Evangeline, had taken too much from him. Phoebe would pay the penance.

With her long, chestnut hair, Phoebe was the right choice. Evangeline's similar hair had been glorious until she withered. In a parody of Miss Havisham, she hid in Glynnholme, safe from the world's gaze. But *he* saw her. Walls couldn't contain her secrets.

Phoebe was Evangeline's latest interest; the frightened and lowly Pip to the haughty Miss Havisham. Hours spent at Glynnholme, researching and talking with Evangeline, gave Phoebe hope. A new project was always her answer to escape the prison she'd created. After discovering a fresh idea, she sapped the life out of it. Masters studies were the first thing to keep her interest. They fed Phoebe little and often, with a hunger she *could* satisfy.

Assessing the damage of a cappuccino, Phoebe tried to stay calm. The dangerous skinny committee in her head stated the calorie count. Determined to stick to the path of recovery, she reduced the volume. The skinny committee dangerously bargained walking could redress the balance of consuming whole milk. Phoebe pressed her fingers against her temples, squeezing out judgement and choosing not to let an eating disorder win. She would focus on her love's company, not restriction. With him, she forgot to use a pedometer or up the pace. He'd given her a reason to walk for pleasure. *He* was pleasure, the clever man she called *Prof.*

* * *

The Professor snarled at Phoebe's laboured strides. Her slowness delayed their arrival at the destination. He exercised patience along with his body as they hiked, reminding himself of the outcome.

As she hauled a leg over a stile, Phoebe stumbled. She paused to catch her breath. Rather than helping, he inhaled her weakness. After taking a few puffs from her inhaler, she rushed to join him.

'Wow, it's beautiful,' Phoebe said as a building came into sight. 'Are you sure no one's in?'

Like a jailer, The Professor swung a keyring around his finger. 'I've already said they've gone away for a while and I can come here whenever I want.'

'You certainly have friends in high places.'

Despite the grandness of the house, he hated Phoebe for equating wealth with value. He was desperate to show the better view of a scene he'd created for her. Over winter, the owners went abroad and a skeleton staff lived out. No one was there at the weekend. While not a friend of the owners, The Professor had a key.

Hoisting the rucksack higher up his shoulder, he seized Phoebe's arm. 'Let's get moving. I can't wait for you to see what I have planned.'

* * *

Phoebe's body lay on the floor. Sunken eyes, shrouded by dark circles, had always been there. Sharp cheekbones would become more prominent as she decayed. The ghostly skin colour wasn't a consequence of blood loss from a head wound. She made for a disappointing corpse, but, oh my, how Phoebe could fly! A shove down the stairs and she hurtled. The satisfying crack of her skull striking the steps confirmed the end.

The Professor carried her to the master bedroom. The resting place reflected the house named Satis in *Great Expectations*. Phoebe became a lady of death, a Miss Havisham copy.

He held her in a perverted lovers' embrace while undressing her. The once-white silk gown she now wore - several sizes too big and yellowed with age - mocked Phoebe's past. Before she met

THE PROFESSOR

The Professor, her fiancé ended their relationship the day before the wedding. When Phoebe shared the story, The Professor knew he'd found his Miss Havisham. Both women had experienced the humiliation of being jilted.

Finally, Phoebe was free from all her demons except him. Time stopped. The watch on a chain, lying by her side, didn't have a battery. The hands were placed at twenty minutes to eight. As The Professor attached a veil and a garland of withered flowers to Phoebe's bloodied scalp, he considered mothers doing this for their daughters' bridal preparations. He laughed. A satin shoe fitted Phoebe, Cinderella style. The other was on a table like when Pip first visited Miss Havisham. By the dressing-table mirror, The Professor had previously arranged a handkerchief, gloves, more dead flowers, and a prayer-book. Every detail was perfect.

Flames nibbled at the hem of Phoebe's dress. The Professor beheld pure white charred black. A man's capacity to destroy a woman mesmerised him. The scent of burning flesh brought him back. Phoebe had to be identifiable so he could take the credit for the destruction. She couldn't be consumed by fire like her Dickens counterpart. Still, it was a fantastic sight. The Professor nodded to Phoebe as thanks for her services to literature. He pinned a quote from *Great Expectations*, complete with his name, to her outfit.

"I saw that the dress had been put upon the rounded figure of a young woman, and that the figure upon which it now hung loose, had shrunk to skin and bone."

The Professor switched off the light.

'Goodnight, Miss Havisham.'

CHAPTER 16

Jane

I offer the usual jokey request. 'Permission to enter?'

'Are you a vampire?' A voice asks from inside the shed. 'If you are, you're not coming in.'

The door bursts open and I startle. Dad appears, shaking his head.

'Sorry, love. That was insensitive considering what happened to that woman from your university.'

I step towards him. 'No harm done, although Fiona's death is bothering me.'

'Why?'

Dad walks past machinery and towards the back of the shed. This building is bigger than our lounge. When the council offered my parents the chance to buy the property they were renting, they jumped at it. The three-bedroom house and garden have a lot of space, but Mum joked Dad should live in the shed, considering how often he's in it.

'Fiona was such a lovely person,' I reply. 'She didn't deserve to die like that.'

'I had to stop reading the newspapers. It turned my stomach. There's no need to write such gory, disrespectful things.'

THE PROFESSOR

He picks up a chisel and starts shaping a piece of wood. Familiar smells of sawdust, paint, and turpentine are comforting. While I'd love to sit in here for ages, I never stay long. This is Dad's territory. Shavings fall on a newspaper spread out over the floor. I don't have the heart to mention Fiona's photo is showing on the front page.

'Promise me you'll be extra careful,' Dad says. 'This murder business is terrible.'

Despite my concerns, I force a laugh. 'I'm fine. Just because Fiona studied at Oxford Carroll doesn't mean I'll die too.'

He crouches to inspect his work. 'Still, two students have died recently.'

'I know. Clementine probably didn't die by suicide, as originally thought. There were literature quotes left at the crime scenes of both students. Everyone's talking about a sicko called The Professor doing it. His name was underneath the quote he'd pinned to Fiona's clothing.'

Dad's nostrils flare. 'I'm worried about you being at that university. Keep your old man happy by being safe. Call me if you ever feel threatened by even the smallest thing. There are some twisted bastards out there. This world is getting more dangerous every day.'

This lecture will continue for hours if I allow it. Anything to do with The Professor makes my stomach churn too.

'What are you working on?' I point at a covered form.

'All will be revealed. Too soon to say at this point, but it might be my best work yet.'

I notice a figure next to the project. Her resin face is pale. Dad's eye for detail is unsurpassed. He hates his figures being referred to as dolls, asserting it diminishes them. Dolls are for children to play with. Dad's figures and houses are exhibition pieces, encapsulating reality. Measured strokes of a tiny brush bring his miniature people to life.

I look at the stricken figure lying on her back. The waif stares, as if searching into my soul.

'She reminds me of Cathy from *Wuthering Heights*,' I say, 'Ghostly and desperate.'

Dad doesn't look up. 'I'll take your word for it. Books are your area of expertise.'

'It's one of my favourite novels.'

'Not to my taste. A bit depressing. I'll stick to listening to Kate Bush singing about it.'

'Do you believe in ghosts?'

'Load of twaddle. Once you're dead, that's it.'

He sits in the rocking chair Mum nursed me in when I was a baby. Sometimes I admire his no-nonsense attitude. I've inherited some of it in how I deal with difficult people. Kate often asks me to deal with irate customers.

Dad fixes his eyes on me. 'Spill it, Jane. You only come in here when you want something or you're upset.'

'Funny how we're talking about *Wuthering Heights*,' I begin, 'as the drama department has asked if you could—'

'No.' He picks up momentum in the rocking chair.

'Hear me out first.'

Dad holds up a hand. 'After what *that* man did, I'm never going there again.'

I'm still annoyed with Henry for ruining everything. Dad was constructing sets for the university's production of *Wuthering Heights*. With me helping, it was a great way to spend more time together. Previously, we'd gone beyond ships passing in the night and were in different ports. Mum wouldn't have allowed it to happen. As the centre of our family, she held us together. Dad fills time doing carpentry jobs, making dolls' houses, or going to the pub. I'm either working in the shop or at the university. I want us to be closer, to honour how Mum prioritised family.

'If I talk to Henry about his behaviour, will you reconsider?' I ask.

The chair propels behind Dad as he stands. 'He had me getting things for him like a dog fetching a ball for its master.'

'Although it's not an excuse, Henry's used to others waiting on him.'

'Sodding toffs and their selfish ways,' Dad grumbles. 'I'm not Henry Glynn's servant! He showed me up in front of everyone.'

THE PROFESSOR

I cringe, recalling how a commotion began while I was painting the set. Henry kept calling Dad, *Larry the Lamb*. I remember Mum calling him the name once in jest. They had an almighty row. Dad shouted that he never wanted to hear the insult - making him sound pathetic and weak - ever again.

Henry didn't need to be in the drama studio that day. He's not involved in the play but insists on checking everything is true to the novel. Throughout the afternoon, he tested how far he could push everyone. For a while, Dad resisted a fight by hammering nails hard.

'I walked away with my head held high,' Dad asserts.

'Henry deserved it. After you went, a drama lecturer told him to get lost. He flounced off in a huff.'

Dad laughs. 'I bet he did.'

'Serves him right.'

The final insult was when Henry handed a black bag to Dad and instructed him to pick up rubbish. I applaud Dad for not ramming the bag into Henry's mouth. If he'd done that to me, he would've needed surgery to remove it from his arse.

Dad points at the covered project 'I've got a lot on at the moment, but I'll do a few bits for the play here if they're transportable.'

He grabs a saw and approaches a plank of wood. I join him. Dad flings the saw down.

'Jane, you know better!'

I hold my hands up and move aside. 'Sorry.'

From a young age, he's warned me to stay back when he's using equipment. I wonder if *I* need a tool to unleash my frustration. Henry won't get away with hurting my dad. We're all we've got. I'll always fight to protect what's mine.

CHAPTER 17

Grace checks her work. She searches for mistakes and, as always, finds many. Perfectionism can wait until tomorrow. She massages her neck and shoulders, feeling the strain of reaching high for hours. The top of the set's walls won't be visible through the stage curtain pelmet. Grace will know if she skimped on it, though.

The *Wuthering Heights* play has become her purpose. She lives, dreams, and breathes creating Cathy's chamber. Even English Literature students couldn't have analysed chapter three in as much detail as Grace has. She takes this as a win for the art students who are often viewed as weird hippies, stoners, and wasters.

Standing at the back of the drama studio, Grace curses its smallness. Those sitting in the front row will notice any flaws in her painting. The bedroom setting is claustrophobic - as the novel demands - but it does perfection no favours. The beauty of sprawling landscapes is more Grace's style. After completing this set, she can't wait to create the moors where Cathy and Heathcliff roam and fall in love. Still, Grace knows she must complete a project before beginning another. She decides to spend the rest of the evening learning more about painting domestic scenes. The room where a ghostly Cathy haunts an unwelcome visitor, Lockwood, will be Grace's masterpiece. Forget the actors. This is her time to shine under the spotlight.

THE PROFESSOR

In her local school's sixth form, Grace was the proverbial big fish in the little pond. Her artistic skills received regular praise. Since starting university, she's a tiny fish who forgot how to swim, drowning in self-doubt. Discovering others in her year group are equally, if not more talented, bruised her ego. Grace's tutor advised her to find her own path and to stop the constant comparisons. Frustration led to paving her way elsewhere by seeking sexual validation. When men desire Grace, she enjoys the approval. Her latest conquests are seductive secrets she'll never share.

Grace regards the window where the ghost of Cathy pleads to be allowed in. Grace would rather be set free. Low self-esteem dictates she has no right to study here. Negative thoughts speak in her father's voice. It's difficult to dazzle in the shadow of a renowned artist. When Grace applied to study at Oxford Carroll, her father was appalled. From childhood, the expectation was for her to follow his famed footsteps at Central St Martin's in London. She needed her own route, though, made by her imprints. Now she questions the decision.

As she returns to the stage, Grace notices litter scattered across the floor. Students can be such pigs sometimes. She fills a rubbish bag, expecting to repeat the process later in the communal kitchen in halls. Although she's the same age as the other residents, Grace feels ten years older. Where is her peers' respect? They're supposed to be the generation who wants to save the planet. Grace fears for the future, left to those who won't empty overflowing bins, let alone knowing which one's for recycling.

Thank goodness for her rescuer. He takes Grace away from all her problems. Their time together makes life more tolerable. He's even arranged somewhere nicer for her to live next term. Thinking of him dissolves her anger. Grace continues to defy her parents by getting her own digs and sleeping with inappropriate men. She's never been good enough for her father, so she might as well live down below his expectations. Trying to live up to them has been exhausting.

As she turns off the lights, an undercurrent of sadness rises. Bubbles of worry and inadequacy threaten to travel from her stomach and burst out of her mouth. So far, she's held the screams at bay. Tonight, Grace will let it all out as if it's her last night on earth.

CHAPTER 18

The next victim isn't an English Literature student. It isn't a failure on The Professor's part. Genius is about to take place.

Wuthering Heights is a novel bursting with brutality. He has an affinity with it, alongside *The Professor* by Charlotte Brontë. The Professor fancies himself as a bit of a Heathcliff. Like Emily Brontë's enigmatic character, no one really knows who The Professor is. While seemingly harmless, he's the master of everything. Violence gets what he wants, especially when masquerading as love.

An earlier viewing of Glynnholme's room named Cathy's Chamber convinced him he can do this. This will be an elaborate murder scene. The Professor won't be hindered by the limitations of a stage set. Unlike Evangeline Glynn, his interpretations of literature can't be contained in small spaces. As in the novel, his Cathy will reach into the bedroom, looking for Heathcliff. The Professor defeats a woman's goal. Dead females can't achieve anything.

Grace slings a black bag into a wheelie bin. Hedges and trees shield The Professor as he watches her behind the drama department building. There are no security cameras here. He's confident most of the cameras on campus and in halls don't work. The university continues putting financial needs above safety. The Professor wishes he could thank the penny-pinching principal.

The library cameras were switched off in the summer holiday, making killing Clementine easy, too.

After banging the bin lid shut, Grace checks her mobile. The screen lights her face in the gloom. She smiles as her thumb swipes up the screen. The Professor creeps forward. Slow, silent steps. His hand reaches out. A tap on her shoulder. Grace turns around. She drops the phone.

'What are you doing here?'

The question is understandable. It's taboo for them to meet here. The Professor doesn't answer. The snapping of Grace's neck is the only sound.

Grace is, thankfully, petite. He barely felt her weight on top of him when they had sex. While carrying her, he considers the idea of the soul leaving the body after death, making it lighter. He'd rather not think about the inner self. Analysing his soul would drag him into a dark pit. There isn't time either. Soon, someone will appear to lock up the drama studio. From previous observations, The Professor knows he has an hour at most. He puts on a balaclava as a precautionary measure.

This victim doesn't have a costume. What The Professor's planning won't need it. When the *Wuthering Heights* play was confirmed, he recognised fate. Not only does he have a ready-made setting, he's also killed its creator. Another female who thinks she's superior to him is gone. Grace pretended not to care about being the daughter of a famous artist. The false humility grated on The Professor.

As he takes Grace to the stage, he recalls Lockwood sleeping in Cathy's chamber, within the confines of a coffin bed. So much death and now Grace is joining in! The Professor runs a scalpel down her arm. Memories of slashing Clementine's wrist mingle with Grace's actual blood. The glory of killing Clementine compels him to continue.

While bringing her corpse to the window of Cathy's room, he admires Grace's work. It's all there, like in the book: a wooden chair; clothes press; an oak case with squares that looked like coach windows; and a panelled bed. The faithful details make him want to weep with joy. The Professor had considered placing

Grace inside the closeted bed. Discovery of the hidden corpse was a delightful prospect, but it's not correct. The bed is the man, Lockwood's, domain. The woman must know her place, shut out of a man's world.

Grace will stand on the outside of Wuthering Heights, with her arm smashed through the window. The Professor hefts blocks to create support, keeping her upright. Sweat pools down his back and face. The balaclava is itchy, but he won't take any chances. He takes a breath. Grace's head slumps forward. Enjoying the effect, he leaves it there, and then balances her arm on the shattered window. Lockwood's frenzied rubbing of Cathy's wrist – to keep her out - against the glass is complete. Blood smears on Perspex remind him of the paint Grace used to apply to a canvas.

As Grace did earlier, The Professor stands at the back of the studio. He beholds the scene. It's not quite right. He's forgotten Cathy's book! From his bag, he pulls out a text. Earlier, he risked using his non-writing hand to scrawl variations of Cathy's name inside, just as she had done. A piece of paper bookmarks a page. Upon it is a quote, detailing Heathcliff's misery at Cathy's ghost visiting Lockwood and not him, "'Come in! Come in!' he sobbed. 'Cathy, do come. Oh do - once more. Oh! My heart's darling, hear me this time - Catherine, at last!'" Of course, The Professor has signed his name underneath.

Heathcliff was desperate for the long-dead Cathy to enter his home and life again. The Professor invites women in too, to their demise. Cathy wanted too much. She paid for it with her life. The Professor brings death to women who seek more than they deserve, too.

From the bottom of the stage stairs, he looks up at Grace and smiles. The Professor is cleverer than Heathcliff. Obsession was Heathcliff's downfall. If used well, obsession can be good. It gives a person purpose. The Professor thrives on fixation, but with caution. In the quiet years where he took a break from killing, losing his identity was unbearable. Now, there will be no more doubt. The Professor is back, doing what he does best.

CHAPTER 19

Jane

Kate turns off the radio and lets out a long sigh.

'What's wrong?' I dare to ask.

She's been stomping around the shop, made more obvious by her tall and stocky frame. Customers often remark when we're standing together on our differing heights and build. Kate tells them firstly not to be rude and to never underestimate me. I may be small, but I'm a tenacious terrier when provoked. My anger simmers for a while. When it reaches boiling point, you'll know about it. Too bad for Henry that he's on my shit list for mistreating Dad and for being misogynistic in the recent lecture on *Dracula*.

Kate counts notes in the till drawer. 'Quiet today. It's hardly worth opening.' The counter rattles as she slams the till shut. 'The last thing I need is to be stressing about the business. I have enough to worry about already.'

'Sam?' I ask.

She nods. 'Sam.'

She walks away. Aware of the routine, I pick up my copy of *Wuthering Heights* and transport to a stifling hot kitchen, with dogs at my feet, and Nelly Dean's narration. Mum believed Nelly was the hero of the story. Sure, she has faults. Sticking her nose into other people's lives is one, but Nelly prospers. While Cathy, Heathcliff, Edgar, Isabella, and Linton are destroyed, Nelly's like the "eternal rocks beneath" Cathy likened her love for Heathcliff to.

Mum said heroes are often those who seem the least likely. True heroism is acknowledging your fears and weaknesses and still being brave. She considered calling me *Nelly,* but Dad was appalled. He thought it sounded silly and no daughter of his would bear the name of a housekeeper. He declared while there's no shame in the job, he wouldn't give me a low station before I got started in life. So I became Jane. Mum still won. I'm a product of our beloved Brontë sisters and named after a strong character, Jane Eyre, too.

Kate appears, carrying mugs of hot chocolate topped with marshmallows. Comfort is inside a cup. I shut the book, leaving Nelly Dean to her stories, and prepare for Kate's latest upset. She places a high stool across the counter. This is our set-up for heart-to-hearts. Sometimes, Kate forgets to move when a queue's forming behind her. When detailing how her children are doing her head in or Sam's being a lazy git, Kate's immersed in annoyance. It isn't arrogance. She's well-liked by our customers. Occasionally, the regulars join in, offering advice.

After setting down the mugs, she pulls out bars of Dairy Milk from her pockets and aims them at me. 'I'm bringing out the ammo.'

'Thanks.'

Before Kate decides she needs both, I take one. I dip it into its liquid counterpart, achieving the peak moment of melting but not becoming sludge. This is an experiment I've cracked over the years.

'Sam's going out most evenings, spouting bullshit that he's working out.' Kate snaps off a chunk of chocolate between her teeth.

'He might be.'

'Is he bollocks.'

Her corkscrew curls shake. Medusa is ready to inflict her wrath with her snaked hair. Sam is screwed. Kate picks up the elastic band ball she's creating, which is currently the size of an orange. Each stretch and snap of a band is therapy. I fear we'll have no bands left if Sam keeps being an arsehole.

'My husband's so cocky that he doesn't bother making up believable lies,' Kate begins. 'I called the gym last night, pretending I needed Sam for an emergency. The bloke on reception looked up if he was there. Sam hadn't checked in. Can you believe the receptionist bloke tried to sell me a gym membership based on Sam not attending for months? The twat said it could give Sam the incentive to exercise if we went together. As if I have time! If I'm not working, I'm tending to the kids. The only time I go to the toilet without an audience is here. I adore my children, but if I had to spend all day with them, I'd go nuts. When I drop them off with Sam's mum, I practically kiss her feet. She loves looking after them. Of course she does. They never act up for Granny.'

'Have you confronted Sam about not being at the gym?' I ask.

After a liberal slurp of my drink, I puff out a breath. Clearly, I need to do more research on the best drinking temperature.

'Not yet,' Kate replies. 'Sam left before I'd woken up. He sent a message saying he was catching up on admin. Another lie. The estate agents are quiet at the moment. He's constantly moaning about it.'

'You *are* going to talk to him, right?'

Kate's chosen to ignore his affairs before. Beyond Sam's cheeky grin and grooming, I don't understand what she - or other women - see in him.

'I have to confront him.'

Kate covers her face with her hands. I hug her as she weeps. Then she takes a tissue from her pocket and blows her nose. The trumpet sound breaks the tension.

'Flaming men,' Kate says. 'You're better off without them, Jane.'

Through the window, I spot a familiar person approaching.

I begin moving away. 'Sorry to ask, but could you do me a favour? Henry's coming. Say I'm not in.'

'Fallen out with your bestie?' Kate calls as I run. 'Did he give you a crap grade on an essay?'

THE PROFESSOR

The door peels from its hinges. Kate considered getting a bell above it but decided we'd never miss a customer, anyway. They have to unglue the door first.

I lurk in the back room. Having a chat with Henry has to happen eventually, but I want to be prepared. He's renowned for manipulating people with his words. When I rip into him for how he treated Dad, I don't want Henry's smoothness to take over.

'Is Jane not working today?' His voice travels. Even basic questions are delivered with gusto.

'Not today,' Kate replies. 'Sorry, it's just me. Want to place an order?'

'Yes, please. How are you, gorgeous Kate?'

'Fine.' Her brashness betrays how much she wants him to piss off.

'You look a little flustered. I love it when a woman blushes around me.'

'I just had a ruddy good bawl, so don't push it.' Hurt overrides politeness. Sam's really done it this time. Kate is never rude to customers, particularly those who spend a fortune.

'Anything I can help with?'

Henry's pervy drawl makes me cringe.

'Not unless you can stop my husband from being a cheating pig.'

Time for an intervention. I'll pretend I'm on an afternoon shift and came in from the back. If I leave Kate with Henry much longer, we'll lose his custom.

Chaka Khan sings about being every woman. The idea of it sounds exhausting. Kate responds to her ringing mobile.

'Hi there. He's what? Really? Yes. I'll be there soon. Jane!'

I inject a bounce in my step as if fresh and ready to start work.

'Well-timed.' I avoid Henry's glare. 'You must've heard me arriving.'

Kate stares at her phone as if it's a bomb set to go off. 'I have to go. Can you hold the fort, lock up, whatever, please?'

'No problem.' I move her aside. 'What's happened?'

She lets out a maniacal laugh. 'I can't believe it. Sam's been arrested.'

'What on earth for?'

'He phoned his mum from the police station because he's too scared to speak to me.' The bitter tone makes me glad not to be her other half. 'Another student was murdered yesterday evening. The police have evidence Sam was sleeping with her and think he killed her, along with the other two women.'

'I… No way. He can't be The Professor!'

Kate grabs her keys and wallet from the shelf and dashes outside.

Fingers click in front of my face. 'I'm still here.'

As my eyes narrow, Henry removes his hand.

'Awful news regarding Kate's husband,' he says.

'That's private.'

His megawatt smile sparks. 'Whisper better, my dear. So, Sam's been a naughty boy. Glad I'm not the only one.'

CHAPTER 20

Jane

I keep busy tidying the till area. Better this than to rage at the person who's financing my studies.

'What does a chap have to do to place an order around here?' Henry taps his fingers on the counter. 'I certainly don't come here for the coffee. That cheap rubbish out of a jar tastes like dirt.'

As I turn to face him, I can't contain it any longer. 'Why are you always so bloody rude?'

His eyes widen. 'I can categorically state I've *never* been disrespectful to you. Where's this anger coming from?'

'The last lecture on *Dracula*, you said some awful things about women. I was ready to thump you when you skirted far too close to supporting sexual violence.'

Henry's laugh is shaky. 'You certainly put me in my place.'

'I reckon it's all a big act with you,' I begin. 'You enjoy playing up to the sexist lothario image, but you're better than that. I know you can be kind, too. Why don't you let others see it more? Are you afraid of others knowing the real Henry?'

His cheeks redden. While he's silent, I decide to unleash all my annoyances.

'Also, you were horrible to my dad when he was constructing sets for the *Wuthering Heights* play. It was kind of him to give up his time. You treated him appallingly.'

'Only banter.' Henry chuckles. 'Isn't that what you people call it?'

'Who exactly are "you people"?' I can feel my nostrils flaring.

Henry checks his watch. 'Must we do this now? I don't want to be late for my lecture.'

'Yes, we must. Here's a lecture for you, Henry Glynn. You're a cruel snob who I don't want to be associated with any further than is necessary. Much as I appreciate the financial support, I will pay back every penny. Consider it a loan rather than sponsorship.'

'Is this the famous working class pride I hear of?'

I try not to slap the cocky smile off his face.

'Oh, piss off. Look, thanks for helping me get into uni and for financing it. When the degree ends and I have a full-time job, I'll make monthly repayments.'

Henry's bottom lip protrudes. 'It's not necessary, but whatever makes you happy. Please accept my apologies for offending your father, too. I let my rude behaviour go too far. You're right. I should be more considerate of other people's feelings. Sorry. I'm a bit of a shit sometimes.'

'A bit?'

'Okay, an enormous turd.' He kneels and grabs my hands. 'Please forgive me, Jane. Please, please. I'll alter my behaviour.'

I release my hand and try not to laugh. 'Stand up, you idiot. Don't think you can worm your way around me that easily. Show you mean what you say about changing. I'll be keeping an eye on you.'

Henry stands and dusts off his trousers. 'Dreadful news about Kate's husband. Do you believe he killed those women?'

Do I? There's no denying Sam's a cheat, but a murderer? Also, his strength is in using his dick, not his brain. Why would he call himself *The Professor* and be obsessed with literature?

'The principal's holding a briefing tomorrow,' Henry says. 'Apparently, the woman who recently died is an art student called Grace.'

THE PROFESSOR

Typical Henry. He's worked alongside Grace for the past few weeks, setting up the play, and didn't acknowledge her existence. Icy fear crushes my chest. I knew her. Sure, she wasn't a friend. Neither was Fiona. I interacted with both of them, though, and saw them alive. Now they're dead.

Henry frowns. 'You're very pale. Are you okay?'

'Not really. If Sam's a murderer, Kate's going to be devastated. If it's not Sam - and I hope it isn't - how safe are female students?'

'Indeed.' Henry fiddles with his tie. 'The university's going to offer self-defence classes. Perhaps you should sign up. Look after yourself. You're a precious commodity.'

'Please don't liken me to an object that can be bargained with.'

'As if I'd dare. Are you still enjoying studying?'

'Yes, despite the killings.'

Images of Fiona, Grace, and a newspaper pic I saw of Clementine enter my mind. They'll never open a book, attend a seminar, or pursue their passions again.

'Your seminar contributions and essays indicate an affinity with Gothic literature,' Henry says. 'Juicy stuff, isn't it?'

I wonder why I'm embracing darkness in my current reading. It's odd for someone who's seized by a numbing dread when considering dying. Maybe enjoying the Gothic will help me to accept death.

'Dear girl,' Henry begins, 'Studying Victorian literature is something you could flourish in. Use me to help you, along with my mother. I've been telling her about you.'

'Why?'

'On rare occasions, Mother takes one of my students under her wing.' He blows a raspberry. 'I must admit, though, what she doesn't know about Victorian literature isn't worth knowing. *Never* tell her I said that.'

'Careful, your mummy issues are showing.'

He leans in towards me. 'Don't *ever* say that again!'

I edge away. 'Thanks, but I'll pass on being your mum's pet project. I don't want to owe your family anything else.'

'You'll be doing Mother a favour. Rattling around Glynnholme bores her. Nothing gives her greater pleasure than sharing her love of books.' Henry offers a business card giving Evangeline's details. 'Email to make an appointment. One of Mother's minions will sort it out.'

Tired of this conversation, I shove the card in my pocket. 'I'll think about it.'

Henry places a typed list on the counter. 'Here's my stationery order. Seeing as I already have heartburn, let's give coffee a miss. Don't miss this opportunity to meet Mother. She'll be most disappointed. Strangers aren't allowed at Glynnholme, apart from those she handpicks. *You* could become Evangeline Glynn's most prized protégé.'

CHAPTER 21
Jane

When I began the degree, the noise in the university library was surprising. Previously, I imagined a respectful silence. As a child, attending the local library was a pleasure, but the librarians made sure people were quiet. While in the uni library, I've learned to stick ear buds in and listen to music. It's a place to chat, debate, or blare out crap tunes. The enclosure of a carrel offers some privacy, although no one sits where Clementine died. Whenever passing it, I try not to search for bloodstains. Since the police began treating the death as murder, the killing spot is spookier. The Professor was here. Surely, he killed Clementine, even if he didn't sign his name at the bottom of the *Middlemarch* quote he left with her body?

A recent safety briefing increased my concerns. A conflict between following the police's advice and keeping Oxford Carroll running was obvious. Throughout addressing Fiona's murder, the principal downplayed the violence and even hinted she was at fault for being out alone at night. To a chorus of jeers, the vice-principal ushered him off the stage, her face full of thunder at her colleague. The drama studio is closed while the police collect evidence. I was shocked we're allowed to come in today, but that's the principal for you.

Leah slams down a mountain of textbooks before grabbing a chair. 'Budge over.'

'Er, personal space,' I say as she nudges up close.

'No such thing around here.' She points at a young woman sitting on a lad's lap. Their arms are locked around each other's necks. Snake tongues flick into their mouths.

'Eurgh.' I mimic retching.

Leah leans in towards my laptop. 'Why are you looking at stuff on Evangeline Glynn? Hey, is she related to Henry?'

'She's his mother. They're the Glynns of Glynns' Confectionery.'

Leah slaps her forehead. 'I should've figured it out. We sell their sweets in our bakery.'

'Since Charles Glynn - the creator - died, those who've inherited used managers to run the business. From what I've read so far, I expect Evangeline keeps a close eye on things, though.'

'You research the hell out of everything. I swear you were born for the academic life whereas I'm winging it.'

Scrolling down the screen, I stop at a particular photograph. 'Wasn't Evangeline stunning there?'

Evangeline reclines on a chaise longue. Lustrous curls a shampoo advert marketing team would be excited about lay on her shoulders.

'She's certainly a good-looking lady,' Leah replies. 'Reminds me of Lizzie Sidall.'

'Who's she?'

Leah scrolls through her phone and holds it up to show a painting. 'I love Pre-Raphaelite artists. Lizzie Sidall was a model and artist in that era. Get a load of that amazing red hair. Evangeline has a similar look, with pale skin, chestnut hair, and not having much meat on her bones. Bet you recognise this painting. Siddall was the model.'

I compare the reclining Evangeline to John Everett Millais' depiction of Ophelia lying in a river, waiting to drown. Both women's images have glassy eyes, but their faces and bodies hint at an unmet passion lurking underneath.

'There don't seem to be any recent photos of Evangeline online,' I say. 'Wonder what she looks like now.'

'Why are you cyberstalking Henry's mum?'

'She wants to meet me.'

'Really?'

'Be quiet!' The girl snake who was devouring her serpent companion glares at us.

Leah stands up. 'Shut your cake hole and get a room! This isn't a hook-up spot.'

Boy snake has the grace to blush. Leah and I give them double death stares. The snakes slither outside.

'Back to Evangeline,' Leah says. 'Why's she interested in you?'

'Henry's been bigging me up as a Victorian literature buff. It's so embarrassing. Victorian lit is the first module. I've hardly started.'

Leah lays a hand on a ring binder full of my notes about the era. 'It's obvious you're really into the Victorian stuff, though. Are you going to see Evangeline?'

'I don't know.'

I focus on the woman glaring back from the screen. Jade cat-like eyes demand attention. The sense of ownership, even from a device, is disturbing. Is the real-life version as commanding?

'Get a load of this.' I click on a tab.

'Woah! Henry lives *there*? The lucky bugger. Glynnholme is incredible, or "reet grand" as my dad says. Whereabouts is it?'

'In an Oxfordshire village called Quillington.'

I share shots of the area. Fields and woods surround a tiny catchment of buildings. Thatched cottages and winding, narrow lanes are the norm.

'Think I'll dust off my walking boots and check it out.' Leah puts her feet up on the desk. I push them off. 'Sorry, boss.' She grins.

I tap my pen against my mouth. How will Dad react if I visit Glynnholme? After the way Henry treated him, Dad won't like it. "Have courage, Jane". It's what Mum said when I was worried or afraid. I'm not scared of Dad, but I hate letting him down. No.

I've begun studying. I'm taking charge of my life. My needs come first now.

'I'm doing it.' I take out a business card from my wallet.

'Good for you,' Leah says. 'Remember, keep your hands in your pockets and don't steal the family silver. The Glynns will be on the alert for paupers. I'll just skulk in the woods nearby as an outcast.' She smacks a hand on her pile of books. 'Got to go. These are well overdue. See you later.'

Engrossed in composing the email, I raise my hand by way of goodbye. I'm only writing a few sentences, but I can't bear the thought of Evangeline finding typos or grammatical errors.

It's done. I'm going to Glynnholme and meeting the mysterious Evangeline Glynn.

CHAPTER 22

Evangeline sweeps her finger along the books and checks for evidence. After decades of service, Rupert is finally paying more attention. She won't abide treasured tomes being covered in dust. It's not as if Rupert has to do the cleaning, just direct the housekeeper, Mrs Patterson. Even that he sometimes gets wrong.

Having an old chum as a servant can be beneficial. It's also somewhat tiresome. Rupert dotes on Evangeline. She loves having people waiting on her. Rupert prefers the title of "companion", even though his employer doesn't seek company. For his loyalty, Evangeline allows the over-inflation of his role. He's stuck by her throughout the worst of times. After a previous housekeeper left in the wake of "all that business", Evangeline needed a discreet ally.

She's aware Rupert becomes loose lipped after too many glasses of brandy. The fool thinks he can hide the bottles. The weakness gives her strength. If he's tempted to share her damning past, Evangeline will fire Rupert under a scandal of alcoholism and worse. He'll also go to prison. Unfortunately, she would be there too. So, she tolerates the infuriating man. Kicking out a lovesick puppy is cruel, even by her standards. For years, she's known he's desperate to have a relationship with her. Evangeline Glynn shacking up with the help? Preposterous.

Men have always been at her disposal. Unlike what many claim, she doesn't hate them. She likes some, particularly those who adored her. The shambles of a past marriage is a good enough reason not to trust men, though. Adding to it her son's bad behaviour, Evangeline's learned to keep the opposite sex in line.

From across the room, the telephone trills. While looking over at what's now an antique, she rubs her temples. The caller isn't giving up. Evangeline stares at the door, considering for the umpteenth time the wisdom of employing a friend. Rupert's movements are often like wading through treacle. She can't tell if it's arrogance or the advancing years are taking a toll.

Finally, he appears. The trolley wheels stick as they hit the edge of a rug. A stooped Rupert kicks the trolley. Evangeline's teeth grind. Maybe she *should* use her mobile. Her patience won't bear another round of telephone jeopardy, hoping Rupert will get to the phone in time. She could do it, but why when she has staff? Besides, she can't move much faster, not that she'll ever admit it.

Hands linked behind him, Rupert waits. An aching back hinders the attempt to stand tall. If Evangeline hears about his ailments once more, she won't be responsible for her actions.

'Well, answer it then!' she shouts.

Rupert stretches his mouth into the enormous smile he always gives her. Whenever he does, Evangeline tussles with guilt and the urge to inflict violence.

Like an actor preparing to deliver lines, Rupert clears his throat. He smooths surviving strands of hair over the top of his head before picking up the receiver.

'Thank you for calling the Glynnholme estate. My name is Rupert. How may I help you?'

Evangeline scowls. He continues to ignore her instructions to ditch the call centre-type welcome. She winds her hand, cranking up her buffoon of a butler. Rupert's nosiness will lead to interrogating the caller. Not today. Evangeline's body demands sleep.

'It's Master Henry,' Rupert says.

'Off you go.'

THE PROFESSOR

Rupert walks backwards as if leaving royalty. He's mocking Evangeline's snootiness, but she lets it pass. Instead, she remembers the boy who played here when his parents visited. She once witnessed young Rupert wetting himself. It still makes her laugh. When his family lost their fortune, she offered him employment.

Evangeline sniggers as Rupert trips over the hem of his trousers. Although the door closes, she knows he's listening on the other side. It doesn't matter. Rupert already knows her most damning secrets. His silence is secured with a generous salary and a cottage on the outskirts of the grounds.

'What now, Henry?' Evangeline begins the phone conversation.

'Charming as always. Why bother having a mobile if it's switched off?'

'Get on with it. How much money do you want?'

'Not a jot. I'm most offended—'

'Spit it out.' Her voice snaps through the line.

Henry sniffs. 'I've seen Jane in the library. Good news. She wants to meet and has sent you an email. Rupert probably hasn't checked yet, the lazy sod.'

Evangeline takes pleasure in thinking of Jane and herself being in libraries, where they belong. Centuries-old texts closet Evangeline when the terrible memories reappear. The university library is no match for Evangeline's, boasting heavy mahogany bookshelves and fleur-de-lis wallpaper. Jane is likely surrounded by steel shelves and magnolia walls.

Evangeline opens her laptop and reads the email.

'Are you there, Mother?'

She scans Jane's wording and nods at the well-crafted paragraphs.

'Mother!'

That boy is so needy and the cause of so much trouble. If it wasn't for him, Evangeline could've continued being a social butterfly. Instead, she beats her wings against the bars of Glynnholme. It's a self-made prison, with Henry as one of her jailers. There is hope, though. Jane is the key to setting Evangeline free.

CHAPTER 23
Jane

I turn up the radio, trying to distract my demanding bladder by singing along. Even though I had a pee before leaving, nervousness has taken over. I'm not sure how much longer I can hold on.

Duetting with Prince isn't working. Instead, I consider what I've learned about Glynnholme. I can't go in unprepared. When I met Henry, I felt out of my depth. As a power house of literary knowledge, Evangeline will undoubtedly be scarier. Scholars still cite her research on Victorian literature, particularly on the Brontës. Evangeline doesn't have any academic qualifications and grew up in an era when women were viewed as inferior. In some areas, unfortunately, we still are.

An interview Evangeline gave in the seventies was a savage burn on the reporter who goaded her. He accused her of using money to be seen and heard. She unapologetically confirmed he was correct. Evangeline had it, so she used it. The interviewer also focused on her recent divorce, digging for dirt on why she left Alfie. She stated the marriage was a youthful mistake intended to irritate her parents. Evangeline was pregnant with Henry before the wedding, causing quite the scandal. In the interview, she detailed Alfie's womanising and gambling. Evangeline gave him time to shape up. He didn't, so she kicked him out. It seems Evangeline's been single ever since. Will I have a similar fate without the riches?

The sign for Quillington makes the need to pee more urgent. I don't want to rock up at Glynnholme, asking to go to the bathroom.

Quillington is an Oxfordshire village I've heard of but never visited. When I looked at a map online, I initially missed it. It only has one shop, hopefully with facilities or a helpful owner. I pass Quillington Store. There are no parking spaces nearby, a consequence of households expanding, while the structure stays the same. I drive in a circuit. Thankfully, the houses have large driveways, leaving more space to park on the road. Getting out of the car, I cross my legs.

'Oi! You can't park there.' A gammon-faced man appears as if from nowhere, arms folded. 'Tharrs reserved.'

The strong Oxfordshire burr is strangely comforting. It's reminiscent of Mum's voice, bordering on West Country with a "Get orf myyy laaaand" farmer vibe. Dad and I teased her when she pronounced it as "couwse" rather than "cows". Mum said we weren't any better, with our cockney tones. Oxfordshire is a weird melting pot of dialects. People outside the county expect us to speak the Queen's English. When I open my mouth, I sound more like an *Eastenders* extra than sophisticated.

I check in front and behind my battered Polo. This was Mum's car. Dad offered to sell it to go towards a new vehicle. I couldn't part with it. Although cutesy isn't my thing, Mum's teddy bears remain on the parcel shelf. Occasionally, I catch a whiff of her perfume in the upholstery.

I address the grumpy bloke. 'There aren't any "reserved" signs.'

He pushes up the peak of his tweed cap and tuts. 'Tharrs because we don't 'ave terr be reserving spaces around 'ere. Locals know which is who's bit. Oive got a delivery comin'. You'll 'ave terr move.'

To avoid an argument, I drive the car a few feet forward. After I slam the door behind me, the parking police shakes his head.

'Tharr there's Glenda's space. No parking there either.'

THE PROFESSOR

My need to pee won't let this stupidity continue. I scribble my name and mobile number on a scrap of paper from my bag.

'If Glenda returns and needs this particular spot on an almost empty road, call me. Sorry, it's an emergency!' I press the note into his hand and run.

The shop door threatens to fall off its hinges as I burst in. A queue for the adjoining post office snakes towards the entrance.

'Excuse me,' I say to a woman holding the handle of a pram, blocking the way.

She apologises before performing an eleven point turn. After being set free, I dash down an aisle of tins and packets. No one's at the till.

A man calls over, 'Margaret's at the counter. You'll have to wait, like the rest of us.'

The groan escaping from my mouth is louder than I expected. A small, grey-haired woman steps out of a booth.

'Sorry, love,' she begins. 'My son who runs the shop is off sick today. Leave cash for what you're buying by the till. I'll trust you.' She turns away to resume her duties.

I walk past the queue. Numerous harsh stares burn into me. I hold up my hands.

'I'm not pushing in. Do you have a toilet?' I try not to whine with desperation.

The woman shakes her skull-hugging perm. 'Try the village hall, but it might not be open. They're probably understaffed too, due to this lurgy flying around.'

People in the line create distances between themselves. A few pull up scarves to cover noses and mouths. A girl coughs and receives filthy looks.

'Thanks anyway.' Wondering just how desperate I am, I eye up packs of incontinence pads on a shelf.

The woman leaves the booth and approaches someone. 'Julie, take over for a minute, treasure.'

'Do I have to?' Julie asks.

Margaret waggles a finger. 'You may be a fancy computer whatsit nowadays, but you once worked here. Never forget your roots, girl.'

Julie mutters, 'Okay.'

Margaret seizes my elbow. 'Follow me. You can use the staff lavvy.'

It's all I can do not to push her aside and run in front.

After flushing the toilet, I turn around in the narrow room and whack my head on a high cabinet.

'Shit!'

After hearing sniggering, I wash and dry my hands quickly. Margaret is outside. She trusted me to pay for goods but probably thinks I'll nick the loo roll.

'Ain't seen you around before.' She scans my face. 'What brings you here?'

I realise gossip will be payment for her helpfulness.

'I'm going to Glynnholme.'

She steps back. 'You've actually been *invited*?'

'Yes, by Evangeline Glynn.'

I hate myself for straightening and puffing myself up.

'Well, I'll never be,' Margaret says. 'Nobody goes there anymore. Used to be teeming with posh nobs, coming from all over the country. Evangeline held fancy dinners and put on balls. Toffs stopped by here to buy ciggies. Snooty buggers.'

'I'm certainly not posh.' I labour my local dialect. 'Cowley, born and bred.'

She nods. 'That's all right, then.'

I've passed the class test. Margaret leads me to a pokey kitchen and flicks on the kettle.

'Why's Evangeline allowing you into her gaff?' she asks.

'I'm a student at Oxford Carroll. Henry, her son, has arranged it.'

Margaret takes two mugs from hooks above the sink.

'No thanks,' I say. 'I'll be late if I have a cuppa.'

The cackling laugh makes me wonder if witches are real.

'I wasn't making you one,' Margaret manages through laughter. 'This is for Julie. Dealing with that miserable lot is thirsty work. Be careful with the Glynns, love. Henry's bad news. He's broken many hearts in this village. Had his way here and then made the university as a playground. Henry ain't being naughty with you, is he?'

'No way! He's my tutor, nothing more.'

Margaret drops tea bags into the mugs. 'If you ask me, the police should've looked more into that business ten years ago with those murders. But what do I know? I'm the simple kind who doesn't read books. All I'll say is wealth covers up a lot. If it was an ordinary bloke, he would've been arrested for what happened to them girls. Henry Glynn, though, always comes up smelling of roses. Now the killing is happening again! The *Oxford Mail* is full of the details. Don't take a genius to figure out the killer's a university boffin. He calls himself *The Professor*.'

I back away, uncertain if there's any element of truth in Margaret's statement.

'Cheers for helping me out.' I grab a handful of sweets to buy to show my gratitude.

'Got a taste for the Glynns' products, too?' she asks.

Bags of Tongue Twister Sour Balls, Honeycomb Pebbles, Sour Saturns, and Chocolate Keys are in the pile. Of course, this shop stocks Glynns' Confectionery. They control just about everyone. Not me, though. I won't ever let that happen.

Margaret pats a hand on my shoulder. 'Go steady, my duck. Glynnholme's a strange place. Bad things happen there.'

CHAPTER 24
Jane

Despite trying to enter Glynnholme calmly, I fail at the first hurdle. Even the black wrought-iron gates amaze me. Golden orbs top the spikes. Fierce gold lions twist in the metal frame, their tails swooping upwards. I consider leaving the car here. The shame of being associated with this wreck is strong. Mum travels with me whenever I'm in her Polo, though. I open the window for some air.

'Hello.'

I look around to trace where the voice is coming from.

'Hello,' a tinny sound repeats. 'Look over to your right.'

Spotting an intercom with a camera makes me groan. Someone's watching me make an absolute twat of myself.

'Sorry,' I begin. 'I didn't realise.'

'Please state your business.' The speaker is a man with an officious tone. It's certainly not Henry. Dealing with visitors would be below him, anyway.

'I'm here to see Evangeline Glynn.'

'Has Ms Glynn sent you an invitation?' the man asks.

'Yes, I—'

'For goodness' sake, Rupert,' a woman snaps. 'Stop that nonsense and let Jane in.'

THE PROFESSOR

I think I've just "met" Evangeline. Now, I'm more terrified than ever.

The gates open at a snail's pace. Finally, having enough room to go through, I negotiate the gravel driveway. Stones flick up and hit the doors, inevitably adding more damage to the paintwork. I wonder how Evangeline feels about it when she's driving one of her posh cars. Perhaps she has a chauffeur. Then I remember she never leaves. Maybe Henry's Aston Martin bears the burden of the gravel instead. Whenever I see it in the university car park, I laugh at how Henry is a crap James Bond wannabe.

A cottage appears on the left. I'd be happy living there, let alone in the mansion. Someone takes good care of their little home. The bushes alongside it are trimmed and the window frames and door appear to be freshly painted. If Evangeline wants a new tenant, I'm in, although Dad wouldn't be pleased with me being in what's probably a staff residence. It's so confusing how he swings from championing the working class to asserting he deserves better than what it offers.

Ahead, teardrop shaped conifers line the edges of the drive. Not a stray leaf or twig dares to disrupt their precise lines. This first time of entering Glynnholme can't be replicated. Silence helps commit the experience to memory. I'll likely never be here again. Evangeline won't find much in me to impress her. How can a student at the beginning of a degree gain an expert's academic confidence? Leah advised me to enjoy it and don't swear. I intend to do my best in both areas.

As I'm wondering if I should've taken the side road, a spectacular sight steals all thoughts. There is Glynnholme. There's no gradual appearance, offering tempting teasers. The house demands to be seen with an instant impact. Metal work similar to the gates juts from the roof. Black swirls topped with arrow points pierce the murky sky. Upside down ice cream cone turrets flank the sides of the building. Time's darkening decay has leeched once-golden bricks. Winter sunlight breaks through, hinting at the Bath stone that created this house. Of course, my extensive research covered the materials used to build it.

This is no stereotypical fairy-tale castle. Disney needn't worry. It's a juxtaposition of eye-catching design, ancestry, and grandeur. The mostly slate grey roof is embellished with occasional rusty red and buttery yellow mosaic tiles. Cylindrical chimneys dart from triangular roofs, towers, and turrets. The overall effect is a cacophony of shapes, colours, and styles.

Charles Glynn dared to make Glynnholme befitting of his fantasy Victorian vision. It has a charm, which doesn't come from architecture. Never has a building drawn me in like this. Before I've even explored it, Glynnholme becomes a being, as real as any person. It's a weary woman, holding on to her glory days, trying to shine once more. I want to shout out to Glynnholme that I'm rooting for her. Excitement rises within me as I ponder over what's inside. I imagine chandeliers, candlesticks, original paintings…

A shadow flits in front of the car. Thud. I get out of my vehicle. A body lies on the ground.

CHAPTER 25
Jane

After the man opens them, dark eyes belonging to a literary villain appear. As if being electrocuted, he jumps up. Hopefully, this means his injuries are minimal. Running over people isn't the best way to start..

'I'm so, so sorry. I didn't see you. Sorry.'

He groans as he straightens. 'You've apologised twice. It's fine.'

Lines crinkle around his eyes as he smiles. As he takes a step, he winces. Blood seeps through a rip in the knee of his trousers.

'Oh, my…'

'There's a first aid kit in my shed, if you don't mind giving me a lift. Then I'll hop out, probably literally.' He picks out some embedded stones from the wound and sucks in air. 'The amount of times I've said the driveway should be tarred is ridiculous. Gravel constantly traps my wheelbarrow.'

'Are you a gardener, by any chance?'

He grins. 'Either that or I'm a weirdo who has a wheelbarrow for a friend. I'm Ed.' He holds out a grubby hand, notices, and wipes it on his jacket. Upon inspection, his palm is still covered in grime. 'Maybe it's better not to shake hands.'

I offer mine. 'A bit of dirt doesn't bother me. I'm Jane. Hop in and you can tell me what I've let myself in for by coming here.'

Ed produces a handkerchief and lays it on the passenger seat. 'Don't want to dirty it.'

I select a gear, or so I believe. The car stalls.

'You probably think I'm a terrible driver,' I say.

'Stop worrying. She won't bite.'

'Who?'

'Evangeline. You're obviously nervous about meeting her. She's an odd one, I grant you, but I've heard she's looking forward to your visit.'

The information doesn't reduce my nerves. As I follow the driveway, I'm silent. Up close, Glynnholme is even more dramatic. Two sets of stairs meet in the middle, forming an impressive frontage. They're reminiscent of the grand staircases in *Downton Abbey* or the film, *Titanic*, where Jack waits for Rose to attend dinner with the first-class passengers.

The steps resemble teeth, preparing to snap visitors into its jaws, and suck them into the mouth of Glynnholme. I take a gulp of "woman up" juice and turn off the ignition.

Ed blows his fringe away from his forehead. 'Must get this mop cut. Problem is, it grows like no one's business.'

'Mine too. That's why I keep it long.'

'Uh, oh, here comes trouble.'

A man dressed in a "monkey suit" scurries down the stairs. The tails of his black jacket flap behind him like penguin wings. He even waddles.

Ed convulses with laughter. 'Rupert's got his best clothes on! I guarantee he's been watching since you drove through the gates. Nosey old bugger.'

While he gives Rupert an exaggerated wave, I roll down the window. Rupert approaches us, throwing his arms up.

'You can't leave that here. It's most unseemly. Vehicles are never in sight, particularly ones that look like *that*.'

As Ed leans over me, I smell earth, pine, and sweat. The closeness is unnerving. He's obviously not bothered about boundaries.

'All right, Rupe,' Ed begins. 'Wearing that cravat so tight is making you more stressful.'

THE PROFESSOR

'Master Edward.' Rupert speaks in a school teacher disciplinarian manner. 'This is most disappointing. You know how the mistress detests anything ruining her view.'

Ed gets out of the vehicle. 'Chill out. I was going to tell Jane where to park before you appeared.'

Rupert puffs out his chest. 'That is *my* job, Master Edward. I'll kindly remind you to stick to your own concerns.'

'Where should I park?' I ask, not only for an answer but to stop them sparring.

'I'll show her,' Ed addresses Rupert. 'Run along and put the kettle on.' He scissors his fingers, mimicking the fast-moving legs Rupert clearly lacks.

Ed turns towards me. 'Ignore him. Rupert thinks he owns the gaff because he's been here ages.' He points to a corner of the house. 'There are parking spaces round the back.'

'Thanks. Why does Rupert call you *master* if you're a gardener?'

Ed's sunny disposition turns *Wuthering Heights*' Heathcliff dark. 'It's complicated. Be careful in there.' He focuses on the house. 'Once you become part of this world, it changes your life forever.'

CHAPTER 26

Evangeline drops the velvet curtain. 'My goodness. You've never mentioned how much Jane looks like—'

'That's because you never asked,' Henry snaps. 'Besides, you've seen photos of Jane.'

'Seeing her in the flesh is different. You could've prepared me.'

Henry considers why he has to do everything. He's worked hard to encourage Jane to study at the university and visit Glynnholme. Every instruction his mother's given, Henry has fulfilled. He's been a dutiful son and still she isn't satisfied. The barbs about his character have increased. Anyone would think Evangeline was a saint considering the horror she expresses at his actions. She forgets Henry knows what she's capable of. Her hands aren't clean. She is Lady Macbeth, trying to wash off the taint and failing.

Evangeline points at Ed hobbling into the shed. 'Trust that boy to get to Jane first. Must Edward always be on the grounds?'

'He is the gardener.'

Henry takes a seat and sparks up a cigarette. Evangeline snatches it from his mouth and douses it in his glass of gin and tonic.

'You're well aware smoking only takes place in the morning room. I will not have The Wildfell Room reeking of tobacco. Also, you'll start a fire with all these fabrics around. We know what happened in *Jane Eyre* and how terribly that turns out.'

'Does it make me the madman in the attic, if I set this lot alight?' Henry teases.

She regards furs and luxurious silks covering a Queen size bed, framed by filmy curtains. Once, she tried sleeping here. The canopy held Evangeline in like trapped prey, also symbolising how Helen from *The Tenant of Wildfell Hall* was trapped in a violent marriage. Every day, the walls are narrowing, forming a Glynnholme cage.

'No one ever comes in here,' Henry says, 'apart from when you're snooping on Ed.'

'It's not snooping, considering the house and grounds belong to me. I can look at them when I want, along with the people in them.'

'Why are you bothered about Ed if you don't go outside?' He taps a cigarette holder against a marble table.

Batwing sleeves of Evangeline's embroidered jacket swish. 'Stop making such a racket! Also, whose fault is it I have a hermit's existence?'

Upon seeing the dragon rage in her green eyes, Henry retreats. With Jane here, stirring Evangeline's anger isn't wise. It wouldn't be a normal day, though, without a few digs.

'The morning room is so dreary,' he begins. 'Why you named it after an American is puzzling. There are many excellent British authors.'

'All the ones you're thinking of are likely men. Get over this annoyance with how I themed some of the rooms after women and Americans. Your temper is such a fragile thing. Read *The Turn of the Screw*. Perhaps you'll learn how angry men always come a cropper.'

Henry slaps a hand against his heart. 'As you well know, I teach *The Turn of the Screw*. There's nothing I don't know about it. I'm not the idiot who named a room after Bly manor - a ruddy great big building - from the book. What's the point?'

'This "idiot" was celebrated for her groundbreaking analysis of the novella, lest you forget.'

He rolls his eyes. 'How can I, with your constant reminders of what an academic failure I am compared to you?'

Evangeline claps her hands. 'I'm bored of this. Come, come! We have a guest to attend to.'

By slow degrees, Henry draws himself up from the chair. He's beginning to like Jane. Now he's led her into the lioness's den. Henry wonders how he can face his student. Guilt at bringing Jane here will surely be all over his face.

CHAPTER 27
Jane

After pressing the doorbell, clanging to rival church bells begins. I resisted using the lion door knocker, although opening its mouth to make it "roar" was tempting. Sometimes I'm heavy-handed. The prospect of landing up with the knocker in my hand is too shameful. I already nearly killed the gardener with my car.

The lantern above sways in the increasing breeze. I step aside, afraid of it landing on me. The arched porch is the waiting area for the main event of seeing Glynnholme in its glory. Finally, the door creaks open. A shiny head, decorated with a few straggles of hair, appears.

'No need to bow, Rupert. I'm not royalty. Besides, we've already met when you told me off for parking in the wrong place.'

There's a cracking sound as he snaps upright. A scowl deepens his wrinkled brow.

'Young lady, I wasn't bowing. I was, well... not to worry. Please enter.'

Rupert stands aside. He leans against a wall, while pulling a foot up. While aiming for a spot of mud on his shoe with a handkerchief, he teeters. I focus on the surroundings. The hallway is lit like the Blackpool illuminations Dad reckons our house resembles when I forget to turn off lights. Glynnholme's lights are much classier than a seaside exhibition. My earlier hope of there being a chandelier is rewarded with one spreading across the ceiling. Diamond droplets twinkle, casting icicles of light to cast reflections.

Rupert's face is tomato red as he bends an obviously frail body. Hopefully, he's not in charge of cleaning the chandelier. It would kill him.

I recall an episode of *Only Fools and Horses* where the Trotters were cleaning several chandeliers in a stately home. Grandad unscrewed fixings for a different chandelier to the one Del and Rodney prepared to catch in a blanket. They could only watch in horror as the expensive item crashed to the floor.

Whenever we watched box sets of the comedy series, Mum shared stories of her dad's escapades. He was a market trader the locals called Bitsa, on account of him selling "Bitsa this and bitsa that". Grampy's wares ranged from screwdrivers to Sindy dolls. While his trading was legal - unlike Del Boy - Grampy had a similar look, wearing a flat cap, polo neck, and sheepskin jacket. Helping on the stall in the school holidays was a treat. The market was a feast for the senses: grocers bellowing about bargain veg; bacon sizzling on the grill from a van; and a rainbow of sweets on the pick 'n' mix stall.

Rupert straightens and something snaps. 'Holy shit. I mean, oh my goodness. That hurt.'

I press my lips together to contain laughter. 'Can I help?'

'I'm fine.' He rubs his lower back. 'Please don't mention my use of profanity to the mistress.'

'Your secret's safe with me.' I point to a painting of a man dominating the top of the stairs. 'He's a grand-looking fella.'

'That's Charles Glynn, master confectioner and creator of Glynnholme.'

Rupert lowers his head. I resist asking if he's bowing again or nodding off. Instead, I study the man in the portrait. Henry has inherited his ancestor's nose and the mass of thick, dark hair. There's none of Henry's boyish lopsided grin there, though. Why didn't people in the past smile for artists? Perhaps serious expressions were a thing, like modern pouts for selfies. Not that

THE PROFESSOR

I'm into posturing. Wearing a dress today feels odd. I thought I should look smart, which I'm now regretting. The gusset of my tights is sliding down, making walking difficult.

'You're not entirely what I expected.' Rupert moves around me, blatantly sizing me up, but for what?

I edge away. 'Sorry to disappoint.'

'No disappointment, only surprise.'

'What do you mean?'

'Rupert, stop monopolising Jane!' Henry's order blasts from upstairs. 'She's here to visit Mother, not you.'

Henry saunters down the red carpet covered steps. The Lord of the Manor act doesn't impress me. I've seen Henry pick his nose when he believes no one's looking. As Dad would say, "He thinks his shit doesn't stink". If Dad could see this get-up, he'd pee his pants laughing. Rupert alone is great entertainment.

I scan the hallway, filled with more paintings of miserable men and beautifully-dressed ladies. There's so much inspiration for Dad's dolls' houses. I visualise tiny portraits hung on richly coloured, patterned wallpaper. Taking photos for reference probably isn't allowed.

Henry approaches me and laces an arm through mine while glaring at his servant.

'Rather than standing there, Rupert, instruct Mrs Patterson to hurry up with the tea.'

'Of course, sir.'

As Rupert leaves, he flicks up a middle finger behind Henry's back. Rupert then winks at me. Despite my best efforts not to, I let out a snort-laugh.

'Something amusing?' Henry asks.

'Just clearing my throat.'

As we approach a door, I read the placard on it. 'The Madam Mina Room, named after the character in *Dracula*.'

'This is the drawing room,' Henry says. 'Mother named all the rooms after various works of Victorian literature. All room titles in this house are capitalised. Mother thinks they're that important. We must allow some of her foibles.' He points to the space behind us. 'We're currently in The Gray Hall named after—'

'*The Picture of Dorian Gray* by Oscar Wilde.'

'You're coming along leaps and bounds with your learning.' Henry grips the doorknob. As if scorched, he backs off. 'Are you sure you want to do this?'

The fear in his eyes is odd. What on earth has he got to be nervous about? This is his home. I'm the person who's out of their depth here.

Henry takes my hand. 'You can leave. I won't think badly of you for it. We'll tell Mother you were taken ill.'

I remove his grip and push the door open.

'That's what I like to see.' A voice comes from an unlit corner. 'You're putting Henry in his place. Welcome, to Glynnholme, Jane!'

CHAPTER 28
Jane

The click of a button illuminates Evangeline Glynn. Her performance begins under the light from a lamp. Research showed this was her favourite way to greet visitors, coming out of the shadows and dazzling with her presence. Saving this act for so long must've been frustrating.

Despite wanting to appear unaffected, I'm impressed. Reclining on a chaise longue - the same one in the photo I showed Leah - is a goddess of feminism, Victorian literature knowledge, and wealth.

Evangeline flicks away snowy-white curls and swings her legs to the floor. The blouse and wide leg trousers are surprising. After reading about her reclusiveness, I'd pictured Miss Havisham. Evangeline is nothing like the rejected bride of *Great Expectations*. For a start, her clothes are modern, obviously designer, and fit her slim and fragile frame. She's smaller than I expected, but her powerful presence dominates.

'Come closer, Jane. I won't bite.'

The baring of her canine teeth makes me think otherwise, but I obey. Evangeline guides me to armchairs by a fire, devouring wood within hearty flames. Sweat forms on my forehead from the heat. Hoping she doesn't notice, I risk wiping my face with the end of my scarf. Before sitting, I place it on the sofa, along with my coat.

'Rupert didn't take your outdoor clothing? Useless man!'

She stabs at glowing coals with a poker and then pulls a tasselled cord hanging by the mantelpiece. A woman appears, carrying a silver tray too overladen for her short arms. I rush to help. The server steps back as if being attacked.

'Oh, no, no, no, my dear. You mustn't. It's not proper guests serving themselves - or so I've heard - seeing as we never have them.'

'No problem.'

I pick up a teapot etched with a filigree pattern, figuring it's the heaviest item. Leah advised not to steal the family silver. If it's all as weighty as this, I couldn't, anyway. Evangeline smiles, clearly enjoying having two people wait on her.

'That will be all, Mrs Patterson,' she says. 'Tell Rupert we'll be having words later.'

Mrs Patterson's cheeks deepen in their redness. 'Sorry, missus. Rupert's having a little trouble. He asked me to keep an ear out.'

Evangeline snarls. 'What's the matter with him? There's always something.'

'Best not to say in front of a guest.'

Unlike Rupert, she hasn't dressed up for my visit. An Aran jumper and jeans are welcome signs of normality in this place where I don't belong.

'Spit it out.' Evangeline smacks a fist on the chair arm. 'I'm sure Jane isn't easily embarrassed.'

'Rupert's got a nasty bout of Farmer Giles.' Mrs Patterson wrings her hands around each other. 'They're giving him gip.'

Evangeline frowns. 'Farmer Giles? Who's that? What's he got to do with Rupert?'

Mrs Patterson concentrates on the ceiling, possibly summoning divine intervention or alien abduction.

'*Farmer Giles* is rhyming slang for *piles*,' I begin, 'or what you might refer to as *haemorrhoids*.'

'I see.' Evangeline remains straight-faced. 'You may leave.'

THE PROFESSOR

Mrs Patterson mouths "thank you" to me before leaving. The dimples in her cheeks prompt me to return the smile.

'And still no one has taken your coat!' Evangeline cries. 'Whatever must you think of us?'

'It's fine. Don't worry.'

'By the way, I know what *Farmer Giles* is,' she whispers.

'Thought you might.' I won't play her game by hushing my voice.

She reaches for the teapot. 'We have more important matters to attend to than the servants' ailments. Shall I pour?'

'Please do.' I extend a hand and congratulate myself for enunciating the words. I'm not sure how much longer I can keep this up, though. Soon, I'll be dropping my *h's* and forgetting my ending *t's*. As for swearing…

The tea's flow is shaky as Evangeline pours. I know better now than to offer assistance. Branches of veins bulge from her pale hands, reaching towards many-ringed fingers. Balancing all the jewels is hard enough. I guess the rich like shiny reminders of what they own.

Evangeline sets down the teapot and wriggles her fingers. 'Everyone has their vices. I adore jewellery. I'm somewhat of a magpie.'

Either she's telepathic or an extremely good reader of people. Both are terrifying prospects. There's no fooling her, particularly with my sorely lacking high society skills. While driving here, I practised my speech. Dad would've had a shit fit if he'd heard it. He's of the "take me as you find me" school of thinking. To be honest, he has a point. Trying to be what you're not is exhausting. For the rest of this visit, I will be me.

Evangeline offers tongs and a bowl of sugar lumps I associate with feeding to horses rather than humans. I'm not a total Neanderthal. In our house, granulated sugar is stored in a canister.

'No thanks. I'm sweet enough already.' I inwardly groan at the crap saying.

After Evangeline sips tea, burgundy lipstick stains a hunting scene, painted on porcelain. She holds up the teacup for inspection.

'That useless housekeeper! I told her to bin this set. I don't care that it's an heirloom. Endorsing the killing of animals is wrong.'

She tosses the cup into the fireplace. Liquid splashes everywhere before the shattering. The cup probably cost more than my outfit. Evangeline watches me, no doubt for a reaction.

'Do you mind if I finish before you throw mine, too?' I ask. 'Hate wasting a good cuppa.'

I don't mention the hypocrisy of deer heads jutting from the hall walls for someone who's supposedly against animal cruelty. I wait for Evangeline's response to my cheeky remark. A booming laugh bursts from her.

'You're an absolute wonder, Jane.'

'I often wonder what the hell I'm doing, if that's what you mean.'

She stands. 'Let's go to the library. It's time to begin your education.'

CHAPTER 29

Ed drains the dregs from his mug of coffee and contemplates having another. A need for caffeine isn't keeping him in the kitchen. Jane's arrival drives the urge to be nearby. Usually, he stays outside as much as possible.

Henry and Evangeline treat Ed like a forgotten shadow. Sometimes they gasp when he appears from the outer edges of their lives. In the right light, though, shadows don't disappear. The Glynns try to keep him in the dark, but he knows where the best hiding places are around Glynnholme. Being short is to Ed's advantage. He's learned how to hide behind Evangeline's many possessions, gliding ghost-like around the house.

As a child, Ed slept in The Hyde Room, named after Henry Hyde from *The Strange case of Dr Jekyll and Mr Hyde*. Next door was Henry's The Jekyll Room. The closeness and lack of privacy were stifling. Even worse were the menacing Janus double-faced mask, stuffed dinosaur-looking birds, portraits of wailing mad men, and Victorian scientific equipment. It wasn't an acceptable space for a youngster's rest and play. Ed felt like a specimen under the Glynns' magnifying glass. For a while, Evangeline refused to allow Ed to live in the servants' quarters. His decision to become Glynnholme's head gardener already annoyed her. Ed won when he moved into a servant's bedroom, anyway. Evangeline still doesn't know because she doesn't care.

As a youngster, Ed enjoyed the stings he inflicted by reminding Evangeline she isn't his mum. Henry regularly shouted at Ed for the ingratitude. Despite the differences in their heights, Ed's always poised to fight Henry. Everything about him makes Ed feel nauseous. Henry never looks directly at him, which is the safest option. Ed avoids the Glynns to protect them - and him - from a burgeoning rage. When Evangeline's awake, he's absent. Some have said he should be grateful to her for taking in someone else's child. He's certain there must be an agenda. There always is with these selfish bastards.

Even after extensive searching for clues, Ed knows little regarding his mother. He's aware Selena was another of Evangeline's chosen scholars. The young student regularly came to Glynnholme for tutoring. Norman Patterson, the former head gardener, told Ed some details about his mum. Selena and Norman chatted in his shed, usually grumbling about the Glynns or Rupert.

Ed wore Norman out, asking what Selena looked like, how she spoke, walked, what was her favourite colour, her favourite feature in the gardens... Norman's loving patience answered most of the grieving child's questions. Yet, it was clear, even to a boy, there were things that remained untold.

Refusing to let the tears come, Ed shakes his head. Whenever he thinks of Norman, the death still hits hard. From when he was an infant, Ed formed a bond with the parental figure. He refuses to use any other tools than Norman's, engraved with his initials. When Ed holds the shears, his role model guides him again. Norm was as close to a father as Ed dared to happen. His real dad remains a mystery no one can or wants to help him solve. He smiles at the photograph of Norman hugging his wife, above the butler's sink.

A hand squeezes his shoulder. 'I still miss him too, love. Now and then, I read Norm's diary entries. It brings me closer to him. In his own way, he was quite the writer.' Mrs Patterson unpins the photo and puts it on the table.

Seeking any leftover warmth, Ed cradles the mug. 'The past three years have gone so fast. When I'm trimming the hedges, I swear I can hear Norm's throaty chuckle. Remember how he tried to surprise me by appearing on the other side of a hedge, the daft bugger?'

Mrs Patterson's body jiggles as she laughs. When Ed allows it, she's a motherly solace. He only calls her *Mrs Patterson* or *Mrs P*, though. The more official titles rather than a first name are comforting. Mrs Patterson is the true keeper of Glynnholme, showing fairness, kindness, and a vast knowledge of the house. Evangeline can't begin to compete. Wealth doesn't buy everything.

'I warned Norm you'd lop his head off if he wasn't careful,' Mrs Patterson says. 'Silly old sod. He was so proud of you, you know that, right?' She smooths a thumb over Ed's cheek.

He remains silent. Ed doesn't deserve anyone's pride. He's full of fury and revenge. Often, he battles with his dead mum, blaming Selena for the choices she made, leading to her death. It's baffling how a clever person allowed herself to become a plaything. There's no doubt Evangeline used Selena. When Ed refused to let the same to happen to him, Evangeline was disappointed. He's convinced she only became his guardian to appear caring to others. She's never offered a scrap of affection.

Nannies, boarding school, and the Pattersons raised Ed. When he was expelled for fighting, Evangeline gave up on him. The scandal of expulsion offered Ed more freedom. Norman took him under his wing, teaching gardening skills and encouraging a love of nature.

Since his mentor died, Ed favours working solo, with occasional help when needed. When the part-timers are on breaks together, he knows they chat about their odd-bod boss. He can't be their friend. Ed has too many secrets, although some aren't his alone. The Glynns, as ever, have to own everything first, particularly the truth. He vows Evangeline will pay for her deceit and neglect.

Mrs Patterson holds up his cup. 'I need to pick up the grandkiddies from school soon, but I can squeeze another coffee in. Do you want one?'

'Yes, please.'

Ed watches her prepare the drinks. Evangeline would have a fit if she knew an electric kettle is in here. Everything has to be authentically antique and exactly as Evangeline decrees. She constantly tells Mrs P off for singing too loudly while cleaning or not serving food on time. Mrs P ignores it, confident replacing her would be difficult. She knows too much, and not just about domestic matters. Also, strangers aren't welcome at Glynnholme, at least not until Jane arrived.

After opening a box of Evangeline's expensive chocolates, Mrs P winks at Ed. She pops Fortnum & Mason's finest confectionery into her mouth and grins. He adores this woman who isn't educated or young. Thankfully, she's safe from The Professor. Ed can't say the same for women like Jane.

CHAPTER 30
Jane

I restrain myself from running to the bookshelves. The four floors of the university library are great, but Glynnholme's The Middlemarch Library is something else. Although smaller, it's more of a book lovers' paradise than an academic space. Oh, that smell! I swear the scent of old books is a drug and I want more.

'Go on then, have a look around.' Evangeline flicks her hands like an owner, letting a dog off the lead.

Unleashing my inner Belle from *Beauty and the Beast*, I regard the books with childish wonder. I follow patterns on the carpet as pathways to shelves along every wall. While I'm darting from one book to another, Evangeline sits in an overstuffed armchair. A marble bust of Queen Victoria on a mini plinth stands next to her, allying two queens, in their own ways.

I watch Evangeline open a newspaper. There isn't a single crease in it. Visions of Rupert swearing as he irons the daily news make me smile. A headline stating a local man's been arrested for the university murders steals my smile. While I'm enjoying myself, Kate must be in hell. He has many faults, but I can't accept Sam's a murderer. Although he's a crap husband, nothing hints at him being dangerous or obsessed with Victorian literature.

Evangeline puts the paper down and glares at me. 'What's the matter? Why are you just standing there? Is it too dark for you? The lights are kept low to preserve the first editions.'

'No, it isn't that.' I focus on the headline, still in view.

She looks down and jabs at the print with her finger. 'This is such a wretched business and so terrible it's happening again.'

By my head, I notice a particular novel, *Hard Times*. Isn't it just for the families grieving their murdered daughters, sisters, and granddaughters?

I reflect upon being in the Glynns' library. While it's incredible, I can't forget Clementine was killed in the Oxford Carroll library. A quote from *Middlemarch* was left with her body. I won't mention to Evangeline that someone I know is in custody, accused of being The Professor. It isn't my shame to bear, but I fear she'll throw me out if she knows.

Evangeline approaches an enormous, faded, half globe set into a table. She opens up the world, revealing bottles and glasses of various shapes, colours, and sizes.

'Fancy a tipple?' she asks.

'No thanks. I'm driving.'

I watch her prepare a drink, surprised she hasn't rung for a servant to prepare it.

'Here's to you.' She raises a glass and knocks back the sherry in one. 'Right, we mustn't ignore these murders any longer.' She nods towards a chair opposite her. 'Take a seat.'

Cracked leather barely covering the armchair cuts into my legs. Engaging my thigh muscles, I manage not to slide off despite wearing tights. Evangeline unrolls parchment, browned and crisp at the edges. It reminds me of a primary school project where we stained our treasure maps with cold tea to age them. The memory confirms I'm the imposter here while Evangeline's the real deal. Her document is definitely not doused in PG Tips.

'This is a map of the house.' Evangeline flattens it out on a coffee table. 'Glynnholme isn't a gaudy place with numerous rooms. Quality over quantity is the Glynn way, in confectionery and in our abode. Forgive me for not offering a guided tour at this stage. We mustn't be overheard. As you can see from the map, this is a small building compared to many ancestral homes. When Charles Glynn visualised Glynnholme, he designed a stunning but cosy place. Better that than one where the occupants have to navigate through mazes of corridors.'

While Glynnholme's splendour is amazing, it's definitely homelier than the stately places I've visited with Dad. He stretches his National Trust membership to the limit by visiting houses across the country. They provide inspiration for his dolls' houses. As a child, I complained about being dragged around muddy grounds in the depth of winter. Looking at artefacts and crusty old buildings bored me, too. Mum took me to a café while Dad transformed what he saw in real life into miniature in his mind.

A long weekend in Haworth, when I was a teenager, unlocked the mystery of Dad's interest in the past. As we walked around the Brontë parsonage, I was entranced. The whole building thrummed with creativity, left behind by the Brontë siblings. The scribblings of the sisters encased in glass were fascinating. That day, I shared with Mum my dream of writing a novel. Her excitement was as strong as mine. I've never told Dad of my ambition. It felt like a secret between Mum and I. When she died, I thought my aspirations died with her. Since I met Leah and have heard her Haworth stories, the sleeping need to write is stirring. Studying the works of Victorian authors has also resurrected my writing desire. Leah's promised a stay at her family home in the summer to unleash my creative ideas.

Evangeline snaps her fingers. 'Concentrate, Jane! What I'm showing you is important. It will mean the difference between you living or dying.'

CHAPTER 31
Jane

The nervous giggle falling from my lips is a weak response. Evangeline's just said my life is in jeopardy. Maybe reclusiveness is driving her mad. Much as she's being a drama queen, it's rude not to let her continue. After all, I'm in her territory.

She points at the upstairs part of the Glynnholme map. 'This is The Wildfell Room, a bedroom. The Professor killed a woman to symbolise Helen from *The Tenant of Wildfell Hall*.'

Although I'm trying to be polite, I yawn. All night, worries whirred in my mind regarding meeting Evangeline, how to conduct myself, and if she'd approve of me. Now I realise it was silly. I can be me. It's enough.

'Please do me the courtesy of staying awake.' Her haughtiness could cut the diamonds on her rings. 'This isn't an architecture lesson. The names of my rooms are significant. I capitalised them because they're so important. That reprehensible beast who calls himself *The Professor* is trying to claim them again.'

Fighting against sleep-inducing heat from the fire, I sit up. The cracked leather of the chair pinches my thighs. This time I welcome it for keeping me alert.

Evangeline continues. 'Murders of female students from Oxford Carroll University happened ten years ago. The Professor seemed to vanish. Now, he's returned. With the recent killings, the first was initially considered as suicide. Does that death, and the quote left with it, remind you of anything?' She swishes an arm in a circle above her head. I understand the links: a library; *Middlemarch*; and Clementine.

'Moving on to The Bly Room,' Evangeline says, 'which is taken from *The Turn of the Screw*. A decade ago, a student's corpse was found dressed as the governess from the novella. A quote was attached to her clothing. Keeping up?'

I nod and become annoyed at myself for being silent. Speaking seems wrong, though. Evangeline's on a roll and I'm learning she doesn't tolerate interruptions.

She taps on a box showing The Satis Room. 'Are you aware of where this comes from?'

I straighten. '*Great Expectations*. Satis is Miss Havisham's home.'

'This is my bedroom. The woman killed and placed in a scene to mimic Miss Havisham, had similar coloured hair to mine. She was also an academic and my tutee. This one was more personal.'

I scan Evangeline's body, comparing it to the healthier appearance I saw online. Of course, she's aged, but perhaps there's something else adding to the physical fragility. Predator eyes fix on me. I swear this woman is a mind reader.

'Just because I'm no longer young and my hair's turned white doesn't mean the murderer won't kill me. *You* would do well to remember he favours a certain type: short, petite, and brunette. Oh, and females studying English Literature, at a certain university.'

Brilliant, I'm a serial killer's fantasy.

She sets her mouth in a grim line before speaking. 'You've likely heard comments some make about me being a reclusive Miss Havisham character.'

'Not at all.' I attempt a passive face and fail.

'Stop fluffing me up. We'll get along better if you say it like it is. My ego's robust enough. The *Great Expectations* killing was a direct message, mocking my misanthropy after leaving society.'

'How do you know so much about the murders? Surely not all the details were reported in the news?'

'Money buys information. You know what? I could do with another sherry.' She nods towards the globe bar. Getting the first drink for herself must've been *so* tiring.

I consider why Evangeline's discussing the killings with me. I thought I was here to learn about literature, not book-related deaths. Does she know about Sam's arrest? The papers haven't named him yet, but she has sources. I'm not Sam's biggest fan, but I will defend him. He's not the violent type and has no interest in books. Kate's still pissed off with him for giving the Kindle she bought him for Christmas to a friend.

'Are you going to stand there all day?' Evangeline shouts.

I take my time pouring the drink to show I'm not her servant.

After knocking back the sherry, she clears her throat. 'Next are the "Goblin Market" killings. Can you find the relevant room on the map?'

I'm a schoolchild being put on the spot by the teacher. Despite my frustration with playing a weird version of Where's Wally? I point at The Goblin Market Room.

'It's a poem by Christina Rossetti about goblin men who offer seductive, addictive fruits to Laura and Lizzie,' I begin. 'Laura eats their wares, making her crave more; mimicking lust or going cold turkey. She nearly dies from giving in to temptation. Lizzie saves her sister by confronting the goblins. They attack Lizzie, pelting her body with fruits. She uses the pulp and juices to feed Laura. Both sisters survive.'

Evangeline's mouth drops open. 'Impressive. Few choose to read the works of Christina Rossetti against more well-known classics. A damned shame. She was a wonderful poet. Of course, her brother, Dante Gabriel Rossetti - an artist and poet - receives all the attention.'

'Mum shared Christina Rossetti's poetry with me.'

Evangeline's eyes narrow. 'Some of it is rather dark for a child.'

I shrug. 'Mum didn't shield me too much with literature. She always explained the meanings and made sure I understood the difference between imagination and reality.'

THE PROFESSOR

'Unfortunately, I fear this killer refuses to discern the distinction. Still, it's heartening to hear your mother brought you up well.' Evangeline looks away. 'She did a good job.'

Spitting embers land on the rug in front of us. Evangeline startles.

'Enough of that.' She gives herself a fortifying shake. 'Let's move on with the summary. Back then, The Professor stopped after the "Goblin Market" murders. Twin sisters, who were studying at Oxford Carroll, were killed. Their bodies were smeared in fruit, and a passage from the poem was at the scene. I told the police it was linked to my estate. They wouldn't listen and treated me like a hysterical fool. I hope they're regretting it now this business has started again.'

I ponder on the recent deaths, along with their literary and Glynnholme connections. Clementine's murder in the university library represents The Middlemarch Library and the novel. Fiona was staged as Dracula's obsession, for The Madam Mina Room. Grace was Cathy's ghost on the *Wuthering Heights* stage, linking with Glynnholme's Cathy's Chamber.

'Note the rooms that are left,' Evangeline says. 'The killer hasn't finished yet. There's The D'Urberville Room for a start. Someone *will* die depicting Tess.'

'Someone I know is in custody.' I can't keep it to myself any longer. Evangeline will catch me out, eventually.

'Sam Bell, your boss' husband. Don't worry. He isn't guilty.'

'How can you be so certain?' While I agree, her evasiveness is grating.

'I have my suspicions about who's doing this,' she replies. 'The Professor thinks he's my intellectual equal, the idiot.'

'You have to tell the police who he is!'

'Stuff and nonsense. We're playing a game and I will win.'

As she holds up the empty glass again, I ignore it. Until she tells the truth, I'm going on strike. Evangeline lets out a dramatic sigh while placing the glass on the table.

'Everything we've discussed is theoretical at this stage,' she says. 'It requires proof, which I will get. The Professor analyses and dissects literature, his victims, and - through that - my home.

Although he's proving to be successful, arrogance will trip him up. I'll be there to ruin him.'

'This is a dangerous murderer, not a villain in a novel. You have to take this seriously. How many more women must die?'

'None if I have my way! Don't think I'm enjoying this. I refuse to be a sitting duck, waiting to be killed.' Evangeline's voice becomes a croak. She coughs. 'Let's continue with how he's using Glynnholme to drive his mission.'

'Why are you sharing this with me?' I finally ask.

Her shoulders drop. 'Because I need you.'

I can't ignore the sudden drop into humility. 'What about The Jekyll Room, The Hyde Room, and The Gray Hall? They're written by men.'

She flicks a hand. 'Don't bother with those. The Professor will never kill men. He believes he's a victim of educated women. We're a threat to his sense of identity and worth.'

'You've certainly done a lot of research.'

'I had to. Look at these two rooms.' She places fingers on different boxes, one upstairs and the other down.

My tongue thickens as I speak. 'The dining room is The Eyre Room. Then there's The Red Room, which is another bedroom.'

Evangeline's frenzied glare feeds on my fear.

'Why did you name two rooms in this house after *Jane Eyre*?' I ask. 'All the other Victorian texts have one.'

'Everyone knows I'm a Brontë buff. *Jane Eyre* is my favourite novel.' She touches her heart. 'Be aware of how important you are. The Professor wants a Jane to complete the Glynnholme set.'

CHAPTER 32
Jane

Under Rupert's watchful glare, balancing a stack of books under my chin isn't easy. He tracks my movements while opening the door.

'So, Ms Glynn has permitted the borrowing of her texts,' he says. 'Consider it a great honour. Be sure to return them in the same condition.'

I pretend to sway and be in danger of dropping the books. Rupert moves faster than he seemed capable of doing. Goalkeeper style, he thrusts out his arms. Laughing, I step aside. As if I'd ever damage something so precious.

'Calm down, Rupe,' I begin. 'I'll wear gloves when reading, so these peasant hands won't leave marks. Oh, by the way, eat plenty of fibre, take warm baths, and drink lots of fluids. Your arse grapes will disappear in no time.'

He splutters 'Well, I never. Show some respect, young lady. You, more than most, should understand the value of domestic staff.'

'Because I'm a lower class than the Glynns?' I roll my eyes.

'Forget what I said. A good day to you, Miss Unwin.' He slams the door.

Considering he's Evangeline's slave, Rupert has a flaming cheek. I regard her books in my arms. After freaking me out by stating I'm probably on The Professor's hit list, Evangeline changed the subject. Her knowing fingers pulled textbooks from the library's shelves, selecting those I absolutely must read. While flicking through one, I tried not to groan at content drier than the Sahara. After noticing my frown, she asserted I need to learn how to analyse literature. She added the initial reaction when reading is the most joyful. However, engaging with different interpretations is important, often to prove them wrong. Her eyes gleamed as she stated how much fun is to be had, pulling apart white male scholars' theories. Evangeline thinks The Professor is terrible for hating women, but it's okay for her to bash the opposite sex.

While placing the book haul in my car, I wonder how I'll get through them all before the next visit. Evangeline wants me to come back. After hearing her theories regarding The Professor's killing agenda, I'm not as excited as I should be. Glynnholme is at the root of the murders. Do I really want to come here again?

'Bugger it!'

I search for the speaker. Near a hedge, Ed kicks away secateurs lying on his foot.

'Shit, that hurt!' He notices me and grins. 'I mean, "ouch".'

'Don't worry. Far worse usually comes out of my mouth.'

'Evangeline hates it when I swear. Even from indoors, she's constantly listening. A window pops open and that plummy voice shouts, "Edward" at me. Whenever she says my name, she looks like she's sucking lemons. Evangeline doesn't appreciate an F-bomb is perfect for certain situations. I should've used it when these bastard secateurs fell on my foot.' Ed picks up the offending tool.

I stifle a laugh. 'Sorry, you're not having much luck since I arrived. I'll go before something else happens.'

'I can get myself in enough trouble without assistance.' He starts walking, stops, and then turns around. 'Are you coming or not?'

'Where?' I ask, hoping it's not inside. Evangeline's intensity is draining. Watching her battle with Ed would completely wear me out.

'You've seen the house,' Ed replies. 'Now, let me show you my lair.'

CHAPTER 33
Jane

Ed's shed is home to a lot of stuff. Clay flower pots are stacked on high shelves, along with seedling trays. Various colours of paint and wood stain tins congregate in a corner. A tower of Glynns' Delights tubs threatens to fall.

'It's true,' I say. 'They do get smaller every year. A few Christmases ago, Dad swore there were fewer sweets in the tub. He refuses to buy them anymore, saying they leave a nasty aftertaste.'

Ed scowls. 'Skimping on things is typical upper class behaviour. If I want Glynn sweets, I have to buy them. No freebies, although I'm allowed their empty tubs. Lucky me. They're good storage containers, though, I suppose.'

He leans against a desk. It seems an odd furnishing choice for a labourer until I spot papers scattered across it. Sketches of plants twist into archways. Ambitious drawings display hedge labyrinths, winding and deceiving those who enter.

'Are these yours?' I ask.

After snatching the design, he shoves it under a glass paperweight, encasing a spray of flowers.

'Just silly doodles,' he mumbles.

'They're stunning! Are you going to use them here?'

THE PROFESSOR

Ed snorts. 'Her Highness, Evangeline Glynn, would *never* allow me to make my mark on her property.'

'Have you shown her these ideas? Anyone can see how skilled you are.'

'When I showed Evangeline my sketches, she laughed me out of the house. Nothing ever changes around here. She's stagnating in the past.' He pulls out a paint-splattered office chair. 'Have a seat. It's old but clean.'

He flips over a crate and sits on it.

'That can't be comfortable,' I say, watching him lower to the ground.

'There's a lot of crouching in my work. I have thighs of steel.' He grins.

I give the chair a spin. It has to be done.

'When did you start gardening here?'

'Evangeline didn't mention me in your little chat then.' Ed's laugh is brittle-thin. 'Not surprising seeing as I'm the poor relation, or what she refers to as her "charge". Thankfully, I'm not adopted and didn't have to take the Glynn surname.'

I stop spinning. 'Evangeline was your guardian?'

Dark eyes remind me of creepy goblins from Mum's illustrated version of "Goblin Market". I look away to hide my shame. Considering we've only recently met, it's unfair to compare Ed to such evil.

'It's obvious what you're thinking,' he says. 'Why would the mighty Ms Glynn take responsibility for the likes of me?'

After taking a piece of wood from a workbench, he produces a curved knife from his back pocket and begins cutting.

'To be honest,' I reply, 'I'm surprised Evangeline would take in *anyone*. She doesn't strike me as the maternal type. Henry's not exactly her biggest fan.'

'Around here, everything's centred on appearances.' He focuses on the mansion, looming over us from the shed window. 'Evangeline couldn't care less about me. She knew my mum. After she died, Evangeline saw an opportunity to appear charitable.'

'Why are you a gardener and not enjoying the benefits of being in the Glynn family?'

A shower of wooden splinters dart from the knife. 'I'm way past eighteen and guardianship. Evangeline's no longer responsible for me. Not that she ever was.'

'Pardon me for saying, but if you're so unhappy, why do you stay here?'

'My mentor, Norman Patterson, was head gardener before me. After he died, I took over. I'm not letting anyone else do this and ruin what Norm started. Besides, me staying around annoys the Glynns. They daren't turf me out, as it would look bad on them. I get on with my stuff and they do their thing. We hardly see each other.

'When I was younger, Evangeline tried forcing me into her mould, but I didn't play along. I dread to think how things would've turned out if I'd been a girl. Evangeline makes out she's a feminist when really she uses women. Mum was another of her projects. Make sure Evangeline doesn't manipulate you. It ended badly for my mum.'

'What happened?'

'After she lost all entertainment value, Evangeline ignored her. I expect a single parent was unacceptable, too. Not that Mum was one for long. She died in a car accident. For some reason no one will share she'd previously signed papers naming Evangeline as my guardian. I was practically a newborn when Mum died.'

'That sounds awful.'

He frowns at the burgeoning creation he's holding. 'I've learned to live with it, although I still wish I'd had family I could've gone to. I guess I'm an *Oliver Twist* type of orphan and this is my workhouse.'

'Oh, is it that bad? Do the Glynns mistreat you?'

'They wouldn't dare. Don't mind me and my stupid jokes. Excuse me. I'm not as educated as the rest of you.'

I face the wall behind the desk. Scribbles are dotted on a map of the Glynnholme house and grounds. This map is more recent than the one Evangeline has in the library. Ed leans over and places a finger on a specific area.

THE PROFESSOR

'Mrs Patterson and I are creating a kitchen garden. Come summer, we'll have an absolute bounty. Mrs P's constantly making lists of what to plant.'

Ed's earlier ominous eyes regain their shine.

'The love of gardening bursts from you,' I begin. 'You're also incredibly creative. Have you considered going to college to learn landscaping and topiary? Is that what it's called?'

Instead of answering, Ed returns to the crate and resumes carving. Grim determination sets his mouth in a straight line.

'I didn't mean to offend you,' I say. 'Maybe formal qualifications could help with getting into landscaping or setting up your own business.'

'I thought you were different.'

'What do you mean?'

'Someone from your background should appreciate not everyone has it easy. We can't all follow our dreams.'

I pick up a pencil and fiddle with it. 'You know nothing about me.'

'Not much gets past me.'

The pencil snaps. 'Damn it. Rookie error for someone who handles these all the time in a stationery shop. Look, I don't believe I'm better than you because of studying. Dad tells me often enough we come from working-class stock. Your working-man's pride reminds me of him.'

'For some of us, it's all we've got.'

Ed approaches a metal case, unlocks it, and pulls the lid open. His body then shields it. Despite the secrecy, I notice a few books inside. He takes out an envelope and removes what appears to be a photo from inside.

'This is all I have of my mother. Apparently, she was humble and wanted to forge her own way ahead. I only got that info from Mrs P because she felt sorry for me. The Glynns are always tight-lipped about Mum. Norman said to leave things behind, but I can't.'

I nod. 'I kind of understand. My mum died when I was eighteen. It's different in that I had some time with her, but I know the pain of living without a mother. Hey, what do you have there?'

He holds up the photograph. 'This is Mum.' The deep lines on his forehead disappear. 'Beautiful, wasn't she?'

Selena certainly was. Glossy, long brown hair reached to her waist. Her wide smile outshone everybody else. She's standing central in a group of people dressed in suits and cocktail dresses. Two faces crossed out with a marker pen are hard to miss.

'Why did you do that?' I try to keep my voice even.

Ed grabs the memento. 'I found this photo in the bin. Once again, the Glynns treated Mum like rubbish. I had a feeling the picture was important, so I saved it. Norman confirmed Selena's in the middle.'

'But marking out *their* faces? That's extreme.'

Gripping the picture, Ed's knuckles whiten. 'That's the least I want to do to Evangeline and Henry. They deserve to be punished for hurting me.'

CHAPTER 34
Jane

Henry finishes drinking. 'Whisky-laced coffee takes off the edge. Downright chilly out there.'

After ripping open a cardboard box, I check the delivery slip, naming the culprit.

'Stupid idiot!'

'Gosh, that's a tad harsh.' Henry sets his mug down on a shelf. 'What have I done?'

'I wasn't talking about you.'

Once again, I curse my colleague's ineptitude. Jaden has ordered a mountain of punch pockets. While I wondered why the courier kept bringing in boxes, I didn't query it. Kate sometimes places bulk orders, but certainly never enough to hold every document in the world. Until now, I haven't disturbed her. Dealing with her husband's arrest for allegedly being a serial killer must be hell. Jaden's got to go, though, and Kate does the firing. Even though he's been here for a while, he still can't operate the till. His eye-watering BO, rudeness, and mostly sitting on his arse, has made me feel stabby. I'm reeling at how he told a regular elderly customer earlier to "Bugger off to WHSmith" when she questioned why we didn't have any notelets. Currently, I'm not sure what's giving me more of a headache: Jaden; this ridiculous order; or Henry's constant pacing.

'Well done for convincing Mother to arrange another visit for you,' Henry says.

'There was no "convincing" involved.'

'Mother's difficult to please. Did she perform the throwing a teacup into the fire routine?'

'It looked expensive. I understand she's against hunting, but what a waste of money!'

He shakes his head. 'Mother couldn't care less about animal welfare. When we used to have visitors, she often pulled that stunt. It's a cheap tea set. Mother likes to shock people and test them out. So far, she hasn't complained about you being a wimp. You passed.'

How dare Evangeline do that to me! She was mocking the relatively poor person who'd be shocked. Thankfully, I kept my composure throughout the party piece. Now, Henry's peacock strutting around the shop further fuels my rage with the Glynns.

'As you can see, I'm up to my ears in it. I've taken your order. Excuse me while I try to sort out this mess.'

He buttons up his camel-coloured - likely cashmere - coat. 'Of course. See you at tomorrow's seminar.'

As he approaches the door, one of my worst nightmares happens. Dad arrives.

'Larry! What a treat to see you again.' Henry thumps him on the back.

After coughing, Dad grimaces and then nods. 'Good afternoon, Mr Glynn.'

'It's *Doctor*, actually, but you may call me *Henry*. Any family of Jane's is a friend of mine.'

Dad looks him up and down. 'Are you leaving, *Mr* Glynn? Don't let me keep you.'

I groan at the likelihood of a verbal shoot out.

Flicking his wrist, Henry takes time showing off his Rolex. It's an obvious power move. 'Got to dash. No rest for the wicked, right, Larry the Lamb?'

THE PROFESSOR

Before he can reply, Henry flounces off. Dad whacks a Tupperware box on the counter, full of the forgotten lunch I prepared this morning.

'That bloody man!' Dad shouts. 'He's lucky I didn't deck him, especially after how he treated me when I was working on that play.'

A pang of sadness rises within me for Grace, the victim on a *Wuthering Heights* stage.

I grab a stool and offer it to Dad. 'Calm down. Henry's a wind-up merchant. Don't let him get to you.'

I can hear his teeth grinding as he sits.

'Why you have anything to do with those Glynns is beyond me.'

'Henry's my tutor and lecturer. Evangeline will help me progress in my studies. It's nothing more than that.'

'Take all you can from those posh bastards. It's time the little people prospered rather than the higher classes.'

'Sit there and read the paper. I'll make a brew in a minute.'

He takes out the newspaper from under his arm and scans the front page. 'Awful for Kate, isn't it?' He points to the headline, *Female Students Finally Free From The Professor?* 'I find it hard to believe Sam's responsible, though.'

Sam and Dad are friendly, which is strange as Dad values faithfulness. He's aware of Sam's indiscretions but asserts there are always two sides to every story. Sometimes, it winds me up.

I notice my novel on the shelf. 'Why did you name me after Jane Eyre?'

He doesn't answer. I yank the newspaper wall away from in front of his face.

'I'm talking to you! Why was I named after Jane Eyre?'

'It was your mum's favourite. We've told you this many times.'

'She loved *Jane Eyre*, but her favourite novel was *The Lion, the Witch, and the Wardrobe*. She said she wanted to call me Lucy.'

'Think you're confused,.' A disembodied voice comes through the newspaper that's back in place. 'All those books you're reading are getting mixed up in your mind.'

I know to give up on a conversation when his focus is elsewhere. My mobile rings.

'Did you get the gist of that?' I ask after the call ends.

Dad is now giving me his full attention. 'Not all of it, but I figured it's about Sam.'

'Kate said he's been released. Witnesses confirmed he was in the pub the night Grace died. Sam was there all evening, playing poker upstairs. Also, he has alibis for the other killings, most of them other women than his wife. There's no way he could've killed anyone ten years ago, either. He was selling time shares in Tenerife. That's where Sam and Kate met.'

Despite how much I dislike her other half, my happiness for Kate is genuine. I only hope others don't think the smoke of Sam being accused of murders means there's an accompanying guilty fire.

Dad smiles. 'I bet Kate's relieved.'

'She is, although she's divorcing him for being a cheating arsehole.'

'Oh, well. Where's that cuppa you promised?'

I wish I could move on so easily. If Sam is innocent that means The Professor is still out there, ready to kill again.

CHAPTER 35

The most important part of The Professor's plan has begun. Jane has visited Glynnholme, setting the next stage into motion.

He could've killed her at any moment. The opportunities are often there, but it would be hasty to act on them. Besides, there's a stumbling block. Sometimes he wonders if he'll ever overcome it. Regularly, he ponders on what must happen. Thought isn't as terrifying as carrying out the final act, though. Time is his ally. With each murder, he gets a little closer to revealing the truth to Jane.

The Professor smiles at Oxford Carroll's website, warning students to be alert. Terror has returned now everyone knows the police got the wrong man. Sam's arrest was a useful distraction, but no one will claim The Professor's title. He's worked hard to prove his worthiness of the name and isn't bothered it comes from a woman's writing. After all, accomplished female authors rely on the masculine aspect of their brains to create genius. When he first read Charlotte Brontë's novel, *The Professor*, it felt like fate. The main character, William Crimsworth, is teased by an older woman who thinks she's superior. Mademoiselle Reuter weakens in resolve and harshness by falling in love with him. *This* Professor is aware of how older women, particularly Evangeline, try to steal from men. Unlike Mademoiselle Reuter, Evangeline's incapable of loving anyone.

He delights in how Brontë's professor gains power over his young, female pupils, and the love interest, Frances. Even better, Charlotte's ominous ending is a delight. William and Frances' son, Victor, is bound to become a hideous progeny even Mary Shelley would fear. The Professor considers the issues of producing tainted offspring. Legacies are dangerous as well as beneficial. He knows better than most.

Charlotte Brontë didn't see *The Professor* published in her lifetime. *This* Professor won't accept finding fame after his death. The thrill of seeing and hearing the public's reactions to his killings makes him feel alive. This is how, once again, he's superior to women. Charlotte may have written a great novel, but she wasn't robust enough - man enough - to seize glory.

Finally, the media are making links between the present murders and those from years ago. A decade of silence was almost unbearable. In that waiting period, whenever he met a female English Literature student, he'd consider for them an appropriate Victorian text, quote, killing method, and scene. While his sharp mind never failed, perfection demanded he wait. He pursued other interests to keep him occupied, mainly seducing women. Unfortunately, whispers began and gossip increased. He reined it in, assured by the knowledge he would return.

Jane will learn how both their lives are rooted in the Glynn empire. Glynnholme helped him to become The Professor. Now, it will be Jane's end.

CHAPTER 36
Jane

Fairy lights flick on across the grounds of Glynnholme. A winter wonderland of frosted pine tree tips and illumination captures my attention. Ed's been busy. Previously, he shared how Evangeline commanded the light show to welcome me on my evening visits. That woman never fails to surprise me.

On my last visit, Ed moaned about untangling the lights, grumbling there's no point considering nobody ever visits. When I reminded him I'm a visitor, he said I'm beyond that as I've been here a few times. I teased it practically made me family. The silence after was awkward. Ed's hostile connection with the Glynns isn't an ideal domestic set-up.

After pressing the doorbell, I wait for Rupert's sour face to appear. I previously advised him to be careful of the wind keeping it that way forever. As always, he glared at me as if I'd sprouted another head.

The door creaks open, reminding me of the opening to Michael Jackson's "Thriller". Instead of zombies, a close second appears. Rupert's given up the pretence of wearing the fancy outfit I call a penguin suit, but the colour scheme continues. I consider if he's taking the piss. A black v-neck jumper, white shirt, and orange tie mimic an emperor penguin's colours. The waddling remains. Maybe those piles are still giving him trouble.

'Hi, Rupert.' I offer my coat and scarf so Evangeline can't tell him off for not taking them, like on my first visit.

'Good afternoon, Miss Unwin.'

'It's Jane.'

He raises his snub nose as if sniffing stinky air. 'Indeed, but one must be formal.'

'Not with me, Rupe. One is most informal.'

Enjoying his pained expression, I breeze past. That bloke needs to chill out. No wonder he's got so many ailments.

After hanging up my outdoor clothing, Rupert rushes to totter alongside me. 'Not the library today.' He steers me towards the staircase. 'Ms Glynn wants to meet upstairs. I said it's improper, receiving guests in a bedroom, but what do I know? I'm only the hired help.'

At the halfway landing point of the stairs, he stops and lowers his head at the Charles Glynn painting. I consider if etiquette commands showing reverence to original owners of posh houses. Dragging my right foot behind me, I curtsey. Rupert pulls me up.

'What on earth are you doing?'

'You were bowing, so I thought I should, too.'

He laughs. 'That's priceless. I was stretching my neck. Think I slept strangely last night. Miss Unwin, you're an absolute comedic delight.'

I'm not sure whether I should be pleased or offended at his amusement. Still, it's nice to see this strange penguin man lightening up a little.

As we walk along the upstairs corridor, I note the names of bedrooms. Each room has a placard with its title. My skin prickles at the thought of how these rooms and Victorian literature are connected to deaths. Rupert halts. I crash into him.

'Sorry.' I bounce away.

The scowl returns. He mutters something before knocking on a door.

'Come in!' Evangeline's voice thunders from the other side.

THE PROFESSOR

Rupert steps in ahead of me. 'Miss Unwin to see you, Ms Glynn.'

Evangeline stokes coal in the fireplace with a poker. 'That will be all, Rupert, unless Jane cares for any other refreshments.' She holds out a hand indicating a teapot, cups, and a stand full of dainty cakes.

I shake my head in response. What's in front of me has stolen my speech.

'Go on then.' Rupert pushes me inside. 'You won't die.'

I turn around. 'Why did you say that?'

'Just a joke.' His eyes linger on me before he leaves.

CHAPTER 37
Jane

I'm somewhere I've only ever pictured. In *Jane Eyre*, her spiteful aunt locked Jane in the red room as a punishment. For me, being in Glynnholme's version, The Red Room, is a treat. Mum thought it odd how much I enjoyed reading about the novel's room. She thought Jane's mistreatment by the Reeds and her imaginings of the ghost of Mr Reed would frighten me. Instead, I perceived the room as a place of change and redemption, where Jane learns she has strength against adversity. She was - and still is - one of my role models.

Evangeline is seated. 'Do look around.'

Under her watchful eye, I go on a little tour. I know every stick of furniture and furnishings from Chapter Two of *Jane Eyre*. Evangeline clearly does, too. The fire competes with the gloom from the drawn blinds. Shadows dance on walls painted a shade of fawn with a blush of pink. I expect Evangeline had the colour specially mixed. Sombre mahogany dominates, from the wardrobe, toilet table, and chairs, to the pillars supporting the bed. The bed! It's all I can do not to jump on it, to test the puffed up pillows and thick mattress. I dare to touch the counterpane of a snow-white bedspread.

'Is this from Marseilles?' I ask.

THE PROFESSOR

Evangeline places her feet on a footstool. 'Of course. In matters of literature, I *never* skimp on the details. Lie down. It's very comfortable.'

I sit on the edge of the bed. Lying down in front of her would make me vulnerable. Evangeline's already making me nervous. I feel my way around. Ready to shield the sleeper, burgundy damask curtains are weights in my hands.

'Pull up a seat and join me,' Evangeline says.

I check my trainers before walking again on the burgundy carpet. Precise hoovered lines remind me of a recently mown football pitch.

'Should I take my shoes off?'

She frowns. 'Why on earth should you do that?'

I guess rich people's carpets are regularly cleaned or replaced. At home, we always remove our shoes.

'You're delighted with what you see,' Evangeline remarks. 'Explain why.'

'I'm not sure.'

'Yes, you are. No need to be coy. Remember, you're here to learn. I can't teach a silent student.'

'I've never been afraid of the red room. In there, Jane understands the world is hard, but she can be harder. That's her turning point.'

Evangeline's face fills with a previously unseen joy. 'How perfectly wonderful! That's how I view this space, too. Henry says it resembles a brothel. What does he know? Actually, he probably does. The redness is everything: passion; ambition; motivation; fight... I enjoy being here and I hope you will too. It's yours.'

'What do you mean?'

'This is where you'll sleep after late studying. Cutting our evening sessions short is such a bother.'

'Thank you, but—'

She holds up a hand. 'No need to thank me. So, have you read *Tess of the D'Urbervilles* as I instructed?'

'I loved it!'

'Good, good.' She nods. 'We must make sure you're ahead of the other students. What do you love about the novel?'

'It's really sad, and I felt like murdering Alec myself. Tess, though, is brilliant. She's naïve and trusting, but that comes from being a gentle and kind soul. Society, along with Alec and Angel, threatens to break her. Even in death, though, she prospers.'

'How can a dead person prosper?'

'Tess dies knowing the truth of who she is and what she refused to become. She'd rather hang than live with the shame of being forced into being Alec's mistress. It's a shame she didn't live longer to discover more of herself, though. Tess had a lot of potential.'

Evangeline sniffs. 'As usual, men stole a woman's options. Thomas Hardy could've given her a happier ending, but he shows the evil that men do with her demise. Also, Angel promised Tess so much: marriage; security; and love. He saw none of them through. Alec cheapened Tess. However, she's cleverer than both of them. Can you relate to her in any way?'

'Maybe. While I'm learning lots, I'm fairly new to it. Like Tess, sometimes I feel like I'm out of my depth. Thankfully, I don't have a dodgy rich family manipulating me.' I offer a cheeky wink.

She lets out a hearty laugh. 'I promise the Glynns won't defile you or lay false claims to an inheritance.'

'Thank fu… I mean thank goodness for that.' I smile.

'Inheritance is a complicated business,' Evangeline says. 'We may not have degenerate men in the family like Alec - although I often question Henry's behaviour - but the Glynn legacy is complicated.'

'How?'

'Charles Glynn and his wife, Margaret, endured a series of stillbirths. Each child was a boy. They were devastated at the losses. When they were finally blessed with a living child, she was a girl. They named her *Mary*. Charles doted on her. Pause in The Gray Hall on your way out. There are many paintings of her there. When Margaret was advised further pregnancies would compromise her health, Charles believed Mary was sent from God. It made him respect females.'

'That's quite something for that era,' I add.

'Indeed.' Her top lip snarls. 'If the men of this family had been more like Charles, I wouldn't have half these troubles. Anyway, he adored Oxfordshire and decided to settle here. He designed and oversaw the construction of Glynnholme. From the beginning, Charles asserted it was Mary's property. He acted as a caretaker before she turned thirty-years-old. In fact, it's written in law Glynn women of that age inherit Glynnholme. That's why I'm the current owner and have been for decades. Everything is meant to pass through the female line.'

'What about the person who previously inherited?' I ask. 'If they're alive, do they have to leave when the next woman comes of age?'

'The previous owner chooses between staying in the house or living in a cottage on the grounds. Charles made sure everyone was taken care of.'

'Wow, that's very forward-thinking.'

Evangeline stands by the fireplace. 'It's wrong how we're surprised women can have things, back then and now. Men have had it all for far too long.'

'What happens if there aren't any women to inherit?'

'A man takes over until the next female is born and reaches thirty. Glynnholme will always belong to the Glynns.'

'So, Henry will inherit everything.'

She stabs a poker into the fire. 'Not if I have anything to do with it! Henry will own Glynnholme over my dead body and I don't mean through inheritance.'

CHAPTER 38

Evangeline is trying to control The Professor. Allowing her to believe she's in charge gives him power. He smiles at her being puffed up, thinking she's made a man to do her bidding. What a wonderful surprise it will be when she learns she's only a player, and a losing one at that.

Each of his killings destroys the joy of Evangeline's rooms. By the time he's claimed them all, she'll be running away from the place she used to love. Murders will destroy paradise.

Every killing is because of Evangeline, Selena, and Jane. They've all taken too much. It's only fair The Professor also takes what he wants. Those three women have ruled his life. Their actions, selfishness, and very being - although one of them is dead - make him do this. Sometimes he wonders if he would've been a more peaceful man if he'd never known the unholy trinity. The idea is ridiculous. The Professor was made to be a murderer.

He watches a young woman swiping on her phone while waiting for a bus. Across the road, he stands at another stop. Snatches of his prey flicker through the passing traffic. He suppresses a rising groan of ecstasy. She's perfect. As she pulls her long brown hair into a ponytail, the action threatens to undo him. He imagines grabbing her hair and pulling her to the ground. Previously, he thought sexually charged violence was over, but for her, he'll make an exception. The riskiness of choosing this person is too arousing to ignore. Besides, in *Tess of the D'Urbervilles*, Tess is violated. The Professor always follows the story and then adds some extra twists.

The target fiddles with her bag strap, held together with elastic bands. Observation has made him aware of her humble roots. Her background reminds him of Jane and her father, toiling for a living. Like Tess, a selfish, wealthy family has seduced Jane. The naivety makes him swear out loud. A girl sitting next to him shuffles further along the bench. Switching on the charm, he apologises. The girl should be grateful she's not a student or Jane.

Damn Jane! She's losing her head over the Glynns. It brings to mind the devilish Alec D'Urberville, forcing sumptuous strawberries on Tess. Similarly, Evangeline feeds Jane lies in a hothouse of secrecy. The Professor suspects Evangeline knows his true identity, but she'll never tell. They both have too much to lose.

A bus blocks his view. It doesn't matter. He's seen enough. The woman has been on his radar for a while. She is perfect. Oh, how his Tess of the D'Urbervilles will suffer.

CHAPTER 39
Jane

Ed pours tea from a flask and then offers the cup.

'No thanks. After being plied with refreshments by Evangeline, I'm drowning in it.'

He takes a slurp and then wipes the back of his hand across his mouth.

'Why does Evangeline hate Henry?' I ask.

'You've met him, right?'

I rub my hands together. The portable heater in Ed's shed is no competition against the low temperature outside.

'Henry can be a dick,' I begin, 'but he's not as terrible as Evangeline says. At least, I hope not.'

Ed twists the thermostat dial. 'It'll soon be toasty. You should've said you were visiting today. I would've warmed it up in here first. The cold doesn't affect me much because I wear so many layers.'

Dropping by his shed after seeing Evangeline has become part of my Glynnholme routine. Aware that she'll disapprove, we've agreed to keep it a secret. I keep protesting that she doesn't own me. It's sad how Ed states Evangeline believes she owns him, though.

THE PROFESSOR

Slipping in here and avoiding detection isn't easy. After leaving the house, I move my car nearer to the woods and sneak along a trail leading to the shed. It's like a discreet date, although I have no designs on Ed. There's no chemistry. The thought of fancying him is icky. He's becoming a friend, albeit a strange one. Despite our chats, I've only touched the surface of who Ed is.

'Oh, I almost forgot. I have something for you.' He unlocks the mysterious metal box I've noticed before.

'This is exciting.'

He blushes as he offers two bundles wrapped in hessian. 'Sorry, I haven't got any wrapping paper. They're something I've been working on.' He reaches into his back pocket and pulls out a curved knife from a leather cover. 'I'm never without my whittling knife. If I can't find any wood to whittle, I'll use other materials. Taking a knife out in public is a bit awkward, though. I'm inspired to create things all the time. You should see my stout little penguins.' He grins.

'Rupert?'

'Who else?'

I unwrap one of the parcels. Smooth wood replaces scratchy material. I'm holding a figurine of a woman wearing a bonnet and shawl. She's holding a pen and sheets of paper.

'This is beautiful! You're so talented.'

'It's a Victorian female writer, whichever you fancy. I don't know their names.'

'This is definitely Charlotte Brontë. She wrote *Jane Eyre*. Mum named me after the main character.'

'Lucky you.' His laugh is brittle. 'I'm the other half of Henry.'

'What does that mean?'

'Think, book nerd. Henry and Edward?'

'Of course! Henry Jekyll and Edward Hyde. Oh, wow.' I wince. 'That's harsh.'

'Yep. I was named after the evil monster.' He grimaces. 'Typical of Evangeline.'

'Surely, your mum chose your name. It might be a coincidence.'

Ed locks the box and moves it aside.

'You have so much to learn about the Glynns. Nothing's left to chance. They make shit happen. Mrs P said Evangeline practically forced my name onto Mum. Evangeline set me up to be horrible from the beginning.'

I place a hand on his. 'You're proving her wrong.'

'Am I? Sometimes, I wonder.' He pulls his hand away.

'There's more to you than you show. For example, you know more about literature than you're letting on.' I point to the box. 'I spotted copies of *Great Expectations* and *Dracula* in there.'

The box rattles as Ed stamps a foot on it. 'Don't ever sneak around in my stuff!'

I aim for the door. 'I wasn't snooping. The bloody thing was open!'

Ed grabs my shoulder. 'Stay, you grumpy cow. Sorry. I'm defensive about my belongings. I don't have a lot.'

I take a seat on the rickety office chair and examine the wooden Charlotte figure.

'You should meet my dad. He makes dolls' houses and the figures. You're both incredibly skilled.'

Ed smiles. 'Thanks. Don't forget the other gift.' He points at the bundle on the desk.

As I remove the packaging, another figure rolls out. I hold her up to the winter sunlight, breaking through the window.

'It's me!'

She has my long, often wayward hair. My usual choice of jeans and a hoodie are her clothing. Ed's even added the dimples that form in my cheeks when I smile.

'Ed, this is amazing.'

'I hope you don't think it's weird,' he mumbles. 'Promise I'm not a weirdo who's fixated on you. I just enjoy making them. Henry says they're creepy, probably because I made one of him and stuck pins in it, voodoo-style.'

'No way!'

I recall the photograph Ed defaced with Evangeline's and Henry's faces crossed out. Suddenly, it's not so amusing.

'Please say you didn't.'

'Chill out. It was a joke. Don't you feel like a doll being toyed with by the Glynns?'

'No,' I snap. 'I'm my own person. No one tells me what I can or can't do.'

He laughs. 'That's flaming obvious. Be careful, though. The Glynns can make people do things they've never dreamed of.'

'Such as?'

Ed's saved by the bell, or rather the ringing of my mobile. It's Leah. Getting Ed's answer to my question feels more important than chatting on the phone. Deciding to catch up with Leah this evening, I end the call.

Ed picks up a shovel. 'Unlike you lazy students, I've got work to do. Send me a message next time you're here.'

'I'd better go home and start dinner.' As I speak, I realise how much progress I've made. 'Stuff it. I'm putting my feet up. Dad can cook for once.'

'Mrs Patterson always prepares a Sunday roast. She needn't bother, considering Evangeline doesn't eat much and Henry's usually out. Mrs P insists on keeping me fed. She's an absolute legend.'

I'm glad someone around here treats him well. Now, he can add me to the list. I watch him walk away. As I head towards the car, my phone rings again. Leah's likely having a meltdown while writing an overdue essay.

'Hi, Leah.'

'Jane… I'm… need…'

Her voice is robotic and distorted. I check the signal. Ed warned getting a connection at Glynnholme is difficult. A freezing fog is settling. Home beckons. I'll call Leah later.

CHAPTER 40

This next murder deviates from The Professor's usual format. While he enjoys wheedling into his victims' lives, with this person, it wouldn't be wise. He wonders why he's never considered this method before. A woman he kind of knows but doesn't have a close relationship with has its perks. Can it match up, though, to the thrill when she realises a friend or lover is a dangerous enemy?

Despite wearing gloves, the chill nibbles at his fingertips. He flexes his hands. Killing tools should always be fit for purpose.

A canopy of trees is an accomplice, offering privacy for the upcoming deed. Hoping she won't break her Sunday routine, he circles the area.

He pictures her in church, singing her heart out and praising God. The brazen little madam isn't as pure as she makes out to be. The Professor has scrutinised every detail. Her mouth is often poised to gossip or judge. Now, *he* stands in judgement and finds her guilty.

The charge: believing she's superior to him because of studying English Literature.

The offence: coasting through the term and barely doing any work.

The punishment: death, *Tess of the D'Urbervilles* style.

He's found the perfect Tess: a country woman; chaste; and naïve. She's also making Tess' mistakes, thinking she's moving on to better things. Everyone has their place in society. If women stayed at the bottom of the ladder, he wouldn't have to teach them the error of their ways.

Jane remains a puzzle he dare not try to solve straight away. Her eventual lesson will be complex. It needs a robust strategy that cannot fail. Frequent visits to Glynnholme compromise her life chances. With promises of more education, Evangeline thinks she owns Jane. No one but The Professor can lay claim to Jane. She is achingly close. If she goes down to the woods today, she'll get more of a surprise than a teddy bears picnic.

The Professor's next victim regularly walks after a church service. Her recently chosen place is the woods near Glynnholme. Killing on Evangeline's doorstep is the clearest message to her so far. Not only will The Professor sully her The D'Urberville Room, murder will blight Glynn land.

Earlier wrestling with risks was intoxicating. The lawns of Glynnholme could be a killing ground. All that separates the wood and Glynnholme are signs stating ownership and fences a child can easily climb over. Sometimes common sense must win. Revealing himself to the Glynns at this stage would be foolish. The copse on the outskirts is more suited to the scene, anyway. Most walkers avoid it in winter. Thick mud and a propensity for dense, icy fog in such weather aren't attractive propositions. Thankfully, it shouldn't deter The Professor's target. She *has* to be Tess. The copse entices her.

The quote he'll later leave with her body is committed to his memory. His body tingles as he accepts the words from the novel as a command rather than the author's moral statement, "Why it was that upon this beautiful feminine tissue, sensitive as gossamer, and practically blank as snow as yet, there should have been traced such a coarse pattern as it was doomed to receive…"

Many readers find this part of the book ambiguous. The Professor knows exactly what it means and how important it is for his task. A woman's body, untouched by a man, will be defiled. He wonders if he can do this. She will scream. The act demands speed and excellence. Arrogance isn't welcome here.

The past "Goblin Market" deaths still haunt him. One of the victim's stubborn will to live - fighting against the wrong dose of a sedative - could've been his undoing. Years of rebuilding his confidence have prepared him. It's not his fault he had to take time out. Women ruin everything.

The Professor grabs a twig and snaps it in half. He imagines it's the sound of bones breaking.

Soon, his Tess will arrive.

CHAPTER 41
Jane

In the distance, someone calls my name. Trying to trace the source, I scan the area. Surely the esteemed Evangeline Glynn isn't bellowing like a town crier?

'I'm aware you've been chatting with that boy,' she yells, 'and I forbid it!'

I stand underneath where she's leaning out of an open upstairs window. An imagining of Cathy, demanding to be let in, flits into my mind. Grace's broken body replaces the image, dead on a *Wuthering Heights* stage. Folding my arms, I look up at a diva.

'Quite the *Romeo and Juliet* set-up we've got going on here, although you're lacking a balcony and the right characters.'

Evangeline flicks away her curls. 'Don't get smart with me, young lady. No more chats with Edward. Do you understand? You're here to see me, not him.'

'My neck's aching looking up at you. Come downstairs.'

'No. I've said what I intended to say.' She reaches for the latch.

'Woah!' I shout. 'Before you go, listen to someone else for once. I won't be told who I'm allowed to spend time with. You're not my mother, not that she ever dictated who my friends could be. While I'm grateful for the support, lay off the commands and stop being so dramatic.'

Finally, she's silent. I consider asking if I've performed a miracle. Instead, I place my hands on my hips, ready for more venting. Tuition be damned. Today, I'm in a salty mood.

'Ed's a lovely person,' I begin. 'It's a shame you refuse to recognise it. You, of all people, should be kinder to him, considering you were his guardian. I *will* continue talking to him. If you have a problem with that, I'll meet up with Ed elsewhere.'

'There's a fire in you. While I applaud the intensity, be aware you're making a huge mistake.'

'How?'

She shakes her head. 'I'm too tired for this. Visit the boy if you insist, but be careful. He's not a suitable match. You must not pursue a relationship with him.'

'He's a man, not a boy. Also, not that it's any of your business, we're just friends. We'd never view each other as anything more than that.'

'At least that's something. Take heed. I know the truth and it isn't pretty. If this goes wrong, it will end in tears for everyone.'

I kick at gravel. 'What on earth are you wittering on about? For once, talk normally rather than in riddles.' This newfound confidence at not accepting Evangeline's bullshit is surprising, but welcome.

The penguin man comes doddering towards me. 'Would you kindly lower your voice?' Rupert is a hypocrite of the command as he shouts. 'Ms Glynn is having a nap.'

I point up upwards. 'No, she's not.'

Evangeline offers a cheeky wave and a grin. Rupert pivots and aims for the house, mumbling about how terribly inappropriate this all is.

'Rupert seriously needs to pull that rod out of his arse.' Evangeline smirks.

I laugh. 'Ms Glynn, such foul language is shocking and most unbecoming of a lady.'

'There's more to me than you think. All you see is a bitter old woman past her prime.'

'Not at all. I… I—'

THE PROFESSOR

She holds up a hand. 'Spare me the flattery. I know who I am and I own it. I *am* a bitter old woman, but I also have a heart. While it's taken a battering over the years, it's still there. One day you might glimpse what's inside. Before we're done, I have plenty more to reveal. Prepare yourself, Jane. I need you to be strong.'

She slams the window shut, leaving me with my mouth wide open.

CHAPTER 42

Leaves crunch under his next victim's boots. The Professor's pulse pounds in his ears. He flexes his fingers again, warming up for this act of *Tess of the D'Urbervilles*, titled "Maiden no More". His Tess unknowingly awaits tuition. In the novel, Alec D'Urberville taught Tess the consequences of naivety. The Professor will do the same with his target.

Leah waits for Jane to answer the phone. A distorted voicemail command begins. Leah leaves a brief message, unsure if it will make sense because of a patchy signal. After deciding to phone her friend later, she continues walking. The woods aren't the moors, but it's a good enough second. She's never happier than when she's enjoying what nature offers. Unfortunately, today there's not much to see. The fog thickens.

At the edge of the copse, The Professor's heart rate quickens. He has one chance to get this right. Leah may be small, but she might be strong. He pulls a balaclava over his head and moves from the hiding place.

Leah places buds into her ears to listen to music. Energetic beats move her along. She feels hope rising. Tomorrow, she'll hand in the overdue essay. Tomorrow, she won't be at risk of failing her degree.

THE PROFESSOR

The Professor slams into Leah. Her feet slide on wet leaves. She falls. Their limbs tangle. He smothers her mouth, braced to scream.

Dragging her deeper into the woods, heady lust consumes him. To stay alert, he presses his thumb and finger together. Leah kicks out, trying to gain traction. He stabs her neck with a syringe. Living but unconscious, she lies still.

He prepares to claim a maiden and make her a ruined woman. Touching Leah's milky-white skin, The Professor visualises his *Dracula* victim. Skill rather than vampire fangs punctured Fiona's neck. The seductive memory of an accomplished murder motivates him. He fumbles with Leah's clothing. While his body is willing, thoughts betray him. For confidence, he reflects on some past successes: Brooke's sleepy death; Clementine's slashed wrist; and Phoebe in a burning wedding dress.

Jane steals his head space. Passion disappears. Not only Jane is to blame. Up close, he now sees Leah isn't fair or sweet. She lacks the underlying sexual allure to match with Tess. Leah fooled him. He won't accept he's made a mistake, but maybe a different quote would've been wiser. *Tess of the D'Urbervilles* is more than a rape scene. Tess endured other miseries he could've used and inflicted.

The Professor kicks Leah's leg. A pathetic groan incites his rage. He must end this. As he leans over, a tear trickles down the side of her face. He turns away. Raw emotion makes him buckle.

'Oh, Jane, what have I done?' he cries.

The Professor tears up the quote, scattering it like confetti. A snap echoes nearby. It's too late to finish what he started. He rises from the ground and runs.

CHAPTER 43
Jane

After the call ends, I stare at my phone. Despite obviously trying, Leah's dad couldn't control his wobbling voice. Talking about what happened to his daughter took courage. Leah asked him to phone me because she was worried I'd think my unanswered calls were a snub. If only I'd been able to speak to her before the attack. Better mobile reception at Glynnholme might have saved Leah from the horror. Knowing she was vulnerable, nearby in the woods, gives me chills.

I flinch as someone touches my head. Looking up from sitting on the doorstep, I smile at Dad.

'Why are you so jumpy?' he asks. 'Come inside. The heating isn't on for the birds.'

While standing up, I cup a hand over my mouth to check my breath. No way am I sharing I was having a cigarette. When I lit up, I thought Dad was out. Although I quit a few years ago, I have an emergency pack hidden in my bedroom. Dad doesn't know I used to smoke. A secret smoker's kit of mints, body spray, and mouthwash covered the "crime". Yes, I'm nearly thirty and can do what I want, but I respect Dad's anti-smoking stance because his father died of lung cancer. Still, after the conversation with Leah's dad, I needed nicotine.

Dad takes out a saucepan from the cupboard. I sit at the table.

'Can you smell a bonfire?' He sniffs.

While he turns away, I sniff my jumper. Smoke clings to the wool. I pull off the evidence and fling it into the washing machine.

'There's a stain on it,' I say as Dad watches. I return to my chair. 'Hey, do you remember my friend, Leah, from university?'

'Would you like a hot chocolate?'

'Yes, please. Anyway, have I mentioned Leah?'

He pours milk into a saucepan. 'Have I met her? This ageing brain isn't what it once was.'

'No, you haven't, but I've mentioned her a lot.'

Dad's mental travelling elsewhere when I talk about my day is annoying. Once again, I wish Mum was here. She loved hearing about what was happening in my life. Dad cares, but he's a hard facts kind of person.

'Yesterday, Leah was attacked in the woods near Glynnholme.' Even as I say the words, I can't believe it.

'That's awful! Is she okay?'

'A man tried to... He threw Leah to the ground and would've hurt her, but he couldn't... well, you know... Thankfully, he couldn't do *that*.'

An angry cloud of burning milk rises over the top of the pan, splashing onto Dad's hand. He places it under the cold tap while I move the pan from the hob. Charred pieces float in milky skin.

'Poor woman. Can we do anything to help?'

'Her dad phoned. After collecting Leah from hospital, he took her home to Haworth. She doesn't want to be in Oxford any more.'

Dad turns off the tap and flicks drips from his fingers into the sink.

'That's understandable. There will be too many terrible memories here. If it was you, I'd take you away, too.'

'Leah shouldn't be denied an education because of a sick pervert.'

'There are other universities. Look, Jane, please be alert for any sign of trouble when you go to university and Glynnholme. I knew nothing good would come of this.'

'The Glynns aren't responsible. Besides, Ed will look out for me.'

Dad sits down. 'Who's Ed? I hope he's not another waster taking advantage of you.'

'You know I've sworn off men for a while. Ed's the Glynns' gardener. He's a friend, nothing more.' I decide not to share the details of Evangeline's previous guardianship. The whole thing is too complicated.

'Keep it that way.'

'Don't tell me what to do!' I blast. 'I'm not a teenager.'

'Don't act like one then.' Dad stretches out reddened fingers and winces. 'Ever since you've begun studying, it feels like we're drawing apart. This private tuition business isn't helping. I hardly see you nowadays.'

I place my hand on his uninjured one. 'You always come first. Henry and Evangeline are only there for my learning. You're family.'

'Never forget it.'

He smiles. I lean over and kiss him on the cheek.

'I'll make the hot chocolate,' I say.

'Be careful, love.'

I laugh. 'Unlike some people, I can make a drink without incident.'

'I meant outside this house.' Dad points towards the window. 'The murders are all linked to Oxford Carroll. It's worrying me.'

'With you by my side, I'll always be all right.'

I give my finest bear hug. Dad pulls away.

'Leave the drink. I've got work to do.'

'Off to your man cave?'

He scowls. 'Stop calling it that. The shed and what I produce in it keeps us clothed and fed.'

'I am grateful, but let me be an adult. I can look after myself.'

'I've never held you back.'

A moment of realisation hits me. *I* have been holding myself back. No more. Now I'm going to be more Jane Eyre and embrace life.

CHAPTER 44

Despite an overwhelming urge, The Professor couldn't return to the copse in the woods. The compulsion to go back was motivated by revenge. He wanted to kill Leah slowly, to make her pay for not being a suitable Tess.

He thought he'd chosen a young woman alluring enough for assault. When it came to committing the deed, he couldn't stoke his desire. Leah ruined everything. The Professor grieves for the destruction of a perfect plan. A selected quote from *Tess of the D'Urbervilles* was set to be pinned to a defiled and dead body. With literature, he enjoys adjusting the plot and making it his own. After all, it's fiction, not facts. While the book's Tess survived after Alec raped her, The Professor's version was supposed to die. Leah wasn't supposed to have the luxury of lying on the ground, waiting for a fog to lift.

Rage continues at Leah waking up and crying had made him careless. He shouldn't have torn up the quote and left it there. The police would piece it together and realise The Professor had failed.

Running away like a coward isn't his style. The snapping sound he heard was probably a creature in the woods. As he ran, he didn't see anyone. He'd become jittery, being so near Glynnholme.

Leah's death was supposed to be a message to Jane about how close he is. Still, the shock at her friend's attack will hurt Jane, but she might be warier, too. No. He won't panic. Jane won't know who The Professor is until he's ready to reveal the truth.

He regards the furnishings in The D'Urberville Room. Before, a painting's pastoral depiction of milkmaids and pastures full of cows eased his stress. Whenever he regarded the maiden at the forefront, he imagined his very own Tess. Now, his thoughts fly to a copse where his sexual potency diminished and the woman won. He picks up a chair by the bedside and hurls it against a wall.

Above the dressing table, a mirror bears his image. He turns away from failure reflected. Instead, he imagines Jane brushing her hair. The strands morph into another woman's locks. Jane becomes Selena. Once, Selena meant so much to him. Then she became a disappointment. Jane will too. He must not let it happen.

The Professor failed the Tess test. Revision and better planning will help him ace the next murder assessment. Nothing less than an *A+* for killing effort is acceptable.

CHAPTER 45

Jane

The dining table with chairs for ten guests harks back to Glynnholme's sociable past. Evangeline insisted on eating here, even after Henry suggested a smaller, more comfortable room. She nearly had a fit when I said I have dinner in front of the television when Dad's out.

After seating Evangeline at the head of the table, Rupert pulls out a chair for me. Henry takes his own seat. In the middle I'm a peacekeeping rose, caught between two prickly Glynn thorns. Evangeline flicks open a napkin like a cracking whip, and then lays it on her lap. She raises her glass.

'To Jane. May your education under my tutorage continue to flourish.'

'May it also thrive at the university where she does her actual studies,' Henry practically growls.

Evangeline rests her chin on her hands. 'Nice of you to join us, Henry, rather than gadding around elsewhere. What's the name of *this* lucky woman?'

'I didn't ask.'

Rupert and Mrs Patterson break up the bitching as they bring in a serving trolley.

'Oxtail soup, to start,' Rupert announces.

Mrs Patterson ladles soup from a silver tureen into bowls. My comprehensive school didn't teach etiquette. Are you only allowed to start eating after the host begins? There's no rush, anyway. I hate oxtail soup. When I was a child, Dad told me the canned version contained real tails. Now, I beg my retching reflex not to kick in. I swill the spoon around the bowl, searching for evidence. Evangeline clears her throat and frowns at me. After I take a tiny sip of liquid, she focuses on Henry instead.

'Henry, do not wear your napkin as a bib!' she bellows.

Her booming voice carries down the table, along crystal ware, silver cutlery, and candelabras. It's puzzling why all places are set. When I came in, I panicked, thinking others were invited to dinner. Dungarees and Doc Martens aren't fine dining attire. If I'd known I was having dinner with the Glynns, I would've made an effort.

Keeping up with the verbal tennis match between mother and son is tiring. My neck strains from supporting my heavy head. My limbs ache too. Maybe I'm getting a cold. Right now, I want to be tucked up in bed.

Evangeline lifts a spoon, holds it there, and then puts it back down. 'Not much of an appetite today.'

Her usual alabaster complexion is verging on grey. With each visit, I've noticed her becoming less vital.

'Do you need to lie down, Mother?'

The gentleness in Henry's voice is surprising. A slight smile escapes from Evangeline's mouth. Perhaps she *does* have some affection for her son.

Evangeline claws the tablecloth with bejewelled fingers. 'Stop fussing. Jane, how is your analysis of *Tess of the D'Urbervilles* coming along?'

It's not only tails in soup that have ruined my appetite. I don't want to talk about *that* book, but Evangeline always expects answers.

'I'm analysing the themes we discussed, although reading is difficult.'

Henry's laughter makes me want to punch him.

'Why on earth do you have a problem with *Tess*?' he asks. 'The story of a young woman taken in by a wealthy family should be right up your street.'

'Don't be so crass.' His mother's frostiness blasts at him.

Henry fixes his gaze on me. 'What in the novel are you finding tricky?'

'This isn't the time or place to discuss such things.' Water soothes my closing throat.

'Poppycock!' Evangeline cries. '*Never* censor literature. We're all adults and can deal with talking about sex, some more than others.' She darts some serious side eye at Henry. 'Is it the rape that bothers you?'

I nod.

'Apologies. I should've thought,' Henry says. 'I heard about what happened to Leah. As her friend, I'm sure you're concerned.'

'Yes, I am.'

I regard the dining area, called The Eyre Room. It's a place where I should be happy, being named after my beloved novel. Nothing can ease my discomfort at the moment, though. Since hearing of the attack on Leah, I've been on edge. It doesn't help I'm probably ill too. Despite sleeping for twelve hours last night, I need more rest.

Evangeline rises from her throne. 'Can't you see? The Professor hurt that young woman. This is a Tess-related murder.'

'But no one died,' Henry adds. 'He always kills.'

She takes her seat. 'I expect he would have killed that young lady. Something went wrong.'

Social niceties can do one.

'That's my friend you're talking about! Leah's a lovely person. She didn't deserve this.'

Henry shrugs. 'Bad things happen to good people. Tess was inherently decent, although naïve. Literature offers no better example of misery being heaped upon someone so undeserving of it. Remember that for your next essay. You'll get a good grade.'

He grins. If I had more energy and fewer manners, I'd wipe it off his face. How can he compare Leah's assault to a learning experience?

Rupert returns with the trolley.

'Not now.' Evangeline doesn't even make eye contact with her servant. 'Delay the next course. We have important matters to discuss.'

Rupert does his usual muttering before leaving.

Evangeline addresses me. 'I assume you're aware of the details regarding Alec raping Tess? Early scholars debated whether it was a sexual assault, but there's obviously no doubt. Hardy titled the section where it happens, "Maiden No More". Does Leah come from the countryside?'

'Her family lives in Haworth.'

Evangeline clutches the pearls around her neck. 'Even worse, this killer is sullying the wonderful village and moors the Brontës cherished! So, Leah fits the criteria of being from a country-type background. Is she a virgin?'

'Mother!'

She swats his indignation away with her hand. 'Oh, do be quiet. Since when have you been coy about carnal matters?'

Ground, please swallow me up. Oh well, let's get this over with.

'Let's just say it like it is,' I begin. 'You think Leah was supposed to be the killer's Tess figure. He would've had his way and then killed her.' My stomach churns.

Evangeline nods. 'Indeed.'

'She's still alive, thank goodness,' I add.

'The attacker was likely distracted or someone was nearby,' Henry says. 'The woods draw in a few ramblers. Leah was a regular.'

'How do you know that?' Evangeline's tone is loaded with suspicion.

'She mentioned it in a tutorial.'

'Of course she did.' Evangeline draws out her words and then turns towards me. 'It's no coincidence Leah was attacked nearby. Tess' rape happened in a copse, too. The Professor tried to tick The D'Urberville Room off his killing list.'

THE PROFESSOR

Henry laughs. 'The Professor is welcome to The D'Urberville Room. It's at the back of the house, Jane, where it belongs; full of Glynn crests and heirlooms. Mother's obsessed with our lineage.'

'It's all we have! The family name must not die out.'

'Good job you're female then!' He knocks over a glass. Red wine leeches like blood into the white tablecloth. 'Sorry I had the audacity to be male and potentially ruin your precious legacy.'

'I'm doing all I can to protect Glynnholme. I'll remind you to play your part, too.'

'Your demands and superiority are wearing me out. Don't forget, you've failed, too.'

A miraculous thing occurs. Evangeline blushes. She turns away, but the stubborn flush is still visible, blooming into her cheeks.

Henry addresses me. 'Mother attempted writing novels set in the Victorian era. It was a complete flop. The rejections kept rolling in. "Awful", "amateur", and "lacks substance" were a few of my favourite criticisms.'

'How dare you! The publishing world wasn't ready for my vision!'

'Funny how you used a pen name. From the start, you didn't have confidence in your ability.'

'Jane doesn't need to hear about this. It's irrelevant.'

'Oh, but it *is* relevant,' he continues. 'Your Victorian-themed rooms aren't love letters to the authors and the era, as is the official line. This house is crammed with your jealousy at being unable to write a masterpiece. Every room is self-punishment for your inadequacy at not measuring up to classic authors.'

'Do you mind if I go?' I ask. 'I'm not feeling well.'

Evangeline approaches me and holds a hand against my forehead. 'You look peaky and you're a little warm, too. Get some rest. Before you go, consider this; The Professor meant to kill Leah.'

'Why are you so certain?' I ask. 'Her dad didn't mention a quote from the novel being at the scene when he called me.'

'It was there, if you search for it,' Henry says. 'The Professor never leaves without making his literary mark.'

CHAPTER 46
Jane

I head for Ed's shed to tell him I'm not up to chatting today. Recently, he's become intense, especially when talking about his mother. While I understand he needs to let out his hurt, I don't have the energy to be supportive today.

'Jane, over here!' Waving fingers skirt above a tall hedge.

I meet Ed on the other side. He's coming down a ladder while holding a strimmer.

'Are you creating one of your brilliant designs?'

He boots the damp grass, leaving a dent.

'I've told you before, nothing of mine will ever be in Evangeline's gardens. How was it having dinner with her highness, anyway?' He nods towards the house.

'She was demanding and annoyed with Henry. He kept winding her up. Standard.'

The weariness in my voice isn't only because of illness. I'm sick of watching the Glynns' twisted performances. Being Evangeline's scholar is losing its shine.

'I've got something to show you,' Ed says.

'Can we do it another day? I need a lie down.'

'That's what being around Evangeline and Henry does to a person. It's why I sleep in the servants' quarters. The further I'm away from those two, the better. Please come with me. It won't take long. The fresh air might do you good.'

I can't refuse that boyish grin. Ed's smiles are so rare they deserve a reward.

'Lead the way.' I try not to sound weary and fail.

We walk across the expansive lawn in silence. Quiet between us isn't awkward. Sometimes in the shed, I read while Ed whittles.

We approach a series of archways, curving over a path. Gnarly branches twist in black ironwork. Leaves will transform this into a more welcoming entrance in the spring. A small set of stairs leads into a sunken garden.

Ed holds out a hand for me to take. 'Tread carefully. The steps can be slippery in this weather.'

A majestic ivory fountain ejects water from its spouts. The spray splashes into the pond below, making lily pads dip and bounce. The flow is a peaceful balm for my headache.

Ed takes a seat on a stone bench. I laugh.

'You'll get piles sitting on that, like poor old Rupert.'

'Old wives' tale.' He pats the space next to him.

We sit and take in the scene before us. A snake coiling from the fountain's base up to the rim dominates its carving. Instead of my usual aversion to the creature, I admire its grace. The swirling serpent flows like the water. This area is a mini paradise, shaded by evergreen trees, closing off Glynnholme and its residents' pettiness.

'You feel it too.' Ed inspects my face. 'It's so joyful here.'

'It really is. I can't describe why.'

'Since Norman died, no one but me comes here. Norm created this garden.'

'He was a clever man.'

'That he was, smarter than Evangeline gave him credit for. She thought because he worked with his hands, he was stupid. You only have to check out these grounds to appreciate Norman was a creative genius. He planned all the landscaping and decorative features. As a tribute, I've kept them going. This area was just mud and neglect before Norman began working on it. After it was finished, The Pattersons always brought me here for my birthday. Mrs P gave me a cupcake with a candle on it to blow out.'

'That's lovely. I hope you still come here on your birthday.'

'Mrs P insists, but it's not the same without Norm.'

I focus on the details of the snake. Petals, replacing scales, cover its body. The longer I inspect my surroundings, the more beauty the garden reveals.

'Norman designed the fountain and a local stonemason made it,' Ed continues. 'See how the snake's formed into the letter *S*?'

'Oh yes!'

'Norman said it was for my mum, Selena.'

'He must've been fond of her.'

'He felt protective of her, and it didn't end after she died. Evangeline and Henry don't know this is dedicated to Mum. Considering there wasn't a funeral or any ashes scattered, at Mum's request, Norman believed it was only right to have some kind of memorial for her. When I asked why he made it here, he wouldn't answer. Often, when I mentioned Mum, he changed the subject. The only time he spoke about her at length was at Christmas, when we'd had too much of his home-brewed beer. It certainly loosened Norm's tongue.'

'What did he say?'

'He warned me not to accept everything that comes out of the Glynns' mouths, and that I deserved the truth. The next day he claimed it was the drink talking and to forget it. But I can't and I won't.'

'What do you reckon Norman meant?'

Incoming night casts colder shadows. The sunken garden dips into deeper darkness.

'I have my suspicions regarding when Mum came to Glynnholme,' Ed says. 'When they think I'm not around, I listen to Henry's and Evangeline's conversations. Servants can often creep around unnoticed.'

'You're not a servant, though.'

'Yes, I am!' he shouts. 'I'd rather be that than a son of Evangeline's. Never liken me to Henry!'

THE PROFESSOR

I stand. 'Look, I get it. You're lost and want to know where you belong in the world. The Glynns have treated you like shit. That doesn't mean you're allowed to yell at me.'

'Sorry.' Ed stares at the fountain. 'Norman made this for Mum. Now, I view it as a message to keep looking for answers. When the Glynns finally spill their secrets, *my* secrets, they'll find out what I'm capable of.'

CHAPTER 47
Jane

A howl tears from my throat. He's here, looming over me! This is the closest he's ever been. Finally, he's taking me to my death. I feel him. I swear I do, even though it's impossible. No escape. A ragged scream rips through my throat. I fling out an arm to fight. Hands grab me.

'Mum! Mum! Help me!'

'It's all right, Jane. I'm here.'

Death's burning grip sears into my skin. I'm not ready to die. Pushing through the groggy line between sleep and reality, I open my eyes. The menacing shape remains. A cloaked figure morphs into familiarity.

'You're okay,' Dad says with a tone so soothing.

This is the routine for my night terrors. Despite how often Dad insists I'm safe, I'll never believe it. Death always returns.

Dad sits on the bed. 'Just a bad dream, love.'

Recently, my mind is working overtime. I'm often a step behind. This hallucination of Death coming to claim me appears when I'm stressed or worried. He seems so real. The scariest appearance was the day after Mum died. Fingers grasping my neck made me jolt awake. As always, Dad saved me from the terror. I have such guilt at always calling for Mum when the nightmares arise, but I can't help naturally wanting her.

Dad touches my cheek. 'You're burning up.'

He offers a glass of water from the bedside cabinet. The staleness makes me cough.

'I'll get a fresh one,' he says.

'What time is it?'

'Lunchtime. You've been asleep since early evening yesterday.'

'Wow, I must be ill.' I try to pick my head off the pillow and drop it.

'Let me look after you for once. I'll heat up some soup.'

After he leaves, I remember the oxtail soup at Evangeline's fraught meal. My fuzzy mind struggles to recall what she shared regarding *Tess of the D'Urbervilles* and how it related to Leah's attack. Something about Henry is niggling at me, too. Ed's hatred of the Glynns is escalating.

Clouds of fatigue snatch my spiralling thoughts. Usually, after Death visits, insomnia sets in. Perhaps being ill is a blessing. At least I won't need sleeping tablets. I hate taking them, but sometimes it's the only way I can settle.

My phone rings. I look at the screen. No matter how ill I am, I have to take this call.

'Hi there,' I begin. 'How are you? Sorry, that's a stupid question.'

'I'm doing okay,' Leah replies. 'Being home helps. I didn't realise how much I missed it. I'm transferring to a local university.' Her voice wobbles.

'I understand, although I'll miss you. Perhaps I can visit in the summer as we planned.'

'I'd love that. Jane, there's something I need to tell you.'

Leah is silent for a while.

'What's wrong?'

'I've remembered more about what happened. The police want it to be kept confidential, but you deserve to know. When that man…' Leah takes a long breath. 'After he injected me with a sedative, I realised he was going to…'

As she cries, I break with her.

She continues. 'While I could hear and see things, my body couldn't do owt for a while. Eventually, the sedative wore off. After the attacker ran away, I managed to get up and find a signal to call the police. When the man *was* there, I wasn't out of it completely. I heard what he said.'

'What was it?'

Deep inside, I'd rather remain oblivious. There are moments when you ask questions that will provide life-changing answers.

'He said, "Jane, what have I done?" It sounded like he was in agony. His voice seemed familiar, but strange at the same time. I'm freaking out. Maybe he was wearing a balaclava because he's someone we know!'

Sleepiness tries to tug me back into nothingness. It's the safest place to be, wrapped up in a dream, rather than this nightmare reality.

'Jane, are you there?'

'Sorry. What do the police think?'

She gives a jaded laugh. 'They reckon I misheard, or it could be anyone called Jane. I mentioned you and they treated me like a hysterical barmpot. It may not be you the fella was referring to, but I couldn't live with myself if I said nowt and something happened to you.'

'Thanks,' I say, while wishing I'd never heard this information. She's done the right thing, though. 'I can't figure out why he'd be calling out to me and sounding guilty. How does he know me?'

'There's another thing.' Leah pauses. 'It has to be the person who's killing students in scenes from Victorian literature. The police pieced together a torn-up quote from *Tess of the D'Urbervilles*, left on the ground. It's from the part where Alec and Tess are in the copse and, he, you know…'

'I do.' I spare her from further, painful explanation.

'The Professor tried to assault me! No doubt he would've killed me, too.'

I cry with her, in sympathy and in fear of my fate. Am I next on The Professor's list? The *Jane Eyre*-inspired rooms of Glynnholme are the only credible ones left for his agenda. Who better than me to complete the set? Evangeline was right.

THE PROFESSOR

'Got to go,' Leah says. 'Stay in touch and be careful.'

I hold my mobile to my chest after the call ends. Dad enters the room carrying a tray.

'Sit up and let's get some food in you.' He places the tray on my lap. 'Were you on the phone?'

'I was watching a video online.'

Worrying Dad isn't wise. He's already concerned about me being at the university and around the Glynns. If he finds out what Leah's told me, there would be one hell of an argument.

I take a long glug of much nicer-tasting water.

'Shall I feed you like when you were younger?' Dad grins as he brings a spoon towards my mouth. 'Here comes the choo-choo train.'

'Don't be so silly.' I stop his hand and tomato soup spills on my pyjama top. 'Damn it. I need to change.'

'No problem. Make sure you eat. Build your strength up.'

Dad closes the door behind him. I fight the urge to shout for him to come back. Loneliness creeps in. Tiredness is stronger. Talking to Leah has drained me. I'll change my clothing later. For now, I'll sleep away the demons.

I look over at a cabinet. The doll Ed made of me is sitting on it. I wish I was as still and safe as her. The Professor has me in his sights.

CHAPTER 48

Henry watches Ed leaving the sunken garden. Whenever he sees the boy going to the special place - he always views Ed as a child - Henry feels pity. The hardships of never knowing your parents and a cherished mother dying soon after your birth must be difficult. Henry can't relate. He's beyond wishing for close family relationships. His father only contacts him when he wants more money. Alfie knows better than to ask Evangeline. By her own admission, she never loved him. When Henry was younger, his parents never argued. They had to be home at the same time for that. Henry didn't even notice Alfie had left until a few weeks later.

Family is complicated, especially when you're a Glynn. Henry's first problem was being born male. If he'd been a daughter, Evangeline would've doted on him. He doesn't mourn what could've been, having seen how she controls her protégés. Thankfully, he's free from that particular purgatory. Not being female is an issue in the Glynn family. Henry's ancestor, Charles Glynn, has a lot to answer for. Fancy giving Glynnholme to thirty-year-old women! Older, bitter females will never enjoy such a bounty. Evangeline is proof.

If this was his house, Henry would strip it bare and start over. No more ridiculous Victorian literature-themed rooms. Evangeline and The Professor have more in common than she dares to recognise. They strive to get the details right, showing off perceived superior literary knowledge. Neither cares about others. Both choose female students, control them, and then kill off burgeoning brains to suit their agendas.

The door pushes open. Evangeline never knocks. Henry balls his fists and then releases them. He won't give her the satisfaction of seeing his annoyance. Coming into his bedroom unannounced is among Evangeline's favourite pastimes. She always looks for proof he makes sure she'll never find.

She points above the unmade bed. 'Where is the Janus mask?'

'I removed it.'

'Put it back. The masks belong in yours and Edward's rooms.'

'No. I'm not having your symbol of a two-faced man and creature hanging over me. It's bad enough you named me after Henry Jekyll and I have to sleep in here.'

As he scans the bedroom, a familiar revulsion burns in Henry's chest. He's given up trying to make his mark. At his mistress' command, Rupert always arranges things back to the way they were.

Clinical white walls and steel shelving are a reminder Henry isn't an inventor, like Dr Jekyll. Evangeline is Henry's creator. She's Dr Jekyll, tampering with lives and experimenting with people's personalities. Refusing to be her lab rat, Henry spends little time here. Under instruction, Mrs Patterson regularly disinfects the room. The acrid smell lingers as he sleeps. Henry opens a drawer, grabs a bottle, and squirts it into the air.

Evangeline's nose wrinkles. 'Did one of your whores give you her perfume as a memento?'

Henry won't confess he bought the scent to remember Selena's signature scent. Evangeline has claimed too much already.

"I refuse to live under these conditions!' he yells.

'Be glad I named you after Dr Jekyll.'

He sneers. 'Robert Louis Stevenson would've been so proud. Lucky Ed got to be the madman, Mr Hyde, which was a message to me, too. Not content with taking Ed from his mother, you coerced Selena into naming him after a murderer.'

'Oh, stop the amateur dramatics. *You* are solely responsible for our misfortunes and we're both paying for it.'

'We have more important matters to discuss. Rupert said Ed still badgers Mrs Patterson for information about Selena.'

'She won't say anything. Discretion keeps her in a job, along with generous bonuses.'

'Thanks to you, everyone's been paid off since we met Selena.' Henry enjoys hearing the sarcasm in his voice.

'Don't you dare judge me, not after what you've done!'

'My mistakes are dead and buried.'

Evangeline waggles a finger. 'Without my help, you'd be locked up. That wretched business, years ago, was supposed to be the end. Yet here we are, back in the thick of it.'

'Why can't you let it lie?'

'Because I've literally had to lie for you, many times!'

'You don't need to do that anymore. Move on. It's over.'

'Don't be ridiculous. With you, it never ends. Jane's getting inquisitive, too. Edward isn't as stupid as he seems. They must never know the truth. Now, let's go over the story and strengthen our alibis. Neither of us could survive prison.'

As Ed stands at the other side of the door, connecting his room to Henry's, he hears many revelations. Many questions are answered and new ones created. Ed will never be the same. Jane needs to hear what he now knows. Their lives depend on it.

CHAPTER 49
Jane

Kate practically stabs at her tablet while inputting a figure.

'The other day, Sam rocked up at the house at 6am, thinking he could see the kids,' she says. 'I slammed the door in his face.'

Instead of replying, I nod. I'm not totally convinced she won't take him back. There's no way I'm getting caught in the middle of this. Potentially being a serial killer's next victim is giving me enough to worry about.

Kate frowns. 'Are you sure you're feeling better? You look knackered.'

'I reckon I've slept more in the past week than I did last year. I'm still tired, though.'

'Which is why you shouldn't be here.'

'I'm not leaving you to do the stocktake alone. Counting every pen and pencil is a nightmare. I can't believe I'm saying this, but I almost miss Jaden.'

'He had to go. I should've known my husband's cousin would be a useless bastard too. Still, Jaden might've been able to at least count things.'

We both shake our heads and laugh.

'Go steady today,' Kate says, 'or I'll have your dad to answer to.'

She raises the tablet to hide her face. I pull it down.

'He phoned you, didn't he? I've told Dad so many times to stop treating me like a child.'

'Larry cares. He's worried you'll overdo it. You're lucky to have such a considerate father. I wish my children did.'

To be fair, Dad was great when I was ill. For once, he looked after me rather than the other way round.

Kate turns up the volume on the stereo and shimmies to "Dancing Queen".

'What I'd give to be only seventeen again,' she says. 'I'd certainly do things differently.'

'I'd have gone travelling before starting university.'

'But you're studying now, which is brilliant. You've proved we're never too old to realise our dreams.'

We sing together about how we can dance, jive, and have the time of our lives. Being free of worries for a minute feels good.

'Sorry to break up the party.'

Kate switches off the stereo and stares at the visitor. 'Trust you to kill the vibe. So, you *do* have a key to this place. Give it to me.' She holds out a hand.

Sam places the key in her palm and then strokes her wrist. Kate steps back.

'Why are you here?' she asks.

'I expected the shop to be open. You'll lose money.'

'We're doing a stocktake. Not that it's any of your business. This is *my* shop. You have no reason to be here.'

She shoves him. He stumbles and quickly corrects his stance.

'Sweetness, all I want is a second chance.'

The pleading tone grates on my nerves, let alone Kate's. She grabs a handful of pens. Biros rain on Sam. He holds his arms up as a shield.

'Stop it! You're hurting me!'

'Not even anywhere near as much as you've hurt me! I've given you so many chances. No more. The divorce papers will be in the post soon.' She finishes hurling missiles.

'I didn't kill Grace,' he says. 'That must count for something.'

Kate fixes a frosty glare on him. 'Don't you dare mention her name around me.'

She means it. I'm banned from reading *Wuthering Heights* in the shop because of Grace's death being related to the novel.

Kate continues ranting. 'That woman may be dead, but it doesn't excuse her for stealing someone's husband.'

'She didn't know that...' Sam bites his lip.

'You shit. Grace wasn't aware you're married, was she? You lied to her, too.' Despite not wanting to be part of this domestic, I have to defend one of The Professor's victims.

Sam stamps his foot. 'Grace wasn't so innocent. She was sleeping around with loads of men. Ask your precious Henry Glynn if you don't believe me.'

'I couldn't care less what he does,' I reply.

Sam snarls. 'Oh, but you should. Grace mentioned he was rough with her in bed.'

'Spare us the sordid details of what your mistresses do in the sack. Isn't it enough you've already broken me?' Kate slumps against a shelf.

'Sorry, but this is relevant,' Sam says. 'Grace shared with me that Henry regularly slept with his students. The university ignores it because the Glynns keep giving them money. I'm surprised Henry hasn't tried it on with you, Jane. Watch out. You're likely to be next.'

'Rubbish.'

I'm certain Henry won't make a move on me. Sometimes he regards me with what I can only describe as reverence. It's weird, considering he's wealthy, knowledgeable, and powerful.

'Jane, you may hate me for what I've done to Kate,' Sam begins, 'but you need to hear this. Henry was arrested as a suspect for the original spate of killings. I bet he hasn't mentioned that he was accused of being The Professor. It was kept hush-hush. I expect he provided false witnesses, too.'

'How do you know about it?' I ask.

'Grace told me. When she tried to finish their relationship, Henry threatened to make things difficult. He added he was once a wanted killer. When he noticed how shocked she looked, he backtracked, claiming it was a joke.'

'Why are you really here?' Kate asks. 'I expect it isn't to warn Jane.'

Sam's dentist-approved grin widens. 'I was with a client viewing a property in the area and thought I'd pop by to see my gorgeous wife.'

She pushes him towards the door. 'From now on, only contact me to arrange seeing the kids, and at a reasonable time.'

He looks over his shoulder. 'Please be careful, Jane. The Glynns aren't the wonderful people they seem to be.'

Kate closes the door behind Sam and locks it. She puts the music on and duets with Madonna. The cracking in her voice betrays the bravado.

I answer my ringing phone.

'Finally,' Ed whinges. 'I've been trying to get hold of you for days.'

'Hello to you too.'

'Are you okay?'

'I probably had flu. Sorry, I saw your messages and forgot to reply. My head's a little fuzzy.'

'There's so much to tell you.'

'Go on then. I have five minutes.'

'Not on the phone. We must do this face-to-face. Can you come to my shed tomorrow?'

Weariness creeps back in. Maybe I've overdone it by returning to work. I need to know what's rattling Ed, though. I'm not scared of him, but his intensity is concerning. Ed's a ball of kindling ready to be set alight and in danger of burning out.

'Okay, man of mystery. Tomorrow morning at ten?'

'Thanks. Brace yourself, Jane. It's explosive stuff. We've both been living a lie.'

CHAPTER 50

Evangeline believes she's in charge, but The Professor's leading her to his conclusion. By stealing her literary rooms, he's destroying her power.

Currently, Evangeline decides on the content of Oxford Carroll's English Literature syllabus. Regular sums of money ensure the same texts in the same order are studied every year. While she lives, everything stays the same. The Professor will change that.

From the beginning, he chose female victims because it felt like he was killing Evangeline and Selena. Then he discovered the pleasure of an expertly executed literature-related murder. He could've used all of Glynnholme's rooms. He could've killed males in a *Strange Case of Dr Jekyll and Mr Hyde* or *The Picture of Dorian Gray* manner. If The Professor murdered men, though, Evangeline would be delighted. No, women should suffer, as regularly happens in Victorian classics.

Consider Tess; abused and made a reluctant killer. In *The Tenant of Wildfell Hall*, Helen is a fool for marrying Arthur Huntingdon, a man too powerful for a docile woman. *The Turn of the Screw*'s governess succumbs to madness when she's supposed to be looking after children. In "Goblin Market" a girl devours the dangerous wares of goblins and leads her sister into danger.

Writers knew what they were doing back then. Misbehaving women deserve punishment.

There are only two rooms left for The Professor's killing agenda: The Eyre Room and The Red Room. Jane is at the centre. She's safe while he considers his options. He battles with deciding on an outcome. Can he kill Jane? Should he choose someone else? The other victims didn't have the same names as their counterparts. No! This is how it must be. Jane *is* Jane Eyre. Finding another victim is a mockery of his work. Any other victim would be a poor imitation. Yet, what will he do with Jane?

There's no place for mistakes. The botched Tess murder involving Leah plays on his mind. He's often on high alert, wondering if the police will find him. A balaclava ensured Leah didn't see his face, but he slipped up, crying out to Jane. Self-hatred at being unable to sexually perform unleashed his desperation. Once again, Jane is his weakness. Calling out to her might be his undoing.

Jane, always Jane. Without her, The Professor can be free. No binding attachments. No more threat of advancing her knowledge beyond his. Removing her from Evangeline's clutches would also be a kindness.

Evangeline, always Evangeline. The name is acid on his tongue. She isn't a retiring wallflower, fading into ageing obscurity. Evangeline enjoys her reclusive role, surrounded by exquisite linens, sumptuous fabrics, and the highest of threads in her sheets. A woman can't be trusted with such riches.

Men are usually business minded. Charles Glynn was a sentimental fool, blinded by love for his daughter. He didn't consider the consequences of his inheritance rules, giving everything to women.

Men don't name rooms after books. They read, analyse, and then own books. The Professor rails against the idea he's imitating Evangeline by creating scenes from literature. His mission is a parody of her interpretations, restricted within four walls. In comparison, he is free. He saunters through the hall, unbothered. Images of former Glynns glare disapproval at his acts. He laughs.

THE PROFESSOR

The Professor offers a nod at The Madam Mina Room. A shiver passes through his body, remembering Fiona's weakening pulse under his strangling hands. He doesn't need to enter. It is done.

He can't venture into the dining room. The Eyre Room tortures him. Jane, always Jane. What will he do? Right now, he must leave.

The Professor progresses to The Middlemarch Library. A fortress of books can't keep at bay delicious memories of killing Clementine. A scarlet book on a shelf reminds him of blood trickling from her wrist. He slashes his finger with a scalpel and flicks blood on the desk. It's not only a reminder of Clementine's death but also a warning he's part of this. The Professor's being is enmeshed in Glynnholme as much as Evangeline's. He moves on from the library. It is done.

The Gray Hall is a study in finer things, from the delicate chandelier to golden filigree frames holding paintings. This masculine space, in homage to *The Picture of Dorian Gray*, is untouched by Evangeline's hand. She doesn't dare to interfere with a man's space. The Professor grins, considering how she has to be in the hall to access the rest of the house. Perhaps she didn't think it through when naming parts of Glynnholme.

Upstairs, he regards The Bly Room. A painting of a governess with a boy and girl sitting at her feet dominates a wall. Of course, as Evangeline commands, the female is central. The Professor stares at the portrait and sees Karin there; a young Swedish woman sent by her parents to England. Karin hadn't chosen to study English Literature, but she was a dutiful daughter. She wasn't a fan of children either, sharing stories about the "brats" she looked after.

The Professor met Karin in a night class. She wanted to do something other than her studies. He pretended to understand. For a while, he thought she could be someone he might care about, in his own way. Then she discovered Victorian literature. When her smile widened while she talked about it, he knew he had to end the relationship permanently.

Karin's white-blonde, short hair was her only flaw. The Professor wasn't too bothered. No brown-haired student matched the governess from *The Turn of the Screw* as well as Karin. She was a needy au pair, haunted by the past, and dominated by a cruel man like the novella's Peter Quint.

A painting The Professor's seen many times seems to alter. *The Turn of the Screw*'s governess usually looks fearful. Now, laser eyes of judgement stare back at him. He grips the scalpel, trembling against the urge to slash the canvas. He slams the door behind him. It is done.

Moving on, he touches placards for the Jekyll and Hyde-inspired rooms. His hands smooth over them. They are already his, these provinces of men.

Like a child playing a game of avoiding pavement cracks, he won't look at The Goblin Market Room or The D'Urberville Room. They will bring bad luck. Today, he seeks courage, not reminders of his mistakes. The Wildfell Room isn't enticing either. Brooke was a spiteful little bitch, undeserving of his thoughts.

Cathy's Chamber looms. Absolute joy at his *Wuthering Heights* memories makes him pause. Whenever The Professor wants to remember the details of Grace's murder, he comes here. As with Cathy, Grace believed she could master men. She slept around. Likewise, Cathy toyed with Heathcliff and Edgar. One man wasn't enough for her. Cathy paid for it with her death. Maybe if Grace hadn't lauded it over The Professor, with her analysis of the novel, she might still be alive. Maybe if she'd stuck to studying art, Grace might have lived. He never dwells on maybes. She was perfect for the *Wuthering Heights* stage. It is done.

Venturing further down the corridor isn't wise. It's not because of respect for The Satis Room. Fury often leads to violence. *Satis* means *enough*. It isn't yet, though. For the time being, he leaves the room untouched. He's already killed one Miss Havisham figure in the shape of Phoebe. How wonderful it will be when he gets to an even better version; Evangeline Glynn!

The Professor returns to a place he keeps avoiding. Now, it demands to be seen. A riot of red hurts his eyes. He turns away from The Red Room, but not on Jane's possible demise. Can he do it? Time is running out. If she survives, it spells the end for him. The Professor will not let that happen.

CHAPTER 51
Jane

A horn blasts. I tighten my hold on the steering wheel. Another driver sticks up a middle finger. I deserve it. I veered over the line and was in danger of landing up on the other side of the road. My mind is fuzzy. This flu won't shift. Whenever it feels like I'm recovering, I fall back. To keep alert, I pinch my forearm. Opening the window, hopefully freezing air will help, too. I consider why I'm driving and if it's worth it. Ed sounded upset when he called yesterday.

My tummy rumbles. The enormous bowl of porridge oats Dad soaked overnight is probably still digesting. I wrote a thank-you note for the gesture, adding I'd gone to Glynnholme. Thankfully, he was out of the house before I got up. The disapproving expression every time I mention the Glynns is tiring. After what happened to Leah, I understand why Dad's worried about The Professor, but I'm being safe.

As per Ed's messaged instructions, I park at the edge of the woods. He obviously doesn't want anyone to know I'm here. Why we have to meet in a draughty shed rather than a cosy coffee shop is puzzling. I wrap my scarf closer to my face. As frosted grass dampens my boots, I reflect on Ed hardly ever leaving

THE PROFESSOR

Glynnholme. He has more in common with Evangeline than he'd ever admit. They're both tethered to this place.

Plumes of smoke entwine and trail from the house's many chimney tops. Evangeline is enjoying a roaring fire, the lucky cow. Thinking of her, I lighten my treads. Her bat ears and eagle eyes are always working. This is ridiculous. I'm even wearing dark clothing to avoid being easily seen. People might think Ed and I are secret lovers. The idea makes me laugh louder than I intended. The shed door bursts open.

'Be quiet! Get in here before someone sees you.'

Ed pulls me inside. I take my usual seat on the office chair. He paces in front of me.

'This is all very cloak and dagger,' I say.

'It has to be. Henry and Evangeline mustn't know I've found out what they've done. Those two have blood on their hands, literally. I'm going to show you how.'

For the first time, I'm wary of Ed. He looks set to kill.

CHAPTER 52

Evangeline's caged heart is prising open. It's Jane's fault. Evangeline prided herself on avoiding affection's touch. Hearts are delicate. They also make the owner fragile.

She regards the religious iconography dotted around The Madam Mina Room. Evangeline seeks evidence of how love can offer power rather than depleting a person. In a painting, the Virgin Mary gazes at her stomach, pondering on the holy life growing inside her. Is she powerful because of the miracle child she carries or diminished by such a huge undertaking?

Evangeline recalls when Selena revealed her pregnancy. The arguments and sense of betrayal blighted Glynnholme. Everyone suffered, not only Selena, who lost everything. Evangeline rubs her chest, trying to soothe the pain of loss. Selena was her greatest scholar and had such promise. Surprise, surprise, a man came along and took what wasn't his. The Professor steals academic women's opportunities to learn more. None of this is a coincidence.

From the first murder, Evangeline suspected it was *him*. He tried to hide the explosive temper, but nothing gets past her. When The Professor's identity is revealed, many will question why she didn't share her suspicions. The fact is, he knows too much of her secrets.

THE PROFESSOR

Every day, Evangeline hates herself a little more for placing women in danger. Loyalty to others means she must be silent. With each murder, she lights a candle and quickly blows it out. What use is it to families who mourn a relative? But she has loved ones too, not that anyone would believe it. Evangeline *is* capable of love. It keeps her alive. Soon, she will pay the price for that devotion. The Professor will eventually try to kill her. She's ready for him.

Mina Harker from *Dracula* scowls from a portrait above the fireplace. The feminist ideal of the New Woman assesses this old woman. Evangeline sits by the window. Shame, her constant companion, takes a seat beside her. She can't claim to support women while letting The Professor murder them. She shakes her head. No, she isn't entirely to blame. Evangeline's given him what he wanted and more. He's enjoyed Glynn money, comforts, and freedom. This is how he repays her! A blaze rises inside her. Coughing becomes a frenzied bark, rattling her body. If the killer doesn't get her, something else will.

'Rupert!'

Flat-footed treads sound even on a plush carpet. Rupert pushes the door open.

'May I be of assistance, Ms Glynn?' he asks.

She fixes him with a deflating stare. 'I know you're listening outside. Must we keep up this charade of you pretending to be elsewhere whenever I call? You'll wear your shoes out with all that pacing.'

His hand flies to his chest. 'Well, I never—'

'Yes, that's exactly it! You *never*. You *never* do your job properly. You *never* give me privacy. You *never* cease gossiping with Mrs Patterson. You *never* have a day without an illness or ailment. You just *never*. Full stop!'

The coughing resumes. Rupert rushes away and returns with a glass of water and a box.

'Time for your medication, Ms Glynn.'

Evangeline takes the tablets and drinks, while considering the cleansing ability of water. She needs to wipe many slates clean and atone for so much. Leaning back, she assesses a picture of Dracula capturing Mina in a seductive embrace. Evangeline finally realises *she* is a vampire. She's leeched the joy out of Glynnholme by stagnating in it. Evangeline has pierced Henry's heart by withholding affection to punish his dreadful father. No wonder her son has turned out to be such a disappointment. As a fresh realisation hits, she holds her aching ribs. Evangeline's hardly any better than The Professor, regarding mastering females. She made her students study literature her way, not letting them discover their own learning experiences.

Rupert stands over her, his furrowed brow deepening. Evangeline now understands she's stolen his life, too. Since they were children, he's loved her. Her repayment was to make him a servant and a criminal. She reaches for him. He focuses on their connection, shaking his head. She grips his hand tighter.

'I'm sorry, Rupert. You've been a dear friend, doing so much for me. There's one important thing you *didn't* do, for which I'll always be grateful.'

'What's that?'

'You never left my side. Thank you. I'll never forget it.'

He forces a laugh. 'You talk as if you're on your deathbed. There are plenty of years left in you yet, Ms Glynn. You'll outlast us all.'

She looks out the window, watching Ed leading Jane to the sunken garden. His scowl and heavy stomping confirms it.

'Every story has an ending,' Evangeline says. 'Mine is almost here.'

CHAPTER 53

In the past, Henry viewed Jane as just a project. Now, she's become so much more.

Henry recalls when he first went into the stationery shop, under Evangeline's orders. Nerves overtook as he approached the building. It took sheer force of will to push open the door. He knew already what Jane looked like. As much as he struggles against it, she's been on his mind for years. Still, when Jane appeared, he forgot how to breathe.

Henry hadn't expected a witty, kind, and clever person. Before, he'd tried not to give Jane too much consideration. He was busy living a lie of a life. Sex, secrets, alcohol, and academia were the ingredients for a melting pot of oblivion. Then Evangeline decided it was time. While Henry knew the day would come, he didn't dare prepare. For decades he foolishly believed he could break free from the chains tethering him to Glynnholme.

He pours a generous slug of whisky into a crystal glass. The fiery sensation as he drinks makes him feel alive against all this death. Glynnholme reeks of it. Fatality nestles in the walls. Morbidity wraps itself in the bed linens, suffocating the sleeper with terrible dreams.

Women have died. Henry can't stop it. Fate does its will. He has to keep playing his part. Growing affection for Jane has led to him making mistakes. No matter how fond he is of her, Henry won't let Jane be his downfall. He's considered becoming a better man. Whenever Jane casts frowns at his careless ways, a knife of disappointment stabs the fragments of his heart. Watching her go to Ed's shed tears Henry apart. He wants to be there too, probably as the focal point of their conversation, but some things never change. Instead, he satisfies himself with behaving badly to feel more alive.

Standing at a window in his room, Henry assesses grounds that should be his. Charles Glynn and the ridiculous inheritance be damned. This is Henry's territory. He'll continue fighting for it, despite the victims it creates.

Henry watches Ed leading Jane towards the sunken garden. Burning guilt competes with the alcohol firing down his throat. Ed's thunderous face is confirmation. He heard Henry and Evangeline arguing earlier. Ed knows the truth. Henry must bring this to an end.

CHAPTER 54

When Jane first visited Glynnholme, Ed felt a spark between them. Not love or attraction. Considering Jane romantically seemed wrong. The connection is of like-minded individuals. They were bound by something seemingly undefinable. Now he knows what it is and must tell her the truth.

The sunken garden is Ed's special place. Once again, the Glynns have taken something precious from him. Not content with stealing his chance of being adopted by a normal family, they denied him a stable upbringing, too. No more. Revenge and hurt propel him forward.

'Careful, you'll rip my arm off!'

Jane sounds afraid. She should be. Ed wonders what else he's capable of, beyond what he's already done. When others try to make him look stupid, a rage ripples inside him. Although he tries to suppress it, occasionally his anger lets loose. Years of Henry's barbed comments about Ed being an idiot have led to this. Henry doesn't know him at all. Ed enjoys reading. Holding a book draws him closer to his mother. He might not study and write essays, but he understands Victorian literature. It's part of him.

Ed often considers how similar he is to Pip from *Great Expectations*. Both were lost children, domineered by women who favour female understudies. Ed is also Will Ladislaw of *Middlemarch*, trying to improve and be more learned. There's a touch of

Peter Quint in Ed's personality, too. No matter how hard he tries, Ed can misbehave, like the servant from *The Turn of the Screw*. Since he can remember, Ed's been made to feel inferior; a caged animal for the Glynns to poke and laugh at.

No more the outsider. Ed has confirmation of who and what he is. He should never have tried to hide from it. A person's true nature will always eventually rise to the surface. Still, Henry and Evangeline will pay for ruining the sunken garden, his oasis of comfort.

Ed looks behind him at Jane. Her face is full of fear. She's right to be scared. This is the beginning of the end.

CHAPTER 55
Jane

Last time we were in the sunken garden, it was a haven of tranquillity. It's not the arctic spray from the fountain or cold shadows that have stolen the warmth. Ed's anger resonates. I feared for my arm coming out of the socket when he practically dragged me here. Now he circles the area as I approach the bench.

'Don't sit there!' He darts over and shoves me aside.

I rub my shoulder. 'Enough! I'm here because you're upset about something. Keep your hands off me! Touch me again and I'll not only kick your arse, but I'll also leave. You'll never see me again.'

'Don't be scared of me!' he cries.

'I'm not.' Despite my annoyance, I make my tone gentler. 'You're obviously passionate about this place, but it's making you behave strangely. Remember, I'm not the enemy.'

'You're so much more than that.'

I blush. 'Sorry. I thought you understood. We're friends, nothing more.'

Ed's laughter is sharper than the frigid air.

'Jane, you're not bad-looking, but you're not my type, particularly now.'

'Oh, I'm such an idiot. I didn't realise you're gay.'

'I'm not, although it doesn't matter if I am. Imagine how horrified my father would be, though, if I was. Definitely not a chip off the old block.'

'You don't know who your dad is.'

Ed pulls out a yellowed piece of paper from his pocket. Repetitive folding and unfolding is revealed in the weakened lines. He offers it to me.

'Take a look at this.'

I scan it. 'Too bad your father isn't listed. It would've given you some answers.'

'What's the point of putting his name on there? This is full of lies, like everything else around here.' Ed snatches the paper, tears it up, and scatters it into the pond.

'Stop!'

After plunging my hands into the freezing water, I lay the pieces on the pond wall.

'You needn't have bothered.,' Ed says. 'It's useless.'

'This might be, but you can apply for a copy.'

'No, I can't. It's a fake.' He looks at the tatters of his birth. 'Eavesdropping around Glynnholme often pays off. From listening to Evangeline and Henry's conversations, I've found out lots of things. Until now, they hid the most explosive facts.'

'Which are?' My tone signifies this is being drawn out longer than a TV talent show winner reveal.

'Evangeline's money buys almost anything, including the services of someone skilled in faking documents.' Ed points at the soggy certificate.

'Why bother with a fake copy?'

He places the quarters together. 'Read it properly.'

'Oh, our birthday is on the same day.' I smile.

'There's a reason for that.'

As Ed stares at me, it feels like he's willing me to come up with the right answer. I shrug. This guessing game is knackering. I'm craving a warm bed and sleep.

'Have you ever seen your birth certificate?' he asks.

'Yes. It's in a file of our family papers. I've used it for identification stuff.'

THE PROFESSOR

He shakes his head. 'Be thankful you haven't been arrested for fraud.'

'What on earth are you blabbering on about? It's a legal document.'

'Your birthday isn't even the date you celebrate. Evangeline had a certificate made for you, too. She kept our made-up birthdates the same, though. I heard her telling Henry.'

I check Ed's eyes for evidence of drug use. He's never looked more lucid.

'This is ridiculous,' I begin. 'Mum and Dad have never met Evangeline. Why would they allow her to falsify an important document about me?'

'Because Larry and Viv aren't your parents.'

I laugh. 'You've lost the plot. Of course, they are.'

Ed reaches for me. I step back. I have to leave. My assessment of his character was wrong. He's damaged and possibly dangerous. I head for the steps.

'This fantasy world you've created is weird. Considering how the Glynns treat you, it's understandable. You need psychiatric help. There's no shame in it.'

'The only help I want is for you to listen.' Ed's voice trembles. 'Afterwards, if you decide to never see me again, I won't argue. But hear me out. That's the least you can do for your brother.'

'What the fuck?'

Ed taps the space beside him on the bench. 'Please sit and then I'll tell you what I've learned.'

I remain standing. 'How can you be my brother? I'm an only child.'

'That's what I believed, too. Turns out we're twins.'

CHAPTER 56
Then

Selena thought that after having his children he might love her. Even her looks, which he used to admire, weren't enough. Previously, he claimed small brunettes were his type. Selena soon realised any woman he could get into bed was his type, particularly students.

Leaning over the double buggy, she smiled at her twins. His coldness towards them was heartbreaking. Just as he'd rejected Selena, he abandoned his children. Even while she was pregnant he slept around. It wasn't the first time he'd withheld sex to control her.

Baby Ed's balled fist shook as he woke. Her warrior son provoked Selena's pride and fear. She needed him to have her courage, but not his father's cruelty. Once again, she vowed to raise Ed to respect women and know they cherished him. He wouldn't follow in his father's terrible footsteps.

As she neared Norman's shed, Selena halted and doubled over. She took measured breaths. After her children's conception, Selena swore to stay away from Glynnholme. She forgot Angeline always got her way.

Selena struggled to negotiate the pushchair on the steps into the garden. Whenever they met, he hid her from sight.

THE PROFESSOR

Their encounters took place in closed rooms and dark places. It was an unnecessary undertaking as their relationship was an open secret. As always, though, he believed he was untouchable.

'Why on earth did you bring them?' He marched down the stairs.

'Because I'm the only parent they have.'

Selena laid her palms on the infants' hearts, transmitting through touch that she'd always be there. They were all she had. As the only child of parents who'd both died in a car accident, Selena had been alone since she was seventeen. Now nineteen years old, she felt so much older.

Assessing the man she'd come to hate, Selena wondered how she fell for him. Before they met, she was smart and independent. He'd made a fool out of her.

'Jane has a cold. I'm worried about her.' Selena searched his face for fatherly concern. 'Ed's bound to catch it, too. They're so close. Sometimes, when they're sleeping, they hold hands.'

'Babies can barely function, let alone form a bond.'

'Don't be so hard-hearted.'

Henry glared at the problematic woman. Brown eyes, silky hair, and a petite frame had lured him in. If only Selena hadn't been so alluring in their first tutorial.

As always, he refused to look at the twins. Henry didn't know how to love. If he became a proper father to Ed and Jane, he'd inevitably ruin their lives. Being a Glynn was enough of a punishment. Partly in thanks for Selena's silence, he turned up at the registry office to have his name put on their birth certificates. More than that, it was necessary as proof of an heir. Until Jane reached thirty, money ensured Selena's discretion regarding his paternity.

'Good afternoon, Selena.' Evangeline's voice carried through an archway. 'I trust you and the children are keeping well?'

'I'd rather they weren't in this mud pit.'

Selena regarded earth and gravel piled next to tarpaulin; some materials to build an area for a fountain and pond. She recalled Norman's animated expression as he shared his plans for the sunken garden. After seeing Henry, Selena always met with

Norman. They'd stopped going to the shed, though. She didn't dare tell Norman why. Currently, he was recovering from having his appendix removed. Not having him around after this inevitably stressful meeting disturbed her.

Strengthened by glancing at her babies, Selena continued. 'Why can't we talk inside? Stop treating us like a dirty secret.'

Evangeline lifted her skirt and grimaced at the mud marking the hem. She considered how it was fitting for Henry and Selena to meet in filth. They didn't deserve the setting of her cherished house. She couldn't decide who made her angriest: Henry for seducing Evangeline's most promising project, or Selena for falling for it.

'We're here to discuss matters, not have a social.' Evangeline was all business. The solicitors concentrated on the legal matters, but she always dictated the terms and conditions.

Jane let out a cry. Ed joined in. Selena smoothed their wrinkled foreheads.

'Shut those brats up!' Henry yelled. 'I have a rotten hangover.'

'A heavy night with another of your floozies?' Selena kept her tone light, knowing making him angry was unwise.

She had given Henry everything. All she asked was for him to be a father, if only in name and for financial support. Sometimes the deceit bothered her, but Selena would do anything for Ed and Jane. After wiping Jane's runny nose with a tissue, Selena beheld Glynnholme's heir. Although she felt nauseous being here, Jane could change this. One day, they'd turn this into a place of love and hope.

Evangeline held out her arms as if separating boxers in a ring. 'Stop this bickering. After the mess you two have made, we're doing this my way. We must consider Jane and Edward.'

'It's all I want.' Selena winced. 'I need to sit down. I'm still getting over the caesarean.'

'This will be quick,' Evangeline replied. 'You'll both agree and then this is over. Selena, you will raise Edward as you see fit.'

The ground underneath Selena seemed to shift. While she was ing from a major operation, the wobbliness was from far

THE PROFESSOR

'Jane too, of course. You forgot her.' Selena's voice trembled.

Evangeline shook her head. 'No I haven't. Jane will be placed under the care of a couple I've chosen. They will do my bidding. Let's face it, Henry's incapable of looking after himself. Imagine him being responsible for a child.' Her laugh became a cackle.

'Here's to you, Mother, and never changing your nasty ways.' Henry raised a hip flask in mock cheers before drinking.

Selena stood in front of her offspring. 'You're not taking Jane! Leave my children alone. I shouldn't have signed papers letting you be a guardian if I die before you. You played on my weakness when I was in hospital, getting over a C-section. I'll do everything I can to make sure I stay alive so you'll never get your hands on them. This is a huge mistake. Keep the money and let us go. I don't want anything from either of you.'

Evangeline approached her. 'It's too late for regrets. Plans have changed. Considering the petty squabbling and threats, Henry and you can't be trusted. Selena, you will give up Jane. If you refuse, I'll make things very difficult. You'll lose your home. Every job you get, you'll be fired from. Any man you meet will be paid off to leave you. I'll circulate rumours so awful no one will come near you. My wealth and influence will make your life miserable.'

'You bitch!' Selena practically spat out the words. 'You can't do that to me!'

'I can and I will. To be clear, in the event of your death preceding mine, I'll become Edward's guardian. I won't have a Glynn living in a children's home or sent to unsuitable adoptive parents. The guardianship papers for Jane to be my ward no longer stand. She will live with the couple, thinking she's their daughter until I'm ready to reveal the truth. You won't know where she lives or have any contact with her. Concentrate on your son instead. At last, Glynnholme has a female heir. Henry's asserted he'll never settle down and have more children. Finally, he's learned to use protection when engaging in sexual activities.'

'Mother!'

'Shut up, Henry. Now, where was I before these constant interruptions? Yes. Thankfully, Charles Glynn allowed for heirs to be born out of wedlock. Jane's our only chance of maintaining the female line. She must be brought up well and shielded from bad influences.'

'I'm not a bad influence!' Selena cried. 'Please, don't take my daughter! This is wrong. I…'

She slipped and then slammed into the ground. The post-op wound flared, but Selena couldn't stay down.

Henry advanced upon her. 'Do as Mother says. I'm losing out too. I can't inherit because of *her*.' He jabbed a finger at Jane.

The vicious gesture incited an unknown rage within Selena. Her babies were pure, not pawns in rich people's games. She'd always fight for them. Evangeline's threats didn't matter. Selena had already been through adversity. She could survive. Her family would never return to Glynnholme.

'I'll bloody well kill you!' Selena dragged herself up and ran at Henry.

Henry believed, despite his many faults, he was chivalrous. Faced with someone threatening his life, he lost his manners. Selena had cashed in on their children by demanding some of the Glynn fortune. She thought by becoming better educated, she was superior to him. Henry would never confess Selena broke his heart. If she hadn't got pregnant, he might have married her. Barrelling at him was someone who threatened to take everything. With a shove against her chest, he took charge.

Selena lost her footing and struck a stack of paving slabs. A sickening sound echoed around the garden. Her skull cracked. In death, Selena's hand stretched out towards her precious twins.

CHAPTER 57

Jane

Now

I'm trying to get my head around what Ed's shared. Perhaps this explains why there's a connection between us. We are twins. No, that's wrong. Larry and Viv are my mum and dad. They brought me up, loved, and cared for me. Their names are on my birth certificate. I glance at Ed's torn-up document, drying by the fountain. Fake. Is my whole life one big lie?

Ed takes my hand. 'You've gone quiet.'

'It's a hell of a lot to process. You're saying my parents aren't actually my parents, I'm a twin, you're my brother, Henry's my father, and he killed my real mother, *our* real mother. Come on, Ed, you're pulling my leg, right?'

'No, I'm not. Sorry, I had to be the one to tell you. Ever since I heard Henry and Evangeline's conversation, I've been reeling. The way they were talking was weird too.'

'How?'

'Evangeline didn't need to go into so much detail, seeing as she and Henry were there when everything happened. I reckon she knew I was listening and wanted me to know everything.'

'It's puzzling why she'd do that after all this time. I'm not sure how to deal with this. This isn't true. It can't be.'

I let the tears I've been holding fall. Whether they're from sadness or disbelief, I don't know. Who am I now if this is the truth? I've always been Jane Unwin. Just as I'm beginning to like her, I might lose her.

Ed offers a tissue. 'I hate upsetting you. If I wasn't so shocked, I'd probably be bawling too. Being Henry's son doesn't fill me with joy.'

'Having Evangeline as a grandmother isn't making me do cartwheels, either.'

'There is some good news. You're the heir to Glynnholme. One day, it will all be yours.'

'Shit. No. That's ridiculous.' Instead of laughing, I splutter over a lump in my throat.

'There's more to tell.'

I force a smile. 'Is Rupert our uncle?'

Ed grins. 'Thankfully, not.' His mouth soon straightens. 'Brace yourself for the biggest shock, though.' A tear trickles down his cheek. His shoulders hitch.

'Are you okay?' I ask.

'Far from it. Our mother, Selena, is buried under this bench.'

CHAPTER 58

Then

Evangeline refused to look at the child. If she did, it would surely break her.

'I expect regular reports on Jane's health, education, milestones, and other matters listed in the documents.' She adopted her usual business-like tone.

Viv was too devoted to her new daughter to reply. Despite the terrible circumstances, she finally had a baby. It was obvious there were more troubling reasons behind Larry and her taking in Jane. Viv had many questions, but she didn't dare ask them. No one would take this child away from her. Viv would stay quiet and always do her best by Selena and Jane.

'The house I've provided is tailored to all your needs,' Evangeline said. 'Being by the sea for a while will be most enjoyable.'

'I'm worried about our place being left empty,' Viv replied.

'Your home in Cowley will be fine.' Evangeline's sneer expressed her snobbish views on the area. 'Rupert will check on it regularly and forward any post.'

Larry stroked Viv's shoulder. 'We have to leave for a bit. There's no way we can claim you've just given birth. Considering you never had a bump, the neighbours will ask questions. We'll have a hard enough time telling our families and getting them to believe it. Tiny as she is, Jane hasn't just been born either.'

'I often find,' Evangeline began, 'people are so self-absorbed they tend not to delve into the details of others' lives. Anyway, we've covered this. You'll say you're moving to Cornwall to work for one of my elderly relatives. Unknown to you, Vivienne was pregnant and found out while there. You didn't share about the pregnancy because of the fear of losing another baby.'

Viv winced at the callousness of reducing her heartache to a motive.

An oblivious Evangeline continued. 'If anyone's suspicious, tell me and I'll deal with it. The fake birth certificate is evidence of your parenthood too.'

Larry frowned. 'What if someone figures out it's a forgery and we're arrested for fraud? Then they'll find out Jane isn't ours.'

Evangeline fixed him with a glare. 'Do not question my ability to employ someone who produces documents as good as the real thing. I've registered Jane with various services in Cornwall and will do so here when you eventually return. My contacts are most discreet. As far as everyone's concerned, until I decide to confirm otherwise, you are Jane's parents. Her falsified birth certificate has your surname and a different birth date so as not to link her to Henry or Selena. I have the genuine certificate for when I choose to tell Jane about her true Glynn identity.'

'Are you sure there isn't any family on Selena's side to contest it?' Viv knew she had to start asking questions.

'Selena was a loner,' Evangeline stated. 'No family, no friends. She was an unfussy woman. Even in her will she stated she wanted an unattended cremation and no memorial service. I found out after I offered to pay for the funeral.'

Evangeline paused. Guilt remained at knowing what had really happened to Selena's body. Using her parents' deaths as inspiration for claiming Selena died in a car accident was awful, too, even for Evangeline. She knew the trauma had haunted Selena. She didn't dare get close to people for fear of losing them. When she came to Oxford to study, Selena began trusting others. The Glynns repaid it with lies and death.

THE PROFESSOR

Tears formed in Viv's eyes as she focused on the sleeping boy. 'Can't we take Ed too? It feels wrong to separate them.'

Larry crossed his arms. 'That wasn't the deal, love. Twins are too much to deal with.'

'I'm Edward's guardian.' Evangeline tried to steady her voice. 'You take Jane or have nothing.'

She wished she could declare how much she wanted to keep the girl. The short period of having Jane after Selena's death gave Evangeline false hope. She'd wondered if she could get it right as a parent this time. Evangeline had considered raising the twins herself. It could never happen, though. Keeping them was harbouring evidence of children related to the woman Henry killed. Worse than that, he'd ruin Jane if he was involved in her upbringing. Edward would stay. Evangeline was an expert at being indifferent to boys. If Edward turned out like his father, so be it.

Henry swayed as he entered the room. 'Oh look, here's my daughter, being rescued from her naughty father!'

The repeating sound of Selena's skull cracking lessened in Henry's head the more he drank. Despite Evangeline banning him from the sunken garden, he'd been there to bid a final farewell to Selena. Most of his heart was already buried with her. What little he had left threatened to shatter at letting go of Jane.

Henry regarded Ed sleeping in a Moses basket. Although the boy was staying, Henry vowed never to show his son any affection. Love would make Henry confess to his terrible deeds.

After Selena died, Rupert and Henry wrapped the corpse in a tarpaulin, dug a deep hole in the ground, and buried her. Throughout, the process was supervised by Evangeline. After, when Henry showered, he realised guilt doesn't wash off.

Thankfully, the head gardener, Norman, was at home, recovering from an operation. Disturbed earth in his treasured garden would've aroused his suspicions. Evangeline instructed the gardening team to wait for his return before resuming work. Every night, Rupert smoothed over mud to make it less disturbed and cover the crime.

'Thanks for the privilege of raising your child, Mr Glynn.' Viv practically curtsied with gratitude.

'Thank Mother,' Henry slurred. 'Good luck being a daddy, Larry the Lamb.'

Larry flinched. 'I've asked you many times not to call me that. Do me the courtesy for once of listening. You may be rich, but if you keep taking the piss, I'll smack you in the gob.'

Henry laughed as he grabbed the other man's bicep. 'So, you're a fighter? Been building up your muscles doing whatever it is you do around here?'

Larry shrugged off the grip. 'I'm the maintenance man. If you bothered to speak to commoners like me, you'd know that.'

'We're not staff anymore, though,' Viv said.

Evangeline nodded. 'Indeed. As per the agreement, you must never mention Glynnholme, Henry, or me to Jane. If questioned by anyone, you'll state you'd rather not talk about this place due to regretting working here. In time, your employment will be forgotten.'

'And you'll have a lot of our cash to make a cosy life.' Henry poured a generous serving of whisky from a decanter, knocked it back, and raised a hand. 'Goodbye, Unwins. Goodbye, Jane. It's all over.'

Evangeline watched him leave. 'Don't mind Henry. He's as upset as the rest of us at Selena's death. This is why we have to let go of Jane. She reminds him too much of her mother.' Evangeline bit down on another lie.

* * *

Henry laid on his bed. He touched his chest, willing his heart to stop beating and end the pain.

Once again, he'd lost against women. Selena became pregnant without his permission. Secretly, he'd loved her intensely. Evangeline stole his children. Although Ed was still there, he might as well have been on a different continent. Evangeline wouldn't let Henry be anywhere near him. Educated women tried to destroy Henry. He decided to use and abuse them more than ever.

CHAPTER 59

Jane

Now

I'm sitting on a bench. My real mother's body is lying underneath. It doesn't feel macabre being here. I want to connect with Selena.

Why would the Glynns lie in the discussion Ed overheard regarding Selena's death? There are too many details for this to be a made-up story. Although I'm not sure how, I must try to accept the truth. I won't give up on the people who raised and loved me, though. Transferring the love I have for my mum, Viv, to an unknown corpse seems wrong. I bend over and touch the gravel. It's all I'm capable of doing. Forgive me, Selena. I can't forget the woman who was *Mum* to me. Give me time.

'All these years I've tried to find out where my mum's ashes were laid to rest,' Ed begins. 'Evangeline claimed she was cremated in a private service. I'm going to the police station. This is best done in person. How on earth can I cover everything in a phone call? I held off until I spoke to you. Sorry I didn't tell you when I phoned, but I couldn't find the right words. I didn't sleep last night, worrying about how you'd react. Is it weird I wanted us to come here so we can protect Mum from *them*?'

'No. I hate the thought of her being alone for so long.'

I can't help but fixate on the burial spot. If it wasn't for the Glynns, Ed and I could've grown up together. My birth mother would be alive. But I wouldn't have known Larry and Viv. This is painfully complicated.

I look at Ed. 'You're my brother.'

He nods. 'You're my sister.'

How do I accept being the child of anyone else but the Unwins? Henry and Evangeline will *never* be my family, not after what they've done. A shadow shifts across me, reminding me of the man, Death, who haunts my dreams. Finally, I realise I'm standing on a grave in a garden of death and lies.

'I need to get out of here.'

I race up the steps. The lawn soaks the bottom of my jeans as I run across it. Ed catches up with me.

'Are you coming to see the police with me?' he asks.

'I can't. I need… I don't know what I need. I don't even know who I am anymore.'

'I'll go on my own, but promise you'll stay away from the Glynns while I'm gone. Remember, they might be relations, but they're nothing to us.'

I grip my head. 'All this has given me one hell of a headache.'

Ed hugs me. 'Stay safe. Now I've found you, I'll never let you go.'

I wriggle free from the stifling embrace. This is too much. I was an Unwin, not a Glynn. I've always been an only child, not a twin. How can I be a different person?

'Evangeline and Henry will pay for what they've done to Selena and us,' Ed says. 'They believe they're superior with their intelligence, books, and estate. The common man and woman win this time.'

'You sound like my dad. Well, Larry.'

'Confusing isn't it? Although you're more of a Glynn than I'll ever be.'

Do I detect envy in his voice? Surely not.

'Evangeline's your mentor. Henry teaches you at university. Soon you'll inherit all this.' Ed holds out his arms.

THE PROFESSOR

'Let's not get into this at the moment. There's already a lot to process, but rest assured, I'm stronger than any of you think.'

'We'll see,' he replies as he walks away.

I watch Ed approach the side of the house where his car is parked. While he's away, I'm going to take action. As Ed and I were talking, a realisation hit me. The Glynns have more than Selena's death and burial on their consciences. I march towards Glynnholme, feeling murderous. I guess it runs in the family.

CHAPTER 60

As with any great book, The Professor's work needs an unforgettable ending. He isn't a fan of cliffhangers, but this time it might be to his advantage. This mission won't have a convenient conclusion in the usual crime novel style, with a killer's identity revealed and their motives explained. The Professor will escape and hide again within a more normal life.

Jane is a pretender to the Glynnholme throne. From a young age, she's been wilful. The Professor watched from a distance as she refused to play games with other children according to their rules. Her enquiring mind questioned the order of things. While he admired the cleverness, her disobedience was an issue. Since Jane started studying, she's become even more of a problem.

The Professor knows she's currently at Glynnholme. He's aware of everything she does. For a while, he allowed these visits to take place. Now they must end.

From the first moment he saw Jane, he's battled between loving and hating her. Love has kept her alive. Sometimes he wonders if he should stop hating and just love her more. No. Love would be the end of him. The choice - as ever - is between Jane and him. In the past, he chose her. Now, he must come first. Hate wins.

Jane knows too much. Soon she'll join her mother, Selena. The Professor smiles at the thought of a deathly family reunion.

CHAPTER 61
Jane

After leading me into the house, Rupert opens his mouth to speak. Determined not to deal with his officious crap, I push past.

'Well, I… How dare you!' He flaps those penguin-wing arms.

Standing in the middle of the stairs, I reel around. 'How dare *I*? How dare *you*? You have blood on your hands. Don't ever question my motives, not after what you did.'

Guilt clearly trips his tongue as he splutters.

'Where's Henry?' I ask.

Rupert tugs at his collar. 'Dr Glynn is out.'

'You better not be lying, considering you're already in the shit. I'm only too happy to shove you further into it.'

'I saw Dr Glynn leave.' A red face betrays Rupert's calm tone.

'What about Evangeline?'

'Ms Glynn is taking a nap.'

'Right then.' I continue heading upstairs.

'No! You mustn't disturb her.'

Rupert *can* move fast when he wants to. He's soon behind me, yanking my shoulder. I push him away.

'If you ever touch me again, I'll end you. While you may have buried my mother, you're not taking me down, too.'

His ruby face begins losing its colour. 'I… It was… I didn't…'

I leave him making up excuses while I aim for my destination. Rupert will no doubt phone Evangeline before I reach her. It doesn't matter. She won't be prepared for what I have to say. Now, I'm in charge.

Upstairs, I march down the corridor, reading the names of rooms I'm apparently set to own. Do I want Glynnholme? It's an absurd idea for someone like me. I've lived in an ex-council house most of my life. If I *did* live here, the named rooms would go. No more of this living in literature. There's a real world out there. Books are an escape - a wonderful place to enter when life is difficult - but we must live in reality too. My books in Glynnholme will be held with affection, not encased within shrines. They won't be artefacts of others' troubled pasts. These books won't reflect Evangeline's failures and obsessions.

Enough. I can't waste time thinking of my inheritance. I'm here for the murdered students. I'm here for Larry and Viv, who rescued me from the Glynns. I'm here for Selena, who would've been trapped in the grounds forever. I'm here for my brother, Ed, who's been poorly treated. I'm here for myself too. No more nice Jane. Prepare for set-free-from-the-Red Room-furious-and-fighting,-Jane-Eyre. I shove open the door for The Satis Room. Evangeline lies in bed, bolstered by pillows. Her hands fly to her head.

'Such rudeness, walking in here as if you own it.' She remains clutching her head.

'Oh, but I *do* own it, well, almost.'

Who is this brave person I'm becoming? I won't let Evangeline see I'm falling apart, too. She's taken too much. I'll never be one of her possessions.

After removing her hands, she reveals another secret. Her scalp is bald apart from a few fine wisps along her forehead. She grabs a white curly wig resting on a marble head and places it on her own.

'Cancer,' she says. 'It's terminal. No more chemotherapy.'

The veins knotting in her hands protrude more than ever as she grips the bed covers and winces. Previous glimpses of Evangeline's fragility tried to expose the truth, but her deceptive skills masked an illness. After what she's done, she doesn't deserve kindness, but I refuse to lose my humanity. Whether I like it or not, Evangeline is my grandmother.

'I'm sorry,' I say.

The customary snarl forms. 'Don't pity me.'

I approach the bed, noting mahogany bedside cabinets shining from a recent polish. Evangeline didn't opt for Miss Havisham's dusty and decaying scenery in this version of the bedroom in Satis House. A grandfather clock ticks in the corner next to a dressing table covered with lotions, potions, and trinkets. Trust the control freak, Evangeline, to change the details of a pivotal scene from *Great Expectations*. While she may be dying, her room doesn't symbolise time halting, like how it felt for Miss Havisham. The Professor and Evangeline have much in common. They manipulate literature to suit their own purpose. The Professor adds plot twists to his murder scenes, like Evangeline's rooms. They're cheats, plagiarising literature and cheapening it. There's nothing literary left that I want to learn from Evangeline. Difficult and grubby as they will inevitably be, I need answers.

Evangeline flings the bed cover back. A midnight blue silk nightdress, edged with lace, enhances the whiteness of her skin. It's not surprising she isn't wearing a yellowing wedding dress, Miss Havisham style. As much as Evangeline values attention to detail, she hates reminders of her failed marriage. After placing her feet on the floor, she wobbles.

'I can do it!' she blasts as I try to help.

'Stubborn cow.'

'Stubbornness runs in the family. I suppose we've got a lot to discuss. You know what happened to Selena.'

'Rupert phoned you then. I'm surprised you picked up your mobile phone, after claiming you hate it. Another of your many lies.'

Evangeline sits by the fire. 'So, Edward figured out he was supposed to hear my conversation with Henry. Edward is cleverer than he seems, although I've known for a while he eavesdrops. Still, my biggest mistake is in underestimating him. Be careful, Jane. Just because he's your brother doesn't mean he's trustworthy. Thankfully, you've escaped from inheriting your father's awful traits. Edward, I'm not so sure about.'

'He isn't a murderer!'

Evangeline fixates on the flames in the fireplace. 'How well do you know Edward? When men don't get what they want, they lash out. Women often receive the brunt of it.'

I take a seat opposite her. 'Leave Ed out of this, and lay off the fighting the patriarchy crap, too. You're no feminist. You're a bitter bitch who enjoys belittling people, particularly men. I bet your husband left because you made him feel inferior.'

'Such impudence!' She slaps a hand on the chair arm.

'You need to hear what everyone else is too afraid to say. You are largely responsible for how Henry turned out. I expect he grew up never feeling loved. Constantly fighting with your son is messed up. Look what happened. He treated Selena appallingly and then killed her.'

'It was an accident.' Evangeline's reply is barely above a whisper.

'Burying a body isn't an "accident". You chose not to tell the police about Selena's death and then ordered your minions to bury her. Separating twins wasn't accidental either. Treating Ed like an outsider - a servant - was a calculated move. Allowing us to grow up, not knowing who our actual parents are, was disgraceful. *You* masterminded it all.'

'Everything was to protect you. I'm still protecting you.'

While trying to get comfortable, Evangeline frowns. Why do these toffs insist on having rock hard chairs? If I furnished these rooms, they'd be full of cosy sofas your backside leaves imprints in.

Evangeline continues. 'After Selena died, I needed you to be as far away from Henry as possible. As the heir to Glynnholme, it was important. You can't deny your upbringing - while lacking Glynnholme's luxuries - was acceptable. Vivienne, particularly, did an exceptional job. The Unwins' reports and my private detective confirmed it.'

THE PROFESSOR

While the lack of privacy makes me want to scream, it will have to wait. I'll focus on how Viv was the best mum ever. Dad has always been by my side, too.

'Why did you make Rupert and Henry bury Selena?' I ask.

'You probably won't believe it, but I love my son. Going to prison would've killed him. Imagine hardened criminals around a rich, weak man. As a mother, I did what I had to do. I've failed Henry in many ways, but not in this.'

'What about *my* mother?' I force the words out. Processing I was born to a different woman than the one I knew is difficult.

'I can't bring Selena back.'

'But you could've shared with Ed and me about her. Even though she's gone, we deserve to know our backgrounds.'

'Don't hold on to the dead.' Evangeline grimaces. 'They stink up the place, trying to stay with the living. Better to concentrate on your enemies and keep them close.'

'Does that include The Professor?'

'What does he have to do with this? I don't know what you're talking about.'

'Stop lying!' I cry. 'Henry murdered those women. You've been covering for him. How could you?'

She doesn't reply. Instead, her eyes widen as she focuses on the doorway. Damn it. I thought I was safe alone with Evangeline. The Professor advances towards us.

CHAPTER 62
Jane

Skirting the edge of the room means I'm not the proverbial sitting duck. As Henry gets closer, Evangeline remains seated. Is it physical weakness or has she given up? The knowing look they give each other confirms a different, more dangerous reason.

'Is this some kind of sick *Friday the 13th* mother and son killing thing?' My voice trembles.

'What has a superstitious date got to do with this?' Evangeline replies.

'It's a horror film, Mother, although I have no idea what Jane's going on about.'

'You two set me up!'

Henry shakes his head. 'I've been at the university all day, trawling through tutorials. How would I know you're here?'

'Telephones are a marvellous invention for such things.' Even under pressure, Evangeline hasn't lost any of her sharp wit.

'Thanks, Mother. That's not in the least bit helpful.'

'Rupert, gave you the heads-up,' I add.

'I haven't seen or heard from him. Blasted fella has disappeared.' Henry scans the area as if the servant is hiding in here.

THE PROFESSOR

'Considering I told Rupert I know he helped to bury Selena, he's probably done a runner.'

The heat of the fire is stifling. Sweat trickles into my eyes. I blink at the sting before wiping my forehead with my sleeve. Henry approaches Evangeline and touches her shoulder. She shivers despite the claustrophobic temperature.

'What do you reckon you know, Jane?' Henry adopts the patronising voice he uses for people he thinks are idiots.

I will my heart to slow its rapid beating. 'You're The Professor! I can't believe I didn't work it out sooner. Selena was educated, brunette, and petite, just The Professor's type. She was someone you had to own because you couldn't bear Mummy having another pet project. Not only did you seduce Selena, you killed her, too. Her death wasn't enough, though. Afterwards, you gained a taste for murder. Working at Oxford Carroll is prime killing ground for such a pathetic man. There, you destroy women who have the audacity to study, particularly Victorian literature.'

Henry's laughter borders on maniacal. 'You should've taken up creative writing. How absurd. If I was a killer, I definitely wouldn't call myself *The Professor*. I have a doctorate. *Professor*, indeed.'

'The Professor aspect isn't necessarily about a title,' I reply. 'I've read more than you think. *The Professor* is Charlotte Brontë's first novel. Did you create a persona based on the main character, William Crimsworth? Do you believe he overpowered the opposite sex by educating, subduing, and occasionally making them fall in love with him? Re-read it and you'll discover William is pathetic. He can't hack teaching boys because he likes to dominate. He pervs over his female pupils and treats Frances like crap.'

Henry raises an eyebrow. 'She still marries him, though.'

'In that era, Frances' choices were limited. If she was real and alive now, she wouldn't touch William or you with a bargepole. Women don't have to take only what's offered anymore. We have many options. We're angry that monsters like you make us fearful. It's about time we had the freedom to walk alone at night or be in a small space with a man without planning an escape route, just in case.

'Frankly, I'm disappointed in you, Henry. Mummy issues are oh-so-very-serial-killer-clichéd. You couldn't even come up with something original when stealing Evangeline's rooms to inspire your killings. And you.' I point at Evangeline. 'Although you haven't murdered anyone, you covered up what he's done. How could you?'

Evangeline's sigh seems to deflate her as she folds into herself. 'Jane, you're so far off the mark. Henry has faults aplenty, but he —'

'Thanks very much.' He pouts.

'Shut up!' Evangeline shouts. 'Once again, I'm trying to save you from prosecution.'

I lean against the mantelpiece when another truth dawns on me. 'Oh my... Henry, you were going to rape Leah. Those willing to sleep with you aren't enough. They're too obedient for your disgusting tastes. I'm ashamed you're my real father.' I catch breaths against the fire's heated desire to steal them.

Henry vigorously shakes his head. 'Of course, I'm not. What utter nonsense.'

'Jane knows everything,' Evangeline says. 'There's no need to lie any longer.'

With his hands held out, Henry edges closer to me. 'I won't hurt you, I promise. After all, I *am* your father. I didn't kill those women and I'm certainly not The Professor. The police questioned me about it ten years ago. I have alibis and witnesses who all checked out. Let's go to the police station. They'll soon confirm it.'

I grab a poker and swing it in front of me. 'Back off! How about I tell them you killed Selena?'

He stands still. 'Perhaps you should.'

Evangeline's arms shake as she pulls herself up from the chair. 'No! We agreed. I won't allow you to drag the Glynn name through the mud.'

'Like we did with Selena's body?' Henry pinches the top of his nose. 'I can't keep living with the guilt. Maybe I should end all this and confess. Jane's aware of who she really is. Let her inherit. Forget about me. I must pay for my mistakes.'

Evangeline stamps her foot. 'I'd rather die than watch that happen. We'll make it go away.'

I turn towards her. 'You paid for those "witnesses" to testify so Henry wouldn't be arrested.'

She turns away.

Henry's eyes widen. 'Why, Mother? I had it all sorted.'

'We have to protect our legacy. Despite Jane and Edward knowing the truth, our plan hasn't changed. It's more necessary than ever.'

They glance at each other and then focus on me. I fling the poker in their direction and run. I need the only person who's kept me safe at Glynnholme. I want my brother. Ed might be in danger, too.

CHAPTER 63
Jane

Ed's shed welcomes me as a usual Glynnholme refuge. I smile at how, as the heir to a grand house and grounds, I'm more comfortable in a small wooden building. Of course, I am. I may have Glynn blood, but I'm still the girl who grew up in Cowley, raised by Viv and Larry. I'm the product of grafters: a woman who served dinners in a school canteen and a man who's a carpenter and creates dolls' houses.

Kate sometimes teases me, saying Dad must have a secret life as a gambler, considering the technology we have at home. I foolishly thought it was because dolls' houses aren't cheap. On reflection, he would've had to sell more than a few each month to buy all the gadgets and gizmos. Ed told me my parents were living off the Glynns' hush money. Did Larry and Viv only want me because of that? No. That can't be true. Mum soothed away my tears at the man, Death, staking a claim. Her smiles, just for me, were genuine. Dad has always done his best for me. The prospect of facing him makes me nauseous, though. I fear the volcano of hurt inside me will erupt at his deceit. It's hurtful how such a principled person kept lying, even after Mum died. I guess he became accomplished at hiding the truth. Still, he's my dad. I'm a

Glynn in blood only. I'll focus on the good that has come from this. I have a brother.

The shed being unlocked isn't surprising. No one's going to steal anything. My hazy mind, rocked by recent revelations, forgot Ed went to talk to the police. I'm proud of how he's determined to find justice for his mum, *our* mother. I should've gone with him rather than confronting the Glynns. Speaking to self-involved people regarding their criminal actions is a waste of time. Evangeline and Henry are more alike than they'll ever admit. Both only care about their wealth, futures, and needs.

A crushing wave of anxiety sucks away my breath. Henry killed all those women. It *has* to be him. My father is a murderer. What am I doing? Jane, stop being an idiotic horror film cliché, waiting to be killed. Move!

Henry probably wants me dead so he can inherit Glynnholme. The prolonged fakery hurts. His low morals were obvious, but we seemed to form a friendship. We were doing things in reverse. I parented Henry, teaching him how to be kinder and less arrogant. Unfortunately, I failed. You can't turn a murderer into a decent person.

I check my phone to see if Ed's left a message. Nothing. There's still no signal. I spot a note on the desk.

Jane,

I was on the way to the police station, but I had a bad feeling you'd confront Henry and Evangeline. Please prove me wrong by being at home or reading this. If you're in the shed, stay where you are. Make sure you lock it. You know where the keys are. I've gone to the house to find you. Be back soon.

Ed.

I can't leave him in there alone. He doesn't know Henry is The Professor. Without working phones, Ed only has me. I have to save my brother. I grab a pair of garden shears I have no intention of using beyond a threat and head for the house of horrors.

The front door is wide open. Rupert would never allow this to happen on his watch. I expect he's done a runner. The loyalty to Evangeline finally wore out. While I want to congratulate Rupert on growing a pair, I'd rather he was in prison. The wily penguin can wait.

I remember Rupert saying I should understand domestic staff are always aware of what happens in the place they work in. I'd taken it as an insult about my lower class to that of the Glynns. Now, I realise he was teasing information on the Unwins being employed here.

As I step into The Gray Hall, my ancestors glare back from their portraits. Charles Glynn fixes me with a stern stare.

'Sorry to disappoint you, Charlie boy, but I'm your only hope.'

Despite the spookiness of the empty hallway, I grin at the *Star Wars* reference. Ed and I are like Luke and Leia; separated twins reunited as adults. Shame we aren't equipped with lightsabers. I could do with one right now.

'Ed.' I keep my voice low.. 'Where are you?'

Although I'm possibly a dick for returning, he could be in danger. Running around, trying to locate a mobile signal is wasting time. Driving to the police station - wherever that is - means leaving Ed. Quillington village is too far to find help. Besides, this feels personal. I have to do this. I'll do my best and then escape. No one else will die. The Professor has claimed too many lives.

The emptiness of downstairs adds to my fear. I look for the telephone, often found in the library. It's missing. Evangeline previously mentioned she makes Rupert wheel it on a trolley to wherever she is. Did he hide it before doing a runner so I can't get help?

In the kitchen, I hover my hand over the stove and then touch the kettle. Both are cold. Mrs Patterson isn't here, which isn't unusual. She works limited hours around looking after her grandchildren.

Stepping into the servants' quarters, I hope Ed might have stopped by his room. This is an area I've never seen, perhaps because Evangeline considers me as family. Glynns don't bother with the space where servants sleep. But Ed is a Glynn too.

I push doors open, holding the shears in front of me. The rooms are worse than those I saw in student halls when visiting

THE PROFESSOR

Leah. Glynnholme's cell-like spaces consist of a single bed, chest of drawers, wardrobe, and a sink. Ed deserves better than this.

I enter his private world. The bedsheets are tightly bound, military style. A coin could easily bounce off the bed. Everything is in its place. There's none of the mess some men create of scattered dirty clothes, takeaway cartons, and toothpaste splattering the mirror. After having a few lazy boyfriends, I certainly know about it. My twin, though, is a neat freak. Navy bedclothes with matching curtains add to the darkness. No wonder Ed enjoys being in his shed. It's where he comes alive.

As I turn to leave, I tread on something. It cracks. Two dolls are on the carpet. They're not the delicate and beautiful figures Ed usually whittles. The unquestionable likenesses of Henry and Evangeline lay like corpses on the floor. Deep slashes scar their bodies. I pick up the Evangeline doll. Her severed head falls from her body.

CHAPTER 64

Back in bed, Evangeline leans against a pile of pillows and holds a fountain pen. It shakes in her hand. Now, she must tell the truth.

After the earlier drama, Henry has disappeared. She hopes he won't find Jane. Glynnholme's continuing glory relies on her.

Evangeline begins the letter with *Dearest Jane,* because she is so very dear. Before, Evangeline didn't realise how precious a grandchild could be. After giving young Jane to the Unwins, she thought she could cope with the separation. Evangeline never has. Decades of taunting Henry and receiving his insults have been punishments for giving up their only good thing. Evangeline can't lose Jane again. The truth is supposed to set you free. All she wants from being honest is reconciliation with her granddaughter.

Evangeline considers the first sentence. Explaining the events of twenty-nine years isn't easy. She will return to the beginning, where poor Selena dared to love Evangeline and Henry. Evangeline had such a fondness for the woman. When Evangeline discovered Selena's relationship with Henry, jealousy bit. By seducing Selena, he stole the daughter Evangeline wished she'd had. When Henry killed Selena, he took Evangeline's granddaughter too. She wouldn't have Jane living under Henry's awful influence. More than that, she had to ensure Glynnholme's lineage by giving Jane a chance to be raised well. Evangeline placed her trust in Vivienne, the dutiful and kind housekeeper. Now,

THE PROFESSOR

Evangeline wishes she had never set eyes on the Unwins. Hopefully, this letter will rectify many mistakes. Jane's anger at the deceit will reduce. Love rather than money will grant Evangeline's wishes. She'll rip open her bruised heart and invite Jane in.

From the second I saw you, I loved you, Evangeline writes.

She continues, detailing time's cruelty of stealing years they could've spent together. Words she struggled to form in her novels flow in letter form. Writing from the heart was the answer. New discoveries come too late. Evangeline's body is failing. Soon, her mind will follow. It's important to reach out to her granddaughter and make it right. Dying unforgiven and never seeing Jane smile again would be unbearable. The fiery pits of hell - where Evangeline knows she is going - are nothing in comparison. Devotion makes her lose herself in words, detailing the wonderful things she's learned about Jane.

'Is that a smile? I didn't think you were capable.'

He is here. She knew he'd return, eventually. Time has run out. Evangeline had tried to write against it and failed.

She drops the pen and paper to the floor, on the side of the bed he can't see. The Professor won't have the satisfaction of reading her true thoughts. He's taken enough. An unknown calm washes over her. For once, she feels no pain. The sense of inevitability is soothing. There's a strange freedom in letting go. She laughs at how all she needed to do was relax.

'What's so amusing?' The Professor asks as he stands in the doorway.

Evangeline is silent.

'I asked a question!'

Instead of answering, she focuses on tree branches reaching towards the window. At night, they often tap at the glass. The ghost of Cathy from *Wuthering Heights* demands to be let inside.

The Professor grabs her shoulder and shakes her. 'Don't ignore me!'

She projects the boldest laugh she can muster. Even to her ears, it sounds like the work of the devil.

'You're getting hysterical in your old age,' he says.

'Dealing with you is enough to drive anyone mad. But my mind's still in full working order.' Evangeline taps her temple. 'You may think you're smarter than me, but I've had my suspicions for a while it was you.'

'Of course you did, but you were too scared to admit it. I've enjoyed knowing that.'

'I desperately hoped I was wrong.' Evangeline's firm tone wavers.

The Professor raises a villainous eyebrow. The stereotypical villain's action disappoints Evangeline. She expected more from someone she almost admired for his ingenuity, not that she'd ever confess it. She mourned every death, not because he stole the joy from of her rooms, but also for the victims. The shame of those women being murdered because of the choices she made haunts her.

After picking up a chair, The Professor places it against the door and sits.

'It's been fun knowing you don't dare expose me,' he says.

'I was going to call the police after I'd taken care of a few matters. Despite this constant charade and fighting between us, I always intended to expose you. I don't care anymore what it will cost us both.'

He crosses his legs. 'Sorry to spoil your moment of glory. Although, I find it hard to believe you would've told the police who I am. The risk to you is enormous.'

Refusing to lie down and die, Evangeline pushes herself up. 'My life is almost over, whether it's at your hand or by other means. Even if I go to prison, it won't be for long. You're killing a dying woman.'

He nods. 'But I got there first. Also, without you, Jane isn't protected.'

'Leave her alone!' A coughing fit overcomes Evangeline.

'I'll deal with Jane as I please. It is my right.'

Evangeline takes a deep breath before speaking. 'Please, I'll do whatever you want, give you anything, just don't hurt Jane.' She places her hands together.

'Praying won't help. God doesn't listen to people like us.'

THE PROFESSOR

'I've given you everything you've asked for. All your needs are fulfilled. If you're going to take a life, have mine! I can be the *Jane Eyre* victim to complete the two remaining rooms on your kill list. Being a Brontë expert and a Glynn makes me the perfect choice. What better prize than the person who owns the house you want to claim?'

A tear snakes down her cheek and then drips from her jaw. It's for Jane, not herself. Jane must live. She is the future of Glynnholme.

Evangeline lets out a cry as he launches at her, slaps her face, and then seizes her wrist. The violence shouldn't be surprising, but it is.

'Your life for Jane's isn't much of a bargain,' The Professor begins. 'Besides, your death has always been part of my plan.'

He walks around the bed. Something scrunches under his foot. He picks up the letter, reads, and then crumples it.

'Jane has really got under your skin.'

'Just like she's under yours. Remember that when you're looking into her eyes as you try to kill her. You won't be able to do it!'

He stuffs the balled paper into her mouth. Her nostrils flare, trying to seek air for weak lungs. Words stick on her tongue - those in the letter and those left unsaid.

'We've reached the conclusion of your story, Ms Glynn.'

The Professor wipes her tears with his glove. Grasping hands reach for her neck. She looks out the window. The wind increases. Branches scratch against the pane. Cathy is coming! As Heathcliff did in the novel, Evangeline begs her to come in.

The wind dies. All is still. For the last time, Evangeline Glynn leaves her beloved home.

CHAPTER 65
Jane

For the first time, I consider how well I know Ed. It's only been a short time since we met. Even if someone's family, it doesn't mean they aren't keeping secrets. The Glynns have shown me that.

The beheaded Evangeline doll Ed created is worrying. I want to trust he's a decent person who has a right to express his anger, though. If Evangeline had raised me, maybe I would've been volatile too. Ed's been cheated with the upbringing he received. Guilt at being born female makes me halt in the upstairs corridor. It's not my shame to bear, though. Ed and I are blameless. He's a troubled person with many positive qualities. We all need an outlet for our hurt. His escape is through venting on dolls he's made of Evangeline and Henry. I guess it's healthier than harming the real versions, but still...

Ed needs a loving environment, not Glynnholme's prison. When this is over, I'll support him. Perhaps he could live with us for a while, although Dad might need persuading. After all, he didn't fight to take Ed when we were babies. Evangeline is powerful, but I wish Mum and Dad had fought for my brother. Things could've been so different.

I creep past The Jekyll Room, hoping Henry isn't inside. The room names and their occupants are a sick joke. Henry should've been called *Edward* - the Hyde monster. From birth, Evangeline set Ed up for failure. Did Selena name her son after Edward Hyde because she was afraid of Evangeline and did what she commanded? Maybe Selena wanted to please the Glynns. Her daughter won't. Like Jane Eyre, I have an independent will. The Glynns won't claim me as another victim. They're not having my twin either.

I touch the door to The Red Room. It is *not* mine, as Evangeline stated. I never chose this.

An animalistic howl travels from the back of the house. It becomes a long wail. Distress is coming from The Satis Room. As I approach, I raise the garden shears I'm holding. My bravery threatens to disappear as the noise continues. I can't stop. Ed might be injured or worse.

After pushing the door open, I stumble over a chair lying on the floor. Henry is sitting on Evangeline's bed. Her snowy curls cascade over his arm as he cradles her. Her head tilts back. Dead eyes stare at me. A necklace of bruises dots her neck. Henry rocks her like a father singing a lullaby to his child.

'Mother, please forgive me! I never wanted it to end this way. I let it go too far.'

I drop the shears. He looks up at me. I bend down to seize my weapon.

'What are you doing? Why have you got those?' Henry sniffs through his sobs.

'You murdered her!' I shout from the doorway. 'I know you hated Evangeline, but killing her is—'

'I didn't do it!'

After he lets go of her, Evangeline's body flops onto the bed.

Henry holds out his hands. 'I found her like this. After you left, I went for a walk to clear my head and to find you to explain things. When I returned, Mother was…' He takes a breath. 'I've never hurt anyone.'

'You killed Selena!'

'It was an accident. I didn't mean to push her so hard. I accept we shouldn't have buried her, or separated you from Ed. I'm going to the police. Being in prison will be nothing compared to the chains holding me since Selena died. I hardly sleep and can barely think. My lectures are the same every year because literature doesn't matter anymore. I drink too much. I need this torture to end.'

'You should suffer. Not only did you kill those students, you've murdered Evangeline.'

My tongue catches on the name. She was difficult, but didn't deserve this. I'd started to see some good in her. Sometimes I caught her looking at me and the softness of her gaze puzzled me. If it was a flame of affection, Henry has snuffed it out.

He stands. I hold up the shears, pointing the blades towards him.

'Don't you dare come any closer!' I yell.

The shock that had rooted me to the spot disappears. I must run. I have an advantage over Henry, who's likely never seen the inside of a gym. Whisky and fine living haven't attributed to an active lifestyle. Still, I'm no athlete either. He huffs behind me, trying to catch up. I dash down the stairs, daring to look back. Henry trips on a step and lands on his backside. Using the banister, he pulls himself up.

As I dart outside, he shouts, 'Jane, I've never murdered anyone! I loved Mother. You've got the wrong person. There's another Glynn man who's full of anger towards academic women. Stay away from Ed!'

CHAPTER 66

Outside, Jane keeps running. The Professor knows when secretly meeting Ed, she parks on the edge of the woods to avoid Evangeline's detection. This is to The Professor's advantage. The woods bear no surprises. Once, he tested the theory by walking through them at night without a torch. Who needs light when your true self flourishes in the dark? The woods have been a background for many of his walks, stamping out fury at Evangeline, Selena, and Jane.

As she was the beginning, Jane is also the end. The Professor has to make an important choice. If Jane lives, he'll have to endure the agony of an unfinished storyline. If she dies, he can tie up loose ends and destroy the Glynns' female line. The Professor's greatest weakness has been his inability to decide on Jane's fate. Now, he pursues her at a leisurely pace. She can't escape him. Jane doesn't appreciate how safe she's been until now. Many times, he's been close enough to snap her neck, just like he did to Evangeline.

The Professor feeds on the thrill of claiming the woman who started it all. Evangeline didn't deserve to die of a terminal illness. He won't allow past acquaintances to gather at her funeral, full of sympathy. Let them gossip about a cruel death for a cruel woman instead. Thankfully, they'll never know Evangeline approached her death with dignity. He'd wanted her to beg for her life, but she pleaded for Jane's.

If Evangeline hadn't interfered, The Professor may never have begun his killing campaign. Perhaps he could've lived a normal, dull existence. From the moment Evangeline decided upon the twins' futures, though, she destroyed many lives.

The Professor considers his relationship with Jane. He battles between guilt and revenge. Love and hate are equal in intensity. So scarily close to each other, he can't differentiate between the two.

As Jane continues to run, he decides to stick with his planned ending. Memories of successful previous murders boost his courage. He can do this. He is The Professor, an accomplished killer. The other women were pawns in the game he played with Evangeline. Jane is so much more. Perhaps this will be his finest murder. Strength comes from letting go of what you love. Love is his kryptonite.

Now the truth is revealed, Jane's opinion of him will change. She's learned some details of who she really is. Once again, an academic woman believes she's better than him. He will be Jane's teacher, showing the error of her thinking.

The Professor lets his prey go. He doesn't need to give chase. The hound knows where to get his teeth into the fox.

CHAPTER 67
Jane

I slide down the front door, hoping it's a suitable barrier against a murderer. The adrenaline that helped me to escape drains away. Driving home wasn't easy. I reverted to being a learner driver, trying to remember what to do. The fear of Henry following me made my mind whirr. The Professor is my father. I'm a serial killer's daughter.

Hanging on a wall in the hall is a framed photograph capturing a moment from Mum and Dad's wedding day. Her head is thrown back in laughter. Dad has a reserved smile on his face. They are my parents: Larry and Viv. Knowing I have Henry's blood makes me want to drain it out of my body. He will pay for his actions and I'll make that happen.

My bag isn't on the floor as I expected. In a fearful state, I must've left it in the car. My mobile is in there. We got rid of the landline years ago. There's no point in having it, considering the only calls were from telemarketers.

I pull myself up. Ed needs me. He could be in trouble. I feel cowardly for leaving, but Henry gave me no choice. Stupid, stupid Jane! If I was reading this in a novel, I'd be screaming at me. I should've called the police when I was driving. Escaping from a murderer who's also my real father was terrifying. Of course, logic disappeared.

I need my phone, which means going outside. After opening the door a little, I take a glimpse. Henry might come here. If he doesn't have it already, he can find my address on the university's database.

I curse my neighbours who seem to have more cars than residents per household. Parking on our road is a case of dumping your vehicle wherever you can. My car is halfway up the road. It's not far, but when you're a killer's target, it may as well be miles away.

As I open the garden gate, a familiar vehicle turns the corner at the top of the road. It carries on past. After parking his pickup truck, Dad – I can't call him *Larry* - walks towards me.

'You look as white as a sheet!' Dad touches my forehead. 'Clammy too. Stop pushing through the illness. You need to rest.'

'I've been running.'

His eyes widen. 'I'd pay to see that. I've asked you to come for a run with me many times. Then you go out on your own, although you're not exactly dressed for it.'

'I was running from Henry Glynn. He killed all those students and now Evangeline. Henry's The Professor! I must call the police.'

Dad puts an arm around me. 'Quick! Get inside.'

* * *

Dad twists his hands around each other. What I've shared is a lot to process, but he knows some of the original story. After all, he's one of the characters.

'Why didn't you tell me I'm not yours?' I ask. 'If I'd known from a young age, I would've come to terms with it. Evangeline didn't have to know you'd told me.'

He continues wringing his hands. 'No matter what, you're our daughter, not a Glynn. We wanted to adopt you. Even though we kept asking, Evangeline wouldn't allow it. As usual, things had to be done her way so you'd inherit.'

THE PROFESSOR

'But I don't want any of it. I never want to see Glynnholme again.' Grabbing a cushion from the sofa, I hold it close. 'I feel set adrift, like I don't belong anywhere.'

'You belong to me. We belong together.'

Dad folds his arms and winces. After inspecting a bruise - another work-related injury, no doubt - he lowers his sleeve. I sip warm milk. It's Dad's cure for everything from tummy ache to heartache. The cinnamon sprinkled on top makes my nose twitch. Even though it was too hot, I glugged the last drink. I needed the comfort.

While Dad was preparing a much-needed second drink and phoning the police, all I could do was stare at a photo of Mum. Six-year-old me sits on her lap with koala arms wrapped around her neck. Guilt pricks at me as I consider how my birth mother is a stranger. I'll never know how Selena took her tea, what her personality was like, or what she thought of me. Am I wrong to love mum, Viv, who raised me, while mourning the mother, Selena, I never had?

Dad notices where I'm looking. He walks over to the photo and picks it up.

'We couldn't have children. It broke Viv's heart. We had so many disappointments. Back then, there weren't loads of tests to find out why things went wrong. You were expected to keep trying or accept it couldn't happen. Before you came along, Viv gave up on having kids. No matter what I said, she was convinced the miscarriages were her fault. When you were offered to us, she was so happy. It didn't matter she hadn't given birth to you. I hope you've never felt like she treated you as anything other than her own child.'

'Never. You neither. That's why this is hard to understand. Mum and you are my parents. It doesn't change. Henry will never be my father.'

Dad slams the photo frame onto a shelf. 'If he comes anywhere near you, I won't be responsible for my actions. Henry's spent too long believing he's superior. When I worked for the Glynns, he treated me like a slave and enjoyed making a fool out of me.'

'Sit down. Getting wound up won't help.'

He keeps pacing in front of the television.

'Soon, Henry will be arrested,' I add.

Dad thumps his fist into the other open hand. 'Evangeline was no better than him. She was so condescending to Viv and me. I made new shelves for that library of hers after the originals had woodworm. When I finished, I offered to put the books on the shelves. She laughed, saying I wouldn't have a clue how to arrange them and to leave literature and learning to her.'

His pacing is almost mesmerising. My head lolls as I track him, moving back and forth.

'It'll take a while for us to work things through,' I begin. 'Don't worry. I'm not going anywhere. I've never judged you and know you're smart. Seeing what you do as a carpenter and making dolls' houses is amazing. While I'm hurt and upset you lied to me, I'm still your daughter.'

He bites his lip. 'Thank you, love. You're not the only one who's shocked by what's come out today. That poor Selena. When she came to Glynnholme, I saw her a few times. She was always friendly. I remember when she first turned up with Ed and you. Henry's involvement was supposed to be a secret, but nothing gets past the staff.'

'What was Selena like?'

'To be honest, I didn't speak to her much, but I promise to share what I know about her later. Let's focus on one thing at a time. The coppers will be here soon.'

As I stand, my legs threaten to give way.

'Woah!' Dad rushes over to steady me. 'Lie on the sofa.'

He places a fleece blanket over me and offers the mug of milk. I take a sip and then lean back. Panic propels me upwards.

'Shit! How could I forget about Ed? We have to check he's safe!'

'Leave it to the police. They're likely to be at Glynnholme now. From what you've shared about him, Ed knows how to deal with the Glynns. He's probably driven away to safety. Get some rest. You'll need it. This is only the beginning of unravelling this mess. I'll wake you up when the coppers are here.'

THE PROFESSOR

I burrow into the blanket. The shock has worn off. A brief nap might help. My police statement will be more coherent after some rest. As I drift, a last thought flitters in my mind as a siren warning. My heart seizes. My breath catches. Sleep grabs the thought and discards it. As I descend into nothingness, I hear knocking.

CHAPTER 68

Henry realises it's more than a door in front of him. Once he enters, his life will change forever. He has a choice: stay outside and keep running, or enter and show Jane who he really is.

On the drive here, he stopped the car. The spectre of Glynnholme loomed over him in the background. He reflected on the miserable building which had given him such pain, grief, and punishment. Worse than that was how Selena haunted him. Everywhere he turned, her frightened face appeared. Only a lot of alcohol could make her disappear, if only for a short while. Not even his beloved books brought him solace.

That day, when Henry looked down on a dead Selena, he recalled Victorian literature's downtrodden heroines, feisty fighters, and lovers. He knew a tragedy when he saw it. More than that, Henry saw the woman he loved. Concerned about being trapped, he had vowed never to confess that. He still had oats to sow and hearts to break. He believed Selena would wait until he was ready. She had until his mother got involved.

When Evangeline discovered Henry's parentage, her initial expression was of horror. As always, it was about the money. She feared for the Glynns' riches. Evangeline should've known Selena better. She never took more than was necessary. Selena refused extra from Evangeline, who liked to spoil her grandchildren after she'd accepted them. Henry admired how Selena stuck to her

THE PROFESSOR

principles. When she offered to pay Evangeline for the tutoring services, he thought he'd die laughing. Working-class people could be terribly dull, but Selena was charming.

When they were alone, she made him want to be a decent man. As they lay together on the grass, looking up at the stars, Henry promised to be faithful. It stabs his heart, remembering her gratitude.

When Selena announced the pregnancy, she expected Henry's anger. He surprised them both as he placed a hand on her stomach and smiled. In an unguarded moment, he imagined their future. He pictured a happy family. Then Selena sullied the idea by worrying about Evangeline's reaction. The reality of his mother's existence stole Henry's fleeting fantasy. While she lived, he'd never have happiness.

Once Evangeline's shock had worn off at the news, Glynnholme's destiny was determined. Jane was the heir Evangeline needed. Selena was set to lose her daughter, not that anyone shared this with her from the start.

Henry played his part in the sunken garden until the moment Selena begged for her children. He lashed out in fear, not fury. He'd spent a lifetime wishing his own mother cared about him. The unconditional love in Selena's eyes for the twins mocked Henry's lack. He wanted to remove the look of adoration from Selena's face, not steal her life.

As they buried her, Henry stopped to vomit a few times. If it wasn't so disturbing, the sight of Rupert standing in a pit would've been amusing. Henry looked away as Rupert rolled a tarpaulin around the body. Evangeline watched from a window at the top of the house. Of course, she didn't do the dirty work that came from her own plan. The thud as Selena's corpse hit the earth undid Henry. Since then, he's unravelled. There's little left on the spool of his rationality. Now, he will let it go.

Jane learning about the inheritance wasn't supposed to happen this way. After Henry and Evangeline had gained her trust, they were going to tell the truth. Eventually, Henry would "guide" Jane to make Glynnholme what it should've been. The impending death of Evangeline might be somewhat sad, but he'd be free to start over. Jane had ruined it. Once again, a woman overpowered Henry. His own daughter, too!

Henry stands at the door. He must go in. Decision made, this is where it ends.

CHAPTER 69
Jane

The man I call *Death*, stands over me. I sense him.

'Mum, help me!'

Even now I need her, although I wonder which mother I'm calling for: Viv or Selena. At the moment, I'd take anyone who can make Death disappear.

I blink, searching for light to cover the dark. Darkness wins. My eyelashes flicker against material that must be wrapped around my head. Possessive fingers squeeze my shoulder. I feel it. Honestly, I do. This is it. He wasn't a dream. Death has been preparing by breaking me down and haunting me. Now he's claiming his prize. His grip presses into my flesh.

No, Jane, no! You're dreaming. You're on the sofa, snuggled in a blanket. Wake up!

Death's hold disappears. A sound like a door closing follows. This is new. Usually, he just vanishes. Usually, though, I'm not wearing a blindfold.

As I try to hurl the blanket off, my hands won't move. Ties cut into my wrists. I press a finger downwards and touch a hard, cold floor rather than the expected carpet of our lounge. Consciousness fights against grogginess. A restraint, likely rope, pushes against my chest as I wriggle.

Competing odours assault my nostrils: paint, sawdust, and methylated spirits. I must be in a shed. It's Dad's shed. The smells are familiar. Pushing against whatever I'm bound to, I try to break free. I hear a groan.

'Who is that?'

As far as I can, I feel for clues. A fellow captive's hands lie still near mine. I brush my fingertips over callouses and dry skin.

'Dad! Are you okay?'

No reply.

'Talk to me!'

Wait, was someone knocking on our front door before I fell asleep? Oh, no! Henry must have overpowered Dad. It appears Henry's drugged, blindfolded, and tied us up. This fuzziness in my mind isn't from waking up. I have no recollection of being moved here either. The same must've happened to Dad. We're The Professor's next intended victims.

'Listen, Henry!' I shout, not knowing if he's close enough to hear, 'you can escape. You don't have to do this.'

Silence.

I push my tethered feet down onto the floor and use my legs and back to shove against Dad. His heavy, sleepy breathing becomes shallower. Hopefully, he's waking up from whatever Henry's doped us with. Please let me be right in thinking Dad's alive. I can't lose him. I'm tied to one father who could be dying or dead, while the other is a murderer. The most elaborate Victorian novel couldn't compete with this plot.

'I'm your daughter!' I cry.

The plea is useless. It's because I'm Henry's daughter he's doing this. He wants Glynnholme for himself. After my death, Henry inherits. Killing Dad is extra sport.

Something creaks. It sounds like the door. Someone removes my blindfold. The light comes on and stings my eyes. It takes a while to fully focus. When I do, I notice a hand pulling away through the partially opened door and closing it. Henry waits outside.

We *are* in Dad's shed. Dolls' houses in various stages of construction are on the benches. Near me a house larger than any

THE PROFESSOR

I've ever seen is under a cover. This is his current passion. I hold back tears as I consider Dad might never get to finish it. No. I won't give up. The Professor won't add us to his list. I lean against Dad, trying to rock backwards and forwards. I need him to be conscious so we can work as a team.

'We've got to get out of here. Henry's nearby. Come on!'

The door opens. He enters. After some initial confusion, I smile. Our rescue is here.

CHAPTER 70
Jane

I continue pushing against whoever's been captured too, hoping they're alive.

'Quick!' I call to our rescuer. 'Undo these ties before The Professor returns.'

The rescuer rubs his watering eyes. He inspects his hand, frowns, and then flicks away tears. Macho men can't cry in front of others. He turns towards a bench, hopefully looking for a tool to snap the restraints. Soon, I'll discover who I'm tied to, although I can guess. Who else could it be? Please let him be okay.

Our saviour lays an arm on top of a covered project.

'Hurry up!' I try to rouse him from a daze.

As he spins around, he whips the sheet off the house. I gasp. I know this building. We all do. Glynnholme.

Like theatre curtains, he pulls open the front panels. Inside, ornately decorated rooms are exact replicas of those Evangeline created. This isn't the most disturbing part of the creation.

'Fucking hell.' My fellow captive's voice is laboured. 'The Professor's victims are in there, made into dolls and how they died by the looks of it.'

Ed!

THE PROFESSOR

'Indeed, they are,' Dad replies. 'I prefer to call them *figures*, though. Dolls are for children. Every aspect of this building is correct and precise. I won't accept mistakes.'

'You're The Professor!' Ed cries. He fights against the binding around our chests. It tightens, biting into my upper arms.

I'm speechless. No. Not him. Not my dad. He *can't* be The Professor.

'Stop trying to escape, Edward.' Dad's menacing voice belongs to someone else. 'I'm experienced in tying people up.' He smacks a hand against his forehead. 'Wow, I've just realised. We've come full circle! I've captured twins again, although you're obviously not exactly like Dinah and Alice.'

'Who are they?' Ed asks.

'They're the "Goblin Market" victims,' I manage to say while my mind struggles to take everything in.

'Edward's probably not aware of "Goblin Market".' Dad overloads the scathing tone. 'Shall I explain or will you, Jane?'

I can't answer. Looking at him is hard enough.

'It's a poem,' Ed begins, 'full of goblin men, fruit, sexual and addiction allegories, and a sister who saves the other.'

Dad's eyes widen. 'Well, well. I'm impressed.'

'You got something wrong,' Ed adds. 'Laura and Lizzie aren't twins.'

'The Professor puts his own spin on things. He takes literature and makes it his own.'

'Those who talk about themselves in the third person are weirdos.'

'Stop baiting him,' I say.

I consider the clues I should've noticed. Dad has the kind of temper that simmers for a while until it explodes. Usually, he avoids reaching volcanic level, but there have been times he's erupted. When I was younger, I saw him take a man outside the pub and batter him for calling Dad stupid. I was terrified. Whenever he argued with Mum, she would go for a walk to give him time to cool down. While she was out, he'd be in the shed, unleashing frustration. I could hear the bangs and crashes from my open bedroom window. I foolishly believed it was a safe way of getting his anger out.

My teenage years were occasionally fraught. Dad and I engaged in a power struggle. I was a stroppy teen, asserting independence. He was an irate parent. Still, I believed he was just being protective. He seemed to become gentler after Mum died. It was probably because Dad was projecting his rage through murder.

He addresses Ed. 'Even if you weren't tied up, you're in no position to fight me. Are you feeling woozy? The sleeping tablets take a while to wear off. They're powerful, right Jane?'

Weeks of tiredness, fatigue, and muddled thinking now all make sense.

'You've been drugging me. I never had flu. Why did you do that?'

He places a territorial hand on the miniature Glynnholme. 'Having this house at my disposal is such a joy. Evangeline tried to keep me out, but she didn't know about this. Jane, your sleeping tablets have often proved useful. It's taken a while to get the dosages right. Crushing tablets into your drinks and food was useful. You were spending too much time with the Glynns. Also, I couldn't have you finding out I'm The Professor before I was ready for the reveal. If it wasn't for Edward turning up, we could've carried on as normal.'

'*Normal* for you is being a serial killer,' Ed says.

'Don't you dare liken me to such predictable people! My work is superior to those who solely kill for kicks. I had a job to do and I did it well.'

The calmness is unsettling. His tears are even stranger. Dad never cries, although I'm no longer the best judge of his character. A murderer lived under the same roof as me. I cooked his dinners, washed his clothes, and slept in a room next to him.

'Why are you crying?' I blast. 'Those women's families deserve to shed tears, not you!'

He swipes an arm across his face. 'I'm crying because I love you. I wanted to avoid this situation.'

'Let us go, then!'

THE PROFESSOR

'I can't. *You* are making this happen. If you hadn't got so involved with the Glynns, we might've been okay. I accepted you'd inherit and we'd live at Glynnholme together. Unfortunately, you gave in to Evangeline's manipulations. She's changed you. Now, everything will be yours, and you'll leave me. Throughout, I've kept you safe. I took ten years off from my mission for you. Believe me, I strived to be a good father. Every day of that miserable decade I had to choose between you or my calling. I hid my literary knowledge despite how desperate I was to share it. You thought a working man who doesn't use flowery language is an idiot. I tried to leave The Professor behind but he's always there, under my skin. If I hadn't scratched the itch, I'd have gone insane.'

'You've already lost the plot,' Ed snipes. 'Naming yourself *The Professor* is fucking ridiculous. You're a carpenter and a dolls' house maker, not an academic. Actually, you're a twisted bastard who gets off on weakening women. That's the work of a thick shit, not a genius. *Professor*? Do me a favour.'

Dad slaps him. I bend over against the impact. The violence is unbelievable but I have to accept it's happening. The horrible truth is Dad didn't unleash cruelty on his family because The Professor had other outlets.

'I strongly advise you keep your gob shut, Edward,' Dad says. 'Seeing as how you're the most unlearned person here, I'll explain it slowly. *The Professor* is the name of Charlotte Brontë's first novel. Heard of her?'

I expect Ed's silence is from stubbornness, not ignorance.

Dad continues. 'I could elaborate on how the protagonist, William Crimsworth's story is similar to mine but it would be wasted on the likes of you.'

'Got it,' Ed replies. 'I'm stupid and you're so clever. You didn't even need to give yourself a made-up title to prove it. Oh wait, you did!'

'Qualifications aren't required to study literature.'

Ed laughs so hard it makes us both shake.

'What's so funny?' Dad asks.

Ed keeps laughing.

'Tell me!'

I close my eyes, preparing for Dad to attack again.

'Bet it eats you up inside that Evangeline and you have something in common,' Ed states.

'No, we don't.'

'Whatever. How about we hear your story, *Professor*? How did you get into the university to kill some of those women?'

'He's worked on campus and in halls.' I say, hating the reality of my answer. 'No one questions why the odd job man is there. The security is crap too.'

'I have keys for most of the buildings,' Dad adds, 'but it was still risky. Proper planning helped. As much as possible, I took my teachings elsewhere.'

'You are one sick puppy,' Ed says.

Dad's villainous laugh is an alien sound.

'Fancy yourself as a bit of a lad, coming here to play the knight in shining armour, don't you?'

'I wasn't aware I had to. I was checking on Jane, not offering myself up to a murderer. He must've laced my tea with tablets, Jane, while you were out cold on the sofa. I thought you were sleeping.'

Dad kneels by me. 'Don't listen to him. I'm all that matters. Since the moment you were conceived, I've been connected to you.'

'What the actual...?' Ed says. 'Were you getting your rocks off watching Henry and Selena having sex? Mind you, considering what else you've done, I'm not surprised.'

I swear I can hear Ed's teeth rattling as Dad thumps him.

'Leave him alone!' I cry.

'I won't be called a pervert!'

A realisation makes me want to tear his face off. 'You were prepared to rape my friend, Leah! You disgusting creature. I'm going to throw up.'

He grabs an empty paint water pot and holds it under my chin. 'Use this.'

Preferring to vomit on myself than rely on him, I turn away and fight against nausea. Why is Dad offering help when he wants to kill me?

THE PROFESSOR

He remains crouching. Then he grips my jaw to pull my head round to focus on him.

'You're so much like Selena it's frightening.' The Professor gazes into the distance. 'Those women had to die. It's all your mother's fault.'

CHAPTER 71
Then

Humidity coated Larry's skin with sweat. Damp air laboured his breathing. He peeled his T-shirt away while glugging water. After testing the varnish drying on the bench with his finger, he smiled. His creations were spread across Glynnholme. This bench was the best yet. The thought of Evangeline's bony arse sitting on something he made was pleasing.

Norman appeared, pushing a wheelbarrow containing weeds. 'Another hot day.'

Norman often started a conversation he undoubtedly knew wouldn't progress. The men always evaluated each other, which was to Larry's disadvantage. The friendly head gardener obviously saw glimpses of the real Larry. Norman's perceptiveness was a skill Larry hoped to develop. He tolerated Norman's chattiness to learn more. Dealing with the older man's intense stare and loaded comments was excruciating. Learning about discomfort, though, taught Larry more about how to inflict it. He tuned out the babble.

Evangeline appeared at her bedroom window. Whenever she gave a petty command, it took Herculean restraint not to retaliate. That morning, she grinned while watching Larry unblock a toilet. Him, a skilled carpenter! He hated being her skivvy.

THE PROFESSOR

His wife, Viv, believed her housekeeper's role was a privilege. She enjoyed living in staff quarters while they saved the deposit for a mortgage. When Larry raged about Evangeline, Viv noted his ingratitude for the maintenance man position. It was created especially for him. He knew it was one of Evangeline's mind games.

Larry wondered if having an easily pleased wife was a blessing or a curse. His respect for Viv was never in doubt. She didn't pretend to be anyone above her station. She loved books, but never wielded it over him as a weapon. Since he was a child, Larry adored the classics. Growing up in a work-oriented family, he hid his novels. His father would've bashed him with them if he'd discovered the stash. The males in the family were made for hard labour. Larry's sister *was* allowed to study. After he began working at Glynnholme, he took books from the library and devoured them. Reading and gaining more knowledge gave him a secret power.

Evangeline opened the window. 'I hope you're both working hard. Thunderstorm coming in later. Chop, chop.' She clapped her hands.

As she slammed the window shut, Larry imagined strangling her.

'Earth to Larry,' Norman said.

He found his smile, hidden in a drawer of attempts at normality, and pasted it on.

'Sorry,' he replied. 'This heat is getting a bit much.'

Norman frowned. 'Is that all? You look angry. Ms Glynn certainly tries the patience of saints.'

'What the lady of the house wants, she gets.' Larry scraped his teeth together.

'On that note, I'm off to the garden centre for the plants she's chosen. See you later.'

Larry locked the fireball inside himself until Norman's truck left. Fire crackled at the other man's passivity. It burned at Viv for forcing Larry to take the job. All he wanted to do was build dolls' houses. Flames of anger set alight as he considered Henry making him an errand boy. An inferno raged at Evangeline's snootiness.

Larry hurled his bottle of water across the lawn. It wasn't enough. He headed for the shed. He decided to damage Norman's tools and piss on his notebooks full of plans for a sunken garden. If questioned, Larry would state he hadn't seen the vandals who'd probably sneaked in from the woods.

The shade was a welcome relief. The sound of car tyres tearing up gravel was not. Larry slipped inside. If the driver was Henry, he feared he couldn't control himself. Another Larry the Lamb jibe was one too many. Henry would learn he wasn't harmless like the vintage *Toytown* character.

Larry approached a desk covered in paper and laughed at Norman thinking he was a horticulture expert. He spent hours after work making researching and making notes. Mrs Patterson regularly grumbled about it. Viv had asked Larry to be kinder to her. The old bag told Viv she wasn't comfortable being alone with him. He promised to behave. Instead, he poured laundry powder into Mrs Patterson's tea and enjoyed watching her spitting it out into the sink.

Heat and light bounded in as the door opened.

'Oh, I thought Norman was here.'

The sun's rays shone through Selena's skirt, highlighting the shape of her legs. The vest top she wore was cut low. Larry appreciated her cunning. Henry couldn't reject her looking like that. No one could resist it.

'He's popped out.' Larry leaned back in the chair, fingers laced behind his head. 'Come in and wait, unless you're off to see Henry.'

Selena stepped in, flicking her hair. Sweaty strands clung to her neck.

'Henry and I are obviously terrible at hiding our relationship,' she began, 'although he hasn't contacted me for weeks before now. I'm such a fool, running as soon as he snaps his fingers.' Her bottom lip quivered.

'That's no way to treat a lady.' Larry stood. 'Have a seat.'

'It's a shame there's a lack of gentlemen around here, apart from Norman and you.'

'I assume you're referring to Henry as the ungentlemanly kind.'

THE PROFESSOR

'Don't tell him I said that. He's annoyed with me as it is. I'm not supposed to talk to the staff either.'

Larry sat on a crate and winked. 'It'll be our little secret. Do you want a drink? This heatwave feels never-ending.'

She fanned her face with her hand. 'Yes, please. Norman has some in the mini-fridge. I'll have lemonade.'

While giving her a can, Larry lingered in looking. Fantasies resurrected of stroking her thighs, kissing her shoulders, and letting his fingers do the talking. There was a side he hid from his wife. Viv was too pure, too good for his desires. For payment, other women tended to his needs. He was tired of always owing women something, though. After all, the best things in life are supposed to be free.

A dribble of lemonade trickled down Selena's chin. 'Oops.' She covered the wet patch on her top with her hand.

Larry picked up a rag and approached her. Selena reached for the cloth.

'Allow me.' He pressed it to her breast.

Trapped by him standing in front of her, Selena pushed his hand away. 'I can do it.'

'Don't be so stubborn.'

He dabbed at her chest, imagining ripping out her heart.

She grabbed his forearms. 'You're hurting me. I need to go.'

'Running off to Henry? He doesn't want you, sweetheart. Change it up a bit. Snooty bitches like you only do it with toffs. You're missing out. Let a real man show you how it's done.'

* * *

Selena laid on the floor. The sun broke through gaps between the walls' wooden slats. It might have been minutes. It felt like hours had passed. Larry looked down at her. She stifled a scream. He had already struck her and covered her mouth to muffle the cries. His looming form reminded her of the nightmares she regularly had, featuring a figure called *Death*, coming to claim her. Selena wished she could go with Death now. Anything was better than being with the bogey man in the shed.

Larry came closer. He thumbed a tear from her cheek and then licked it. She squeezed her eyes shut. Seeing him so near would undo her. Earlier, keeping her eyes closed as Larry raped her was for endurance. She didn't want to deal with the memory of his leering face forever.

As Selena considered what he'd done, she chose to live. Death could wait. Survival took over. Previously, she believed if someone tried to attack her, she'd fight. Sadly, Selena had learned sexual assault can make your body freeze and that it wasn't her fault.

The attacker's arms pulled her to stand. With a perverse, gentle touch, Larry placed her on the chair.

'Open your eyes.'

She couldn't. She wouldn't.

Reflexes betrayed her against the slap. Her eyelids snapped open.

'Don't even think of telling anyone about our afternoon of passion,' Larry said. 'Henry won't be pleased to hear you're sleeping around. I'll tell him you've been having sex with Norman, too.'

'Norman's my friend!' Selena discovered her voice.

'Henry knows you set out to seduce him. I heard him laughing with some guests about the pathetic student he's shagging. Apparently, you're a shy girl who becomes a tiger in bed. Henry says you'll do anything to get a good grade.'

'That's not true! I love him.'

Larry cradled her jaw. 'I know your type. You try to overpower men with your looks and brain. No more. If you ever share what happened here, I'll kill you.'

She looked into his eyes and knew he'd enjoy every second of killing her.

'I won't say a word. Please, let me go.'

Larry pointed towards the door. 'Fly away for now, little bird, but don't forget, birds can be caged, too.'

His kiss on her cheek as she walked past threatened to break her. She faltered as the gravity of the assault flooded her mind. Still, Selena pushed forward while fearing she'd never leave the horror behind.

CHAPTER 72
Jane

Tethered together, Ed rocks us as he tries to stand. I can feel his feet are sliding. It's impossible to rise with the weight of each other.

'You raped my mum, you sick bastard!' he yells.

Dad grins. 'Selena was gagging for it. Women often cry "rape" because they regret acting like sluts.'

The matter-of-fact tone and cruelty are disturbing. When he disciplined me as a child, there was never any malice.

He continues. 'Selena tried to be coy, but she soon gave in. Throughout, she didn't protest. That's not rape.'

'She was obviously terrified!' Ed shouts.

Dad folds his arms. 'If someone's being attacked, they say "no" or call for help, not lie there.'

'Selena froze with fear,' I state. 'The body and mind can almost paralyse in a flight response.'

I recall a similar sensation I feel whenever the man, Death, visits, although that experience is nowhere near as sickening as rape.

'Jane, don't listen to that lad. Ever since you met Edward, he's tried to own you.'

'I'm not a possession!' I blast. 'There's no defence for what you did. No matter what you claim about it being consensual, it's obvious you attacked Selena. While describing your "connection" you couldn't keep that disgusting grin off your face. Selena might not be able to testify against you, but I can read between the lines of what happened. You may have fooled me for a long time, but I heard it in your voice. I could hear the glee at your conquest. Also, you were going to rape my friend Leah. It's clear you have form for sexual assault. You sicken me. Mum would turn in her grave if she knew she was married to a rapist and murderer.'

The wooden floor reverberates as he stamps towards me. The power I associated with a gentle giant is powered by evil.

'How dare you talk to me like that, you ungrateful bitch!' His nostrils flare. 'I've looked after you and paid for everything.'

'I think you'll find Evangeline did that.' My imitation of Evangeline's "eat shit and die" tone is new. I kind of like it.

His hands fly to my neck. I dig my heels in and thrash against Ed as the hold tightens.

'Leave her alone!' Ed cries.

Dad releases his grip.

'Never forget that I am your father, not Henry.'

'Before this, I thought we'd be okay,' I rasp. 'Despite finding out Henry's my father, you and I could've continued as before. We could've found a way. Not now, though. The Professor will never be my dad.'

He clenches his hands against his temples. 'Do I have to spell it out? I'm your biological father. You're *my* children.'

Hysteria builds inside me at the shock of realisation. Convulsive laughter wracks my body.

'Stop laughing at me!' Dad shouts.

My hysterics won't end. I struggle to breathe. A slap soon makes me silent. Dad has never hit me before.

He looks at his offending hand. 'I had to. You were losing it.'

'Seriously, you're apologising for slapping me, after drugging and tying me up?'

'What's so funny about me being your father? I'm worth a hundred of Henry Glynn.'

His self-pitying whine goes right through me.

'I've had enough of your ego, you pathetic excuse for a human. It's hard enough keeping up with things. One minute you're my dad, then Henry's my father, and I've got a brother. Now, you're my dad again.'

'Where's the proof we're yours?' The complacency in Ed's voice is unexpected. I expected more sarcasm. Clearly, he's tired of all these lies too.

'Henry was ignoring Selena for weeks before she and I had our secret tryst. To be certain, though, when home DNA testing kits were introduced, I sent Jane's and my swabs to a lab.'

'Isn't that taken from inside the mouth?' I begin. 'I've never done that.'

'Your sleeping tablets are very strong,' Dad replies. 'You didn't feel me taking the sample after you had a tablet-laced drink.'

'You had no right!' I choke on a sob.

'Larry doesn't care about consent,' Ed goads. 'At least he didn't have to bother knocking me out, too. I think we can safely believe we're twins.'

'More's the pity,' Dad replies. 'I could've done without you. To put your minds at rest, though, Henry paid for Selena's private antenatal and labour care. Evangeline gave us access to your medical records. Twins were confirmed.'

I find my voice. 'Did you tell Mum about the DNA test?'

'No. Viv got what she wanted. It was even better for me because you're mine. The test results just confirmed what I'd always suspected.'

'How could you fool Mum into taking in your illegitimate child?' I ask. 'I can't understand what she saw in you. Then again, you're an accomplished liar. I've lived with you for nearly thirty years and would never have believed you're The Professor.'

'The problem with you, Jane, is your life is too narrow. You've been staying at home, scared to venture afar. The desires lurking within us all are terrible to you because your world's only black and white. Also, you think being at university makes you superior to me.'

'I've never treated you in any other way than a loving daughter.'

'Eventually, you'd try to dominate me.' Dad focuses on Ed. 'Selena isn't the wonderful mother you believe she would've been. Selfish cow couldn't even be bothered to control a vehicle well enough to stay alive for her kids.'

'She didn't die in a car accident.' Ed struggles to keep his voice level. 'The Glynns lied to you too, then. Henry killed Selena. He shoved her. She hit her head and died. Mum's buried in the grounds of Glynnholme.'

Dad's mouth drops open, and then a sly smile forms. 'Well, well, naughty Henry.'

'While I hate him, it sounds like Henry pushed her harder than he intended,' I add. '*You* willingly murdered because of a twisted agenda with educated women and Evangeline's rooms.'

He ignores my comment as he approaches the miniature Glynnholme. 'As you can see, I'm rather good at creating things. First, there were you two, although I'm not so sure about Edward. You've allowed the Glynns to walk all over you.'

'I bloody well haven't!'

'Temper, temper. This rage is interesting. If I'd raised you, we might've formed a partnership.'

Ed straightens his back against me. 'I'm nobody's student, particularly a serial killer's. Besides, you've never wanted me. No one did.'

My heart hurts at the rejections he's endured while I was the golden girl, albeit unknowingly.

'Viv wanted you,' Dad says to Ed, 'but only Evangeline's precious Jane deserved a decent upbringing. Evangeline thought I was a safer choice than Henry! When we last met, she confessed she'd finally figured out I was The Professor. She was hardly caring, leaving Jane with me.'

'You weren't a killer then,' I reply. 'Evangeline trusted you for a while. What happened?'

Dad scratches his chin. 'Evangeline's faith was mainly in Viv. I haven't changed. I'm just an expert at hiding my true self. For a while, I kept a lid on my impulses. Mundane life doesn't suit me, though. All I needed was a reason to be the real me. The reasons used to be Selena and Evangeline. Then you came along; the final and best reason.'

'No matter how difficult she was, Evangeline didn't deserve to be killed,' Ed says.

'Don't pity these kinds of women. They use sympathy to draw us in and make us weak. Jane's obviously done so with you.'

I glare at him and then smile as he turns away.

'I made friends with Ed,' I say, 'like normal people do. You duped me into believing you're normal when really you're a psychopath.'

'Spare me the amateur psychology, sweetheart. I've researched psychopaths and know I'm no such thing. I'm better than that. You can't even begin to comprehend what I've learned. Keeping my intellect a secret was challenging. Consider how clever I am, erasing women with my litcrary knowledge. Behold the beautiful scenes I created.'

He sweeps a hand across the dolls' house. Tiny likenesses of Clementine, Fiona, and Grace are staged in the modes of their deaths.

'Are you…going to…kill me?' I manage to ask.

I'm trying to hold on to a hope that some of the person I loved is still there. Earlier, Dad cried. Surely, not all the years we've known each other were faked.

He points at Ed. 'He has to go. Edward's always been collateral.'

Ed is silent. I touch his fingers with mine.

Dad continues. 'Your death, Jane, is the hardest choice I've ever had to make, although it would be glorious. Edward *must* die.'

'How can we carry on as family if you kill your son?' As an apology for the callous wording, I nudge Ed's hand.

'It will be tricky, but you inheriting Glynnholme would soften the blow. We'll live there together. That's why I let Henry believe you're his child.'

'I'm not accepting an inheritance that isn't legally mine.'

'Nobody has to know. If you don't become the owner, you're leaving me with only one option.'

He removes the fabric covering one room in the dolls' house. In The Red Room, a small figure lies on the floor. Her similar slightly frizzy brown hair is the bane of my hairdresser. The Jane figure's blood seeps into the scarlet carpet.

Here is the scene of my impending murder.

CHAPTER 73
Jane

Dad picks up the Jane figure and cradles her in his palm.

'You were supposed to be just a financial transaction,' he says to the figure. 'Evangeline's monthly payments were useful. Now she's dead. I'll miss it, but at least I've got some savings. It's better that Evangeline no longer has a hold on me. I only allowed you to go to university because she threatened to stop the cash flow otherwise.'

'In case you haven't noticed,' I begin, 'I'm over here. Also, I'm not a kid who needs your permission.' A thought comes into my mind. 'Evangeline was on the phone that day, telling you not to deter me from going to university. It wasn't a bloke called Stan from the pub, was it?'

'Isn't she clever, Jane?' Dad continues addressing my figure. 'Stan's an alcoholic who can barely form a coherent sentence. As if I'd take advice from him. Evangeline wanted you to attend Oxford Carroll under Henry's watchful eye. The Glynn heiress had to be a Victorian literature buff. I kept asking Viv not to read those books to you when you were younger, but she wouldn't listen. She said they were part of your Glynn heritage. Think yourself lucky she adored you. One parent loved you unconditionally. There were always conditions for me. I've loved and hated you in equal measure.'

'But I didn't ask to be born!' I raise my voice to get him to talk to me rather than an effigy.

Dad finally looks at me. 'Nor did I ask for your birth, but here we are. All those women died because of you.'

'How the hell can you blame Jane?' Ed asks.

'Your existence was killing me,' Dad tells the Jane figure. 'Every passing year was another closer to you inheriting Glynnholme. I feared you'd ditch me and reject my plan to live there together. Viv's death - much as it pained me - was a blessing. The angel on my shoulder forcing me to behave was gone. Rather than killing you, sweetheart, I channelled my murdering urges towards others.' He grips the doll's neck. 'I could've killed you sooner and destroyed Evangeline's dream of a female heir.'

'Oi! Real Jane speaking here. You shouldn't have killed anyone. Take responsibility for your actions.'

'Would you rather it had been you who died? That was always the choice: them or you.'

I can't speak. I wish I hadn't tried to get his attention. His hateful stare threatens my bladder with releasing.

Ed whispers. 'Don't let him wind you up. It's what he wants.'

'Shut up!' Dad shouts. 'I'm talking to Jane. She's mine, not yours.'

'I made a Jane figure too,' Ed says. 'Mine are wood. I whittle. Have you ever tried that? It can be tricky at first, learning how to use the knife.'

Dad laughs. 'Do you want a fatherly pat on the back for your hobby? Are you trying to find similarities between us so I'll let you go? Distractions won't work. You can't come between my daughter and me anymore.'

'Just saying how much I enjoy whittling,' Ed adds.

He clasps my hand behind him and squeezes it several times.

Dad strokes the figure's hair. 'You forced me to love you, with that smile and being so caring.' Over and over, he slams her against the bench. 'You weren't allowed to do that! Viv would be so disappointed at you leaving me behind to study.'

THE PROFESSOR

'I'm not having this!' I yell. 'After Mum died, I did everything for you. So what if you have to cook a few meals and occasionally wash your own pants. I want a life too! Mum certainly deserved a better one than being with you.'

He glares at me and I wither. This snarling creature is not my dad. It's Larry. He is The Professor. I'll never call him *Dad* again.

'Viv had the ultimate escape, though, didn't she?' The Professor raises an eyebrow.

I push against the restraints. 'If you murdered my mum, I swear I'll wrench free and pull your heart out of your throat!'

He lowers in front of me. 'As you well know, Viv died of a pulmonary embolism. You're obsessed with her. After your nightmares, you'd call for her. I was always there, Jane. So close, you could've touched me.'

'You? You're the man, Death?' I gasp for air.

'Breathe slowly,' Ed says. 'In for four and out for four.'

Like a pair of lungs, we breathe together.

'Stop being such a drama queen,' The Professor says. 'I needed you to understand badness exists. A Death visitor did just the trick in preparing you for your future, or, indeed, your end.'

'By sneaking into my bedroom and scaring the shit out of me?'

'To a degree, it worked. But you never called for me. Even now, you still cry out for Viv.'

'Subconsciously, I must've figured out you're evil. How do you disappear so quickly every time?'

'When Viv was alive, I hid under your bed until she left and you went back to sleep. After Viv died, I'd take advantage of you slowly coming to and be extra gentle so you'd know it was your dad. Still, even if you were coherent, you'd never have believed I was the man haunting your dreams. '

'You absolute bastard! If Mum had found out what you were doing, she'd never have forgiven you, least of all for scaring me.'

'Viv wasn't really your type, right?' Ed begins. 'They had to look like Selena or at least be studying at the local uni.'

The Professor shrugs. 'Whatever. Consider instead the brilliance that devised the killings, and the skill that built *this* Glynnholme.' He points to the dolls' house. 'I planned the murders and made them in miniature, ready to loom large. Marvel at my expert knowledge of literature for choosing suitable passages for my victims. No wonder you wanted an education, Jane. It's in the genes.'

'You're nothing to me.' I reply.

The Professor snarls as he twists off the head of the Jane figure.

CHAPTER 74
Jane

I take in a last sight of a shed I was often deterred from entering. The Glynnholme dolls' house explains why. I refuse to focus on the figures made to resemble their dead counterparts. They aren't those women. They were people with lives stolen by The Professor. He may have treated them as toys, but I won't. Every victim's memorised face gives me a renewed resolve. I must live. No one will know what Larry did if Ed and I die. The Professor cannot prosper any longer.

I am Jane Eyre - strong against adversity, and as good as an orphan.

I am Jane Eyre, not a bird to trap and kill.

I am Jane Unwin - daughter of Viv, a mother motivated by love.

I am Jane Glynn - a name on a document offering a promising future.

I am Jane. Whatever happens, I am enough.

The Professor is occupied at the back of the shed, no doubt preparing our deaths. Unmasking the man, Death, has diminished my fear of dying. I take courage from my twin. We connect with touching fingers and hopefully having the same idea. I whisper that Larry may be a killer, but he was my dad. He's our father.

Ed doesn't reply.

The Professor approaches, holding a medicine bottle and a cloth. 'As you grew together in the womb, now you're linked in death. Apologies, I haven't prepared a quote. Edward forced us into this position and men aren't my usual targets. Oh well, I'm flexible. Don't worry. You'll breathe this in and then it will be like a deep sleep. You won't feel a thing.'

'Look at me,' I say to The Professor.

He stares at Ed.

'Look at me,' I repeat.

He can't do it. I'm The Professor's weakness. I always have been. This is my strength.

'*Dad*, please look at me.'

He concedes to love. As he turns towards me, his hands tremble.

'Don't, Jane.' His voice quivers. 'It has to be this way. You've left me with no choice.'

'I love you, Dad.'

The bottle slips from his grasp and rolls away. He chases it.

Flicks of a knife cut the ties around my wrists. I set Ed's hands free and pass him the knife. He releases the bindings from around us.

'Run!' he shouts.

Confusion makes me freeze. Instinct tells me to escape. My role in this scene should be complete. We're not living in The Professor's version of literature, though. This is real life with all its complicated, painful decisions.

Outside, I place an ear against the wooden door. A cry penetrates through pine, straight to my heart. I run to him before our connection ends.

While singing one of Mum's favourite lullabies, I place his head in my lap. I hold the man, Death. Now he's gone there will be no more nightmares. A blade protrudes from The Professor's chest. It's the whittling knife I slid from Ed's back pocket.

Ed holds out bloodied palms and focuses on them. I understand what his actions have cost him. Neither of us will ever be the same. We are The Professor's children and his killers.

'You had to do it,' I say.

My calmness is frightening. Why am I not breaking?

'Believe me. I didn't want it to end like this. I only wanted to threaten him with it, to keep him away, but he kept coming at me.'

'He was going to kill you, right?'

I shouldn't have to ask, and yet. Something niggles at my morality and mind.

Ed nods and then lowers his head. I keep my muddled thoughts locked inside. Ed's all I have left.

Literature will help me to survive. From memory, I recite a line from *Jane Eyre*, "'It is not violence that best overcomes hate - nor vengeance that most certainly heals injury.'"

'See, Dad?' I stroke his hair. 'I can choose a suitable literary quote for a death too.'

CHAPTER 75

Jane

Eleven Months Later

Ed pours tea from a flask. It spills onto a workbench. I look around at the new shed, which is part of our new beginning. Knowing what happened to Selena in the old one, we burned it to the ground. Something hasn't changed, though. Ed and I often sit in a shed, even though Glynnholme's house, grounds, and fortune are at our disposal.

Reader, I inherited it.

Perhaps some of my father's deviousness is in me after all, but I deserve a good life. So far, it's been based on lies. I lived with seemingly normal, occasionally boring parents, but that wasn't the truth. I could feel guilty about using illegal documents - like Evangeline - to get what I wanted. Maybe I'm just a fast learner. I used my "real" birth certificate Evangeline left with a solicitor. It states I'm Jane Glynn, daughter of Henry and Selena. Evangeline included a letter and probably falsified records confirming Ed and I are Henry's children.

After I instructed the legal team to find a loophole in Charles Glynn's will, they succeeded. He hadn't considered twins. The solicitors found nothing to dispute me giving Ed half of everything. It's only fair he has this after the way the Glynns treated him.

I'll never know if Evangeline really believed we're her grandchildren. Perhaps she was so desperate for an heir she ignored what Larry did to Selena. Not much got past Evangeline. It makes me uncomfortable she might have concealed a rape and let a violent man raise me. How on earth would being brought up by The Professor be preferable to Henry? Evangeline remains a puzzle I can't solve.

I understand why Selena lied to Henry by telling him he's our father. After the way he treated her, she deserved anything she could get for herself and us. Selena loved her children so much she was willing to make us Glynns. Unfortunately, she paid for it with her life.

Henry hasn't contested the will, influenced by awaiting trial for killing and burying Selena. He turned himself in. When I visited him in prison, he confessed to dithering by the police station door for a while. I'm glad he finally grew a set of balls. Henry wants Ed and me to stay in touch. We won't. Now we've got each other, it's all we need. Henry took our mother's life. It's only right we take everything from the Glynns.

Rupert, the wily little penguin, is in hiding. Eventually, we'll find him, with help from a private detective. I can't wait to look into his terrified eyes.

Selena's church burial was a strange event of grieving an important stranger. Ed, Mrs Patterson, and I were the only mourners. In contrast, Evangeline's funeral was ridiculously overblown. Many of Quillington's residents lined the main road, watching the car carrying her coffin. It was as if a royal had died. People from high society crammed into the church. As I was leaving, Margaret, the owner of the shop and post office, gave me a wave. I scuttled away like a criminal. I'm still working on my feelings of guilt by association.

At Larry's funeral, I was the only person to attend. Only when I was trying to save myself and when he was dying could I call him *Dad*. I never will again. He's now Larry or, when I'm feeling particularly angry, The Professor. A family liaison officer keeps in contact. As The Professor's last intended victims, the media constantly pursued Ed and me. Larry's service was private, so they couldn't get a money shot from me being there. Ed refused to attend. Whenever I mention Larry, Ed changes the subject. I've suggested he have counselling, like I'm doing. He insists working with nature is good enough therapy.

My aunt, Ivy, hollered at me down the phone for inviting her to Larry's funeral. She said they hadn't spoken for years. Ivy detailed how he made her childhood miserable. He tore up her school work and bullied her, using negative names associated with the studious. Ivy couldn't wait to leave for university. Larry's parting gift was to spike her drink at her leaving party, laughing at her confused distress. Everyone assumed she was drunk. She said she'll never forget Larry whispering in her ear as she tried not to fall unconscious. He called her a snobby bitch who deserved to die for thinking she's superior to him. Ivy was proud to secure a university place; a huge achievement back then for the daughter of working-class parents. Larry continued trying to ruin it until she stopped going home in the holidays. Her parents viewed it as snobbery, accepting Larry's lies that Ivy had snubbed them. Larry the lamb cast his innocent sister as the black sheep of the family.

When she was alive, Mum insisted we saw Ivy without Larry knowing. I admired Ivy's feistiness, knowledge, and the full bookshelves in her home. When I was a teenager, Larry found out about our visits. I stayed in my bedroom while a storm rumbled underneath in the kitchen. Mum later came into my room, mascara streaking her cheeks as she shared we wouldn't see Ivy again. Despite that, we sometimes phoned her when Larry was out.

Why didn't I recognise the signs? Larry always craved control. My counsellor says families of criminals are often distressed. She specialises in this type of therapy. No matter what she says, though, I keep searching for clues. I'm punishing myself, looking for something I should've spotted. Previously, when I've read articles on those who didn't suspect a relative was a killer, I groaned at their stupidity. How can you not know you're living with a murderer? The answer is they're very skilled in deceit.

THE PROFESSOR

Occasionally, I look at pictures of The Professor's victims I've put in a scrapbook. I ask them for forgiveness. If I'd noticed something off in his habits or personality, perhaps I could've stopped him. No one knows about my scrapbook or how I've begun studying the psychology of murderers. When your father was The Professor, you'll do anything for reassurance the madness isn't genetic.

The Professor's ego was his downfall. The police found a leather-bound notebook containing detailed accounts and sketches of the murder scenes hidden in his shed. Along with the Glynnholme dolls' house - complete with figures of the victims and rooms showing their death scenes - the police had plenty of evidence. It's a shame Larry was never punished for his crimes. Death seems too easy.

I wrestle with being The Professor's child. There are moments I cry for the father who taught me how to ride a bike without stabilisers and tended to my grazed knees. Other days, I wish I'd plunged the blade into his heart. Ed and I never discuss it. The shame remains, although the legal system deemed Ed's actions as self-defence.

I can't tell Ed my concerns regarding how much I can trust him. I thought he understood the plan was to use his whittling knife to snap the restraints and then we'd escape together. Staying behind and killing The Professor was Ed's decision. I want to believe he was protecting himself from an attack. I want to believe I wasn't clear enough about what we should do. The alternative is… No. I won't go there.

'I thought I'd miss my old house,' I say, 'but being here is a relief from the neighbours twitching their curtains and the press on my doorstep.'

'It's been challenging, but I understand why you held off from moving here. Aren't you sad about leaving? You've been there most of your life.'

Ed stayed with me while I summoned the courage to move into Glynnholme. For a while, it didn't feel right. One day, I woke up and knew it was time to go.

'The house is just full of terrible memories now,' I reply. 'Packing Mum's books had me in floods of tears, but I remembered what she wanted. She told me to follow my dreams. I let her down by staying at home after she died and looking after that man. All those years I wasted on such a sick and—'

'Don't let him harden your heart. You're better than that. You're the best of us both.'

'You're a good person too.'

'Not really,' he mumbles.

'We'd better go. The interior decorators will be here soon.'

He jabs me in the ribs and laughs. 'Get a load of you with your posh new ways.'

'Kate would never forgive me if I didn't make this place fabulous. Actually, she loves me even more now we're discussing my investment in a chain of stationery shops she can manage.'

Ed and I stand outside the shed and regard Glynnholme. When I'm finished, every shred of Evangeline and Henry will be erased. Ed can run free with his designs and be a master of the landscape. We have to look to the future, not the past. Victorian literature will always be one of my passions, but it's not everything. I'm continuing my English Literature degree, but I'm living in the present too.

A familiar panic arises. 'Say again how it's okay we've lied about being Glynns.'

Ed takes my hand. 'I won't tell if you won't. Come on, let's go home.'

CHAPTER 76

Ed

Eleven Months Later

Ed is certain Glynnholme should belong to them. It's their birthright. Jane and Ed are already tainted by being The Professor's children. Jane deserves this, Ed even more so for what he's endured. Finally, he's won.

'Something lovely?' Mrs Patterson asks, while stirring a casserole.

'What do you mean?'

'That smile must mean you're having lovely thoughts.' She takes the potato peeler from him. 'There's no need for you to do that. You're not a servant, love, particularly not now.'

'I'm still doing the gardening.' His tone is harsher than intended. 'I want to do it, for me and Norman. If you don't need me here, I'm going to Mum's place.'

Mrs Patterson nods. She understands the sunken garden is his chosen memorial spot for Selena. The lad's preoccupation with death is unhealthy, though. He says he's fine, but those ever darkening eyes state the opposite. She will keep an eye on Ed. It's what her husband, Norman, would've wanted. Whenever he expressed his fear that apples never fall far from the tree, his face visibly dropped. She thought he was referring to Henry's influence on Ed. Now she knows it's The Professor. Ed's not the only person who snoops around Glynnholme.

* * *

'Hello Mum.'

Ed takes a seat. Rubble covers most of the area after it was dug up to remove Selena's body. When he was allowed to, he put the bench back. Ed sits in the ruins, hoping he hasn't created his own ruin from a deadly choice.

He opens the diary. Soon, it will disappear in a bonfire's flames. No one questions a gardener about burning things.

Ed considers damning words for the last time. Trying to subdue rage, he re-reads Norman's diary. Ed will be eternally grateful to Mrs P, though, for giving it to him. After his death, she kept Norman's possessions and confessed she'd read the diaries for comfort. Unfortunately, she got more than she bargained for.

Ed recalls Mrs P turning up at Glynnholme to the chaos of Evangeline being dead and Ed looking for Jane. He won't forget the desperation in Mrs P's face as she demanded he take one of Norman's diaries. After finding Jane's address from Rupert's records, Ed ran. Mrs P shouted to him to immediately read a specific date from ten years ago. Sitting in the car, desperate to rescue his sister, Ed wondered if he had time for nostalgia. Henry - Ed believed at the time - was likely at Jane's house, preparing to murder her. A voice inside Ed's mind, sounding like Norman, told him to pause and read. So he did.

Now, Ed skims over the entry. The details are still hard to digest. Selena trusted her friend, Norman. She cried as she shared how Larry raped her and the twins were his. When Norman begged her to tell the police, she expressed fears of further harm Larry might inflict. She also had a plan. Her children would be raised as Glynns. Jane could inherit. It was the least Henry owed Selena after the way he'd treated her. Also, she hoped it would keep Larry away from Jane and Ed.

Norman's sentences twist and tussle with the morality of the decision Selena and he made. He wrote of his devastation after

THE PROFESSOR

Selena's death and when Jane left. Norman suggested to Evangeline he could raise the twins with his wife. She laughed at the silly old man, believing he was worthy of parenting Glynns. When Norman offered to take Jane from the Unwins, Larry threatened to kill him if he ever graced his doorstep again. Norman never forgave himself for not fighting harder. Instead, he did what he could to make Ed's life better under the shadow of Glynnholme.

Ed speaks to the ground directly underneath his feet. 'I did it all for you, Mum.'

Larry didn't attack Ed as he'd led Jane to believe. Crumpled on the floor, Larry held the Jane doll to his mouth and sobbed. It ignited Ed's anger. That man had stolen his mother. He wouldn't have his sister any longer.

Ed's whittling knife sliced into his skin. Larry gasped. Ed grinned as he twisted the knife deeper into Larry's heart.

The Professor smiled as he spoke his final words. 'Well, well, Edward. You really are my son. I'm so proud of you.'

LISA SELL

ACKNOWLEDGEMENTS

Thank you for reading *The Professor*. Readers are the reason why we write. Mine are obviously better than the others… Please leave a rating and/or a review on Amazon. They are like gold dust for authors and help with sales. I've got to keep the cats in treats, after all.

Thanks so much to my beta readers: Holly; Kate; Belinda; Sian; and Helen. You gave me the courage, eventually, to publish this book that nearly didn't get published. Your advice and support, as ever, was invaluable.

Thanks also to my proofreaders: Holly; Kate; and Mel for trying to root out those pesky typos. There will always be escapees, but you did a brilliant job.

Well done, Emmy, for another amazing book cover! You never fail to make me happy each time I see the finished product.

They'll probably never read this book or even remember me, but it's only right to acknowledge my A-level English Literature teachers. I was an English teacher once too. I understand how challenging it can be. I also know how rewarding it is when you light a spark in a student for loving literature. Thank you, Peter Norman and Jeanette Mackie, for doing that for me.

Dave, you get the final, but forever, thanks. Writing and life in general would be rubbish without you. Thanks for being there and always in my heart.

Bloody hell. That got soppy. As we were…

LET'S GET SOCIAL!

Facebook: www.facebook.com/lisasellwriter/

Instagram: www.instagram.com/lisasellauthor/

X: www.twitter.com/LisaSellAuthor

Website: lisasellauthor.co.uk

Printed in Great Britain
by Amazon